Also

Romantic Comedies
The Event
The Move
The Plan
The Dream
Relatively Normal
Relatively Sane
Relatively Happy
The Reinvention of Mimi Finnegan
Mimi Plus Two
Kindred Spirits
She Sins at Midnight
Going Up?

Non-Fiction Humor
Motherhood, Martyrdom & Costco Runs

Thrillers
See No More

Middle Reader
Wilhelmina and the Willamette Wig Factory
Who the Heck is Harvey Stingle?

Children's Books
The Friendship Bench

Love is a Battlefield

Whitney Dineen

This book is a work of fiction. Names, characters, locales (except Missouri really is a state), and situations are the work of the authors overactive imagination and voices in her head. Any resemblance to people living or dead, events, etc. is purely coincidental. And I don't mean maybe.

Copyright © by Whitney Dineen in 2020; all rights reserved.

No part of this book may be reproduced, copied, scanned, photographed, or distributed in print or electronic form without express permission of the author. But let's face it, if you love it, she'll probably let you share small portions. You still have to contact her first.

Made in the United States.

September, 2020
ISBN: 9798680246184

https://whitneydineen.com/newsletter/

33 Partners Publishing

Acknowledgements

I'm thrilled to finally be writing a series set in Oregon. The last eleven years living here have been full of all the things that matter in life: family, friends, gardens, chickens … Alas, no camping to date, but I'm seriously considering giving glamping a go.

So much love to my family for their constant encouragement and support. You guys are my heart and foundation.

Many thanks to Becky Monson for yet another fabulous cover. Girl, they just keep getting better and better.

To my editor and proofreaders, Celia Kennedy, Paula Bothwell, and Melissa Amster, you gals rock my world.

Many thanks to my author friends who support and encourage my career, you know who you are. I wouldn't be anywhere without you.

Heartfelt love to my attorney and Hollywood daddy, Scott Schwimer, we'll walk that red carpet together, yet!

To my readers, you guys are the ones who make my dream gig possible and I heart you for being so awesome! I read every single one of your reviews, emails, and posts on Facebook. Thank you for being a part of my journey.

This book is dedicated to every single one of you that has survived this crazy year.
Keep your spirits up, keep your light shining, and help each other wherever you can.
Together, we can do anything!

Chapter One

The Mothers

Libby Cooper is busily deadheading her hot pink double fiesta impatiens when she hears the familiar riff of "You're My Best Friend" by Queen. She picks up her phone and excitedly greets, "Ruby!"

Her best friend since their first day at Oregon State University announces, "I still think he's perfect for her."

Loving Ruby's enthusiasm and pie-in-the-sky optimism, Libby kindly warns, "Addie's never forgiven him for all those pranks he pulled on her when they were kids."

"Maybe not, but that doesn't mean she never will. The question is, can you get her to set foot in Oregon?"

With three quick snips of her gardening shears, Libby replies, "Of course I can. My daughter isn't as tough as she wants the world to think she is. Is she a bit uptight? Yes. But she's really a big softy when she thinks someone needs her help. That's the card I'll play."

Ruby's familiar giggle is quickly followed by, "Excellent! Let me know when you'll be here."

Addison

"There's only a four percent chance my vacation to the Cayman Islands will be canceled due to a weather-related incident. That's a ninety-six percent chance I'm going to be lying around in a bikini being pampered," I tell Eliza, or Elle, as she's been called since graduating from high school. Her smiling face beams out of the laptop sitting on my bed, where she's helping me decide what to pack for two sun-filled weeks on Grand Cayman. That's where I'll be celebrating the opening of Bainbridge Caribbean.

"You're so lucky you got to decorate the most exclusive resort in the Cayman Islands," she says with borderline envy.

"Luck had nothing to do with it," I reply honestly. As I sort through a pile of sarongs, I tell her, "I worked my butt off to show Roediger that I was the best person for the job. I put weeks into my pitch, convincing him that going with anyone else would be a waste of his time and money."

"Roediger Bainbridge," Elle says wistfully as she twirls a strand of her glorious auburn hair around her index finger. "Did you know that Forbes rated him the third wealthiest hotel magnate in the world? That's impressive considering he isn't even forty."

Zings of pride still shoot through me when I think about how he chose me to design the interior of his hotel. The fact that he's single, charming, and super easy on the eyes also plays a part in my enthusiasm for seeing him again. Not that I'm shallow, but no woman with a heartbeat is immune to a package like Roediger.

"He's like the lead in one of those romantic comedies from the nineties," Elle sighs.

While I totally agree with her, I feel the need to add, "Real life is never like the movies. More's the pity." Then I add, "I wish you could come with me."

"As much as it pains me to say, taking your mom for her sixtieth birthday is the right decision."

"Speaking of my mom, I'd better get moving if I want to get downtown in time for our reservation."

"I love how Libby comes into the city every time your dad is away on business."

"It's a great excuse for some girl time with her only child. Plus, the shopping upstate pales in comparison to Madison Avenue."

"Does Your Mother Know" by ABBA blasts from my phone. It's the song my mom programmed for her calls.

I shoot Elle a questioning look as I answer, "Hey, Mom, what's up?" I wonder if she's already at the restaurant and is checking to see if I'm almost there.

"I'm downstairs, let me in," she orders.

"You're here? At my apartment? Why?"

"Just let me in and I'll tell you," she says.

I call down to the front desk. "Emilio, the impeccably dressed woman with the shoulder-length silver bob is my mother. You can send her up."

The doorman pauses before he informs me, "There's a beautiful lady with a ponytail and blue jeans. Would that be who you're talking about?"

Emilio is new so he doesn't know my mom wouldn't wear jeans into the city. Yet, I distinctly hear her say, "Tell him to let me in, Addison."

"That's her, thanks." I turn to Elle and announce, "My mom is wearing jeans."

"In New York City?" my friend asks in alarm before offering, "Something must be wrong."

"There's only one way to find out. I'll call you back later tonight and let you know."

Elle shoots me a thumbs up before I flip my laptop shut. Then, I hurry to unlock the front door before the woman who gave me life has a chance to knock. She claims that once she's been announced, I should watch her walk down the hall from the elevator. She likes to make an entrance.

My mom is not wearing her trouser-styled Ralph Lauren jeans. She's in her gardening jeans, full-on with the holes in the knees and the grass stains that illustrate how she got those holes.

"You can't go to Gramercy Tavern looking like that," I shout down the corridor.

"I'm happy to see you, too," she says in a tone dripping with sarcasm.

As soon as she's within arm's reach she hands me a large bag from Happy Happy Wok Wok. "You brought Chinese? What's wrong?" Not only does my mom not dress casually in the Big Apple, she only eats Chinese food when there's a crisis. It's the only time she can justify putting MSG into her body.

She pushes me through the doorway. "Let's dish up and I'll fill you in."

My mind is running a million miles an hour. "Is Dad leaving you for a younger woman?" I demand.

"What? No. Why would you even suggest such a thing?"

I fling my hands out, spokesmodeling her current ensemble.

Pulling two plates out of the kitchen cabinet, she announces, "Are we still going to the Caribbean on Friday?" *Why wouldn't we be?* As my stress level climbs, she informs me, "I heard it's a bad hurricane season. I'd hate to get stuck on some tropical island so far away from home."

"Mom, I've been flying back and forth for the past year and you haven't once been concerned about hurricanes." It's much more her style to suggest that there are worse things than being stranded in paradise.

She sighs like she's trying to fill a hot air balloon in one breath. "Honey, do I ask for a lot of favors?"

Uh, oh, something *is* up. "No," I answer hesitantly before adding, "which I totally appreciate." Hint, hint, don't ask for any now.

She fills a plate with my favorite shrimp. "It's because I love and respect you too much to infringe on your life for anything less than a dire emergency." *Crap.* She's laying it on thick so I can't say no to whatever bomb she's about to drop.

"Thank you, Mom. I can't tell you how nice that is to—"

She doesn't let me finish. "I talked to Aunt Ruby this afternoon. She's having an exceedingly difficult time right now."

"I'm sorry to hear that," I say, suddenly losing interest in the *kung pao* shrimp on my plate. What could her hard time possibly have to do with me? Even though she and Mom make it a point to get together every year, I've barely seen her in the last fifteen.

"Ever since Tom died last year, she's been running the Willamette Valley Lodge single-handedly and she's in a real bind right now."

"Thank goodness she has children then."

"Yes, well, her kids don't specialize in the kind of help she needs."

No sense hinting around that they should be the ones coming to her aid, not me. "Are you by any chance suggesting Aunt Ruby is having a life or death decorating emergency? Because Mom, regardless of what those shows on HGTV try to tell you, there's no such thing."

Seriously, people survived laminate countertops for generations before they were told that marble and granite were the only civilized options. Not to mention the seventies. That whole decade is what I imagine an acid flashback looking like.

"Ruby's been trying to decide if she should keep the lodge or if she should sell it. The stress has been taking its toll on her physically."

"If it's affecting her health, she should sell it and live off the proceeds," I say bluntly.

"Addison Marie, that business has been in the Cavanaugh family for three generations. You don't bail on longevity like that."

"Why not? If it's getting to be too much for her and her lazy ass sons won't help, then there's nothing wrong with her walking away." Brogan and James Cavanaugh are not my favorite people on the planet. I haven't seen them since we were teenagers, but the memories from shared family vacations during our formative years have scarred me for life.

"James is busy running his farm and, as you know, Brogan has his hands full being a successful author. I hardly think they're slacking. More like preoccupied with their own pursuits."

"Uh-huh." I don't dare ask my mom where I fit into her

friend's *trouble* for fear she'll tell me.

"Don't you want to know what the crisis is?"

"Not even a little bit." Knowing where I fit in will only cement my mom's intentions that I come to her friend's rescue like some kind of decorating Wonder Woman sans the bullet repelling bangles on my wrists.

"She needs to make some renovations to the inn. Bookings have slowed down as new lodgings are opening all the time in their area. She has to do something to redirect interest back to her place."

"She should throw a big party or get a Hollywood movie studio to film something there," I suggest.

"Before she does anything like that, she needs to make sure everything looks its best. That's where you come in." And there it is, the other shoe dropping. Right on me.

"Have her call my office and talk to Chloe. I'll see what I can do about scheduling a consultation with her sometime in the spring."

"The spring will be too late, honey. She needs to be ready by Christmas."

"Christmas? That's completely unrealistic, Mom. It's already the middle of August. If that's her deadline, there's no way I can help. I'm booked solid through March."

"That's not strictly true," she says, gaining strength for her cause.

I hand her my phone. "Call Chloe and ask her. I promise she'll verify the busyness of my schedule." I shouldn't have to point out how in-demand my skills are to my own mother.

"You're taking a month off starting next week," she says matter-of-factly.

"Yes, but I'm going to Grand Cayman with you, and when I come home, I'm going to have a couple of things done here at my apartment." I've been putting off laying hardwood floors and updating the paint for over two years. I don't want to wait two more years until I have the time to oversee it.

"Your apartment is perfect as is, and I'm sure your client will be happy to reschedule our trip when you tell him a family emergency has come up."

Of all the nerve. "First of all, Mom, while I love Aunt Ruby, she isn't family. Secondly, I've already explained that dire decorating emergencies don't exist."

"You yourself said that I don't ask for favors," she says. "But I'm asking now. Ruby is my dearest friend and when she calls me in tears needing help, I will move heaven and earth to come to her aid."

When I don't say anything, she hurries to add, "A lot of people die within a year after losing their spouse. I can't bear to think about that happening to my best friend."

I ignore her and pick up my phone. "Hey Google, what percentage of women die within a year of losing their spouse?"

"According to studies by the Bereavement Center for Mental Health, seventeen percent of women die within a year of losing a longtime spouse," Google announces.

"Seventeen percent," I reiterate. "And I'm willing to bet ninety-eight percent of those are a heck of a lot older than Aunt Ruby."

"My friend needs me," my mom states plainly.

Historically, once my mother has made up her mind, there's no changing it. But I have to try. "Then *you* should definitely help her."

"I don't have the skills, but I intend to come along to offer moral support. That way we'll still have our getaway together for my birthday."

Oh, no, she didn't. Playing the birthday card is the cherry on the guilt sundae she just served.

"What about the opening of Bainbridge Caribbean?" I practically whine. "I want to go on vacation."

"There are plenty of fun things to do in Oregon when you're not consulting on decorating."

"Yeah, goat yoga and mushroom foraging," I grumble. They've probably added a master class in how to macramé your own rain poncho. Oregon is not my idea of a vacation. The last time we were there, I was forced to fish for my dinner. I don't like fishing, and I sure as heck don't have any desire to do a downward dog next to an animal that's liable to head-butt me into the next decade.

"Addison Marie Cooper, do you remember when I picked you up at the police station when you ran that red light and decided not to stop for the traffic cop?"

"I was sixteen!" I try to defend. "I was scared."

"Yet, I picked you up and promised to never tell your dad. I never have, you know."

I hand her my phone. "Go ahead and tell him."

"That's not how this is going to go down. You promised that day you owed me the mother of all favors. You can't renege on that now."

"You have got to be kidding me. I've already booked our flights. We have a beautiful suite being gifted to us by my client."

"The flights were on frequent flier miles. You won't lose

those, and your client will surely invite you back another time."

"No, Mom. Just no."

"And yet, a promise is a promise. I'll call Ruby and tell her we'll be there Friday afternoon. I'm so grateful to have such a lovely and helpful daughter."

Ignoring her blatant attempt at manipulation, I demand, "How in the world can you make up for missing a trip of a lifetime?"

Instead of answering my question, she says, "You won't regret going to Oregon. Trust me."

She knows how I feel about the Pacific Northwest. She knows I'd rather walk over broken glass followed by a stroll through a nest of cobras before returning to the scene of *the incident*—the final nasty prank in a long line of practical jokes that traumatized me for all further outdoorsy activity, short of a nice, sedate horseback ride or lying on a beach drinking rum cocktails, that is.

Libby Cooper has something else up her sleeve and I don't want to know what it is. Unfortunately, I don't think there's any way to avoid it.

Chapter Two

The Mothers

"Well, how did it go?" Ruby Cavanaugh demands the moment Libby answers the phone.

"She's not happy, but she'll be there. How's it going on your end?" Libby wonders.

"I've started acting preoccupied whenever I talk to the boys. It won't be much longer before Brogan shows up wondering what's wrong."

With the cell phone wedged between her shoulder and ear, Libby pours half a bottle of white wine over her freshly roasted herb chicken before putting it back into the Viking oven. "Maybe we should just set Addie up with James. He lives right there in Spartan. Hang on a second," she says as she places her phone on the counter and hits the speaker button.

"Addison has always hated Brogan way more than James. And you know what they say about love and hate. Don't forget Shelly Smitton and Zane Cox."

"We were surprisingly good matchmakers in college," Libby agrees. "I just never anticipated we'd be doing it with our own kids."

"It's not like we haven't given them plenty of time to figure out their own love lives. Let's face it, once you hit your thirties, a motherly intervention is past due."

"I can't wait to see you, Rubes!"

"Me too, my friend. It's been too long."

Brogan

"Yo, Bro, have you talked to Mom lately?" James asks by way of greeting.

I closed the blackout curtains before going to bed, which leaves me lying here trying to figure out if it's day or night.

"Brogan, are you there?" my brother persists.

"What time is it?" I croak as I sit up looking for the bottle of water I keep on my nightstand.

"Dude, it's six o'clock in the morning. The day's a wastin'."

"James, I didn't go to bed until after two. As far as I'm concerned, it's still the middle of the night."

"What were you doing up so late?" he wants to know. "Did you have a hot date?"

I wish. "I promised my publisher I'd send some preliminary notes for the sequel to *Crime Garden*. They signed me on for two more books once it hit the *New York Times* Bestsellers list."

"Props, man, congratulations!" James is way the hell too cheerful for me right now.

"Thank you. Now why are you calling at this ungodly hour?"

"I wanted to know if you've talked to Mom. She's not acting like herself."

"I'd be surprised if something wasn't out of whack. Dad's

only been dead for a year."

"I don't think it's that. She started behaving strangely about a week ago."

"She's got a lot on her plate with the lodge. I'll call her later," I tell him.

"Maybe she's working too hard."

"It's good for her to have a distraction," I say.

"Just check on her. Then call me back."

"I'll do it as soon I wake up. I'm going back to sleep for a few hours."

"Don't forget."

I hang up without replying. Then I turn off my ringer. I lie still for a few minutes hoping sleep will take over, but once my writer brain turns on, it's off and running.

I love my job. It's the perfect occupation for a person who likes a quiet life. The only problem is that I regularly lose track of time, which can make interacting with the rest of humanity a bit challenging.

My mind drifts to my mom as I get out of bed to grab a couple of aspirin. She's only sixty, nowhere near the age anyone would have expected her to be widowed.

None of us have had an easy time accepting Dad's sudden death, especially because he was in such amazing shape when it happened. He worked out at the gym five days a week, hiked and swam all the time, and ate a healthy diet. Dying from a heart attack in the prime of his life knocked us all off balance.

Back in bed, I decide to go home and spend some time at the family fishing cabin. I was planning on waiting until the new year to start the sequel to *Crime Garden* anyway. This way I can keep an eye on my mom and still enjoy some solitude.

At noon, I wake up feeling good about my decision to get out of Dodge for a while. Grabbing a cup of coffee, I head out to the deck so I can watch the surf crash against the Oregon Coast while I talk to my mom.

She answers after five rings sounding tired and distracted. "Yes."

"Hey, Mom, it's Brogan."

"Hi." Dead air.

"How are you doing?" I ask.

"I'm fine," she says, sounding anything but.

"I talked to James earlier today," I tell her.

"That's nice." I'm starting to get nervous. My mom is usually thrilled to hear from me and asks a million questions before I can get a word in. These short and to the point answers are not her style at all.

"James is worried about you. He says you're not acting like yourself."

"Huh." That's it, *huh*? Warning bells ring in my head like a five-alarm fire is consuming an entire city block.

"Mom, I've decided to come home for a bit," I tell her, knowing this information will garner some excitement. "Is the fishing cabin open?"

"Unless Billy Grimps has taken up residency." Billy is a semi-homeless, semi-employed older man who's been squatting in our cabin on and off since my grandparents owned the inn. My family would have happily given him steady work, but he prefers not to be tied down. He claims life is about communing with nature and not about slaving away for "the man." He works only when he wants to. That way, having a regular job won't interfere with his calling.

"I don't care if Billy's there as long as he promises to shower regularly."

"I suppose you could stay with me." She doesn't sound too excited about the idea.

"Okay," I reply. While I usually stay in the cabin, I'm starting to wonder if I should be closer until I know what's going on with her.

"On second thought, you'd better stay at the cabin, I have company coming."

"Really? Who?" My mom usually puts her guests up in one of the ninety guest rooms that make up Willamette Valley Lodge's main building.

"Libby Cooper."

If my mom's best friend is visiting from New York, she must be worried, too. "Good," I tell her. "I'll be fine in the woods."

"All right, I'll see you when I see you," she says before hanging up. No declarations of delight that her oldest child is coming home. James is right, something is going on and it can't be good. I hope Mom isn't clinically depressed or something. I'm definitely going to have to keep a close eye on her.

Chapter Three

The Mothers

Libby: I apologize ahead of time for my daughter's cranky disposition. 💩
Ruby: Uh-oh. Bad flight?
Libby: Bad everything.
Ruby: I'll make sure to have something nice planned for when you get here. Let's see if we can turn her around before she decides to hate Oregon all over again.
Libby: You're the best. We just got to the car rental place. We should be there in about an hour.
Ruby: 😍😍😍

Addison

Portland's motto is "Keep Portland Weird." That's right, an entire city has dedicated their existence to staying weird. By the looks of some of the people at the airport, they're succeeding beyond all mortal expectations. And believe me, I'm from New York, I know weird when I see it.

I pass a girl in her early twenties wearing cutoff jean shorts over a pair of ripped fishnet tights. While hiking boots and a flannel shirt complete the look, it's the hot pink mohair beanie worn over her purple and black streaked hair that says it all: *I have no fashion sense and my armpit hair is tie-dyed.*

While my mom is bouncing along next to me, excited to see her friend, I'm dragging one foot in front of the other like I'm shuffling toward my own execution. Seriously, Gregorian monks are chanting hypnotic tones in my head, lulling me into calmly accepting death.

As we pass the Made in Oregon store, I ask, "What is it about this state that they're so enraptured by the things they make?"

"They're proud of their accomplishments," my mom answers. "They want to support the local economy." Not that vegan energy bars, handmade soap, and homespun yarn aren't good things, they are. But come on, would it kill them to be a little less nutty crunchy?

"Do you want to grab a bite to eat before we get the car?" my mom asks.

"I'd rather just get out of here." I'm hoping some fresh air will clear the skunky stench of marijuana out of my nostrils. The two man-buns in front of us positively wreak of ganja.

One of the stoned hipsters just told his friend, "We had a rad sesh, man. All the vibes. All. The. Vibes." While these guys are probably around my age, there is nothing about them that suggests they're upstanding citizens. I'm guessing they still live in their parents' basements and dream of starting a garage band to save the ringed seals of Finland. Of course, they haven't done that *yet* because they're too high to get off their butts and be productive.

My mom shoots me the side-eye and warns, "Turn your mood around, Addison. It's not going to make this trip go by faster and we aren't going to be of any use to Ruby if your panties are constantly in a bunch."

"All I said is that I didn't want to eat in the airport. What about that makes you think my panties are in a bunch?"

"That look on your face says you're suffering some kind of existential angst." My face does tend to give away my emotions.

Nodding my head toward the aromatic men-children in front of us, I explain, "I just need some fresh air. I'll be fine as soon as we get outside."

Once we have our luggage and get settled into a mid-size sedan, I really do feel better. I usually enjoy air travel, but today's flight was packed full and nearly five hours of non-stop turbulence. Not that I would have minded had we landed in the Cayman Islands, but Oregon is not my idea of a decent reward for suffering such a rocky journey.

My mom pulls out onto the freeway and declares, "This is such a beautiful state. Your dad and I have so many wonderful memories of going to college here."

"How you two East Coast kids ever wound up going to school on the other side of the country is beyond me," I grumble.

"Your dad and I like to think of ourselves as world citizens. We bonded over our love of exploring this beautiful planet we live on."

I look around at all the trees and the blue sky full of puffy clouds and I'm hard-pressed not to agree. "Oregon *is* pretty." I don't offer more. I mean, it's not white sandy beaches and palm trees.

Mom turns on the radio and finds an oldies station playing "Come Sail Away" by Styx, one of her all-time favorite bands. She belts out the lyrics for all she's worth at the same time following Google Maps lady's instructions.

I close my eyes and practice a calming breathing technique while visualizing myself lying in a hammock on the beach. I'm blissfully swaying in time with an imaginary breeze, when I'm startled back to the present.

"Sheep!!!" my mom yells.

My eyes pop open, half expecting to see a herd of lamb chops flying toward the windshield. "What sheep?" I demand when it becomes clear we aren't in imminent danger.

"Over there," she points to a field to her left. "Will you just look at them all? White sheep, black sheep, baby sheep ..." she starts to enumerate.

For the love of God. I close my eyes again and try to get back to the beach. I'm almost there when she yells, "Cows!"

"Mom, there are sheep and cows in upstate New York. Why are you so excited about seeing them here?"

"They just look so much more peaceful here. You know, relaxed and happy."

I start to wonder if my mom picked up a contact high from being so close to those potheads at the airport. *Maybe I should drive.* Before I can suggest it, Google lady says, "Take the next exit and turn left on Christmas Tree Road."

"It won't be long now," my mom enthuses. She's positively radiating excitement.

"Didn't you just see Aunt Ruby over the summer?" I ask.

"I did, but it was only for a quick overnight. She was in New

York for the launch party of Brogan's latest thriller and couldn't spare much time before she had to get back." Then she adds, "You might remember that she invited you to join us, but you were too busy."

"I would rather walk naked through Time Square during rush hour than to go to any party honoring Brogan Cavanaugh." But the truth is, I really was busy.

"You'd think you'd be over that little joke by now. It has to be over twenty years ago," she admonishes.

"It was seventeen years ago, and he put honey in my shampoo bottle while we were camping," I remind her. "The only place I could get water to wash my hair was from the river nearby and that water was freezing cold. If you'll recall I was a sticky bug magnet for days." It's impossible to heat enough water on a camp stove to sufficiently wash out that much honey.

My mom laughs—laughs!—before saying, "You have to give the boy credit. That was a particularly well thought out prank."

"I would think you'd be on my side, Mom. Imagine if it had happened to you."

"Addie, dear, you need to lighten up and have a sense of humor about yourself. A couple weeks in the Oregon countryside is exactly what you need to gain some perspective."

"Perspective on what?" I demand. I'm suddenly so annoyed I consider jumping out at the next intersection and hitchhiking back to the airport.

"Honey," my mom tries to sound soothing, "you work too hard and you're always on the go. You need to breathe the fresh air and let your hair down a bit. You know, trade in your Louboutins for some sneakers and go for a long walk."

"I was planning on going for a lot of walks … on the beach," I remind her. I'm the one doing her a favor here, and I do not appreciate her making me out to be some priss with a nature allergy. Plus, it's her fault I hate Oregon. If she hadn't forced me to visit here every year until I was a junior in high school, I'm pretty sure I'd be ambivalent on the subject of the Beaver State. Heck, I might have even liked it here.

Chapter Four

The Mothers

Ruby: Brogan is going to stay in the fishing cabin. I'll give Addie a nice suite and pamper her for a couple of days before she even lays eyes on him. 😁
Libby: Good thinking. That daughter of mine needs to chill out.
Ruby: Are you almost here?
Libby: We just parked.
Ruby: I'll meet you in the lobby. 🎉

Brogan

With a quick glance at my watch, I realize that in the hour I've been home I already feel the calming effect of the Willamette Valley infusing my soul. I love living by the ocean, but it gets busy during the summer months with tourists taking over the beaches and all local thoroughfares. I finish settling into the fishing cabin before going to see Mom.

The fishing cabin is best described as rustic, and that's being kind. The shower is outside, so if you're staying up here in cold weather, you've got to be prepared to either get in touch with your inner animal and embrace a more organic aroma or walk two miles to the lodge.

James and I stayed up there for the entire month of July one year when we were teenagers. Ripe doesn't begin to describe the stench of two adolescent boys who used only the creek and river for bathing. Mom considered burning the place down until Dad offered to install an outdoor shower. After that, she would have let us stay in the cabin the whole summer if we'd wanted to.

Though we never did because by then we'd discovered our family's resort had become the hot spot vacation destination for families with daughters who kept our breaks from school interesting.

Never underestimate how bored teenage girls can get vacationing with their parents or how willing those parents are to let their daughters spend their days zip-lining or hiking with boys around their age. When it came down to hanging out with them or with my stinky brother, there really was no choice.

Entering the lobby of the inn is as impressive as ever with the thirty-foot stone fireplace and exposed wooden beams highlighting the vaulted ceiling. My dad used to joke that it's how he envisioned the check-in desk of heaven looking. *I wonder if he was right.*

"Hey, Chris," I call out to the middle-aged hotel manager behind the concierge stand. Chris has worked here for the last twenty-five years and is as close to being family as if she were blood.

"Brogan, is that you?" she replies while executing a near sprint to throw her arms around me. "I didn't know you were coming for a visit."

"I'm staying up at the cabin for a while to recharge my battery. How's business?" I ask.

"We're fully booked through October and only have a short break before we fill up again for the holidays."

"Mom must be pretty busy. Is she doing okay?" I'm hoping Chris will give me the inside scoop.

"You'll have to ask her," she says, maintaining loyalty to her longtime friend and employer. "Things aren't the same without your dad running around here, though. We all miss his smile and laughter."

"I know what you mean. I pick up the phone to call him all the time before remembering." A heavy knot forms in my chest like I swallowed a five-pound weight. It happens every time I remember my dad is no longer here.

Chris squeezes my hand. "Life has a way of sucker punching you, doesn't it?"

I nod. "Just when you think you have it all figured out, something like this happens. I thought we'd have him for another twenty or thirty years."

"Your dad was never one to sit back and accept what life threw at him. He got out there and forged his own path. I'm sure he's still doing that."

"I like to think so," I say. Emotion starts to clog my throat, so I switch topics. "I'm worried about my mom."

"Your mom's a fighter. She has her bad days, but she's a lot like your dad. She rolls up her sleeves and plows through the rough patches."

Chris makes it sound like Mom's doing fine, which is not how James sees it and certainly not how she acts when I talk to her on the phone. I hope she isn't on the verge of a breakdown or something. A few years ago, while doing research for a book, I read an article that said not all people show signs of mental instability until they round the bend. One minute they're fine and the next, not so much.

"Do you know where she is?" I ask her.

Looking up at the clock, she answers, "It's almost four, so my guess is she's in the restaurant checking to see what the dinner specials are going to be. Do you want me to call over there for you?"

"Nah, that's okay. I'll just wait by the fireplace and catch her when she walks by." I give my old friend another hug before heading toward the great room. My eye is immediately drawn to the floor to ceiling picture window that overlooks the valley below.

I've traveled the world over and can't imagine living anywhere but Oregon. Our little corner of paradise is balm for whatever ails you. In the Willamette Valley there are rolling hills, rivers, creeks out the wazoo, forests, and farmland. Depending on which direction you go from here, the ocean and mountains are only an hour's drive. What more could you want?

James has been after me to sell my beach house and find a place in Spartan so I can be closer to him and Mom. I've been seriously considering it since Dad died. Life is too short not to see the people you love on a regular basis. I just wish I'd embraced that thinking sooner.

My formative years were spent in this room staring out onto the rugged elegance of the land. I also played a lot of board and card games with James and whichever guests we could talk into joining us.

There are six mission-style rocking chairs in front of the fireplace and various seating areas scattered throughout. I sit down on a leather couch and keep an eye open for my mom.

From my vantage point, I have a clear view of the lobby, which is buzzing with guests. The end of the summer is always full of families trying to fit in their final adventures before the pace of life picks up again in the fall. Between zip-lining, boating, horseback riding, and world class biking paths, there's enough here to keep them busy for weeks.

A beautiful woman walks through the front door and immediately catches my eye. You don't see many people checking in here wearing business suits and high heels. She's about as out of place as "tits on a bull," as Billy would say.

Her hair is silky and shiny—she looks like she just walked off a fashion runway. Ever since Emma, I haven't so much as smiled at a blonde woman, such is the bitter taste my ex left in my mouth. But this one has an elegance about her that I find very appealing.

I stand up and slowly wander over in her direction. I'm not sure what I'm going to say, but I feel drawn to introduce myself. I'm practically at her side when I notice the woman standing next to her.

"Aunt Libby?" I ask in disbelief.

She looks up at me and enthusiastically declares, "Brogan!" Throwing her arms around me, she says, "Your mom said you might be here."

The beauty next to her states, "You never told me that." This is said like I'm Satan's first born and heir to the Kingdom of Hell.

There's only one person Aunt Libby could bring with her who has that particular opinion of me. "Addison Cooper, is that you?" I open my arms and invite her into my lair.

"Don't. Touch. Me." Each word is articulated like it takes a Herculean effort to get out.

She glares at her mom. "Why didn't you tell me he was going to be here?"

"I only found out when I called Ruby from the airport. It doesn't matter though, because you're here to help *her*."

I look down at the gorgeous Addison and smile at the unexpectedness of her presence. "It's been at least fifteen years, Addie. You can't still be mad at me."

Instead of answering, she turns her back and marches toward the front desk. My visit home has just become a million times more interesting.

Chapter Five

The Mothers

> *Libby: It's on, my friend. We just ran into Brogan in the lobby.* 😳
> *Ruby: Darn it. I was hoping Addison would have a chance to get settled first.*
> *Libby: You were right to pick him. The sparks positively flew when they saw each other.*
> *Ruby: Where are you now?*
> *Libby: By the fireplace. We just checked in, but we wanted to say hi to you before going up.*
> *Ruby: I'll be right there. FYI, you're staying with me in my quarters. The room is for Addie.*
> *Libby: This is going to be one fun trip!* 🎉

Addison

I wish my mom had warned me about Brogan being here. I do my best to ignore him, but it's hard. That thick dark hair and five o'clock shadow—at three forty-five in the afternoon, no less—chiseled jaw, and intense blue eyes are knocking me off my game. Had we not had such a sordid past, he's definitely the kind of guy I'd be interested in. I need to make sure to keep reminding myself what a good-for-nothing heel he is.

The lobby and great room are more gorgeous than I remember from childhood. Of course, I only saw them a couple of times as I was always dragged away to sleep in a tent. My parents, along with Aunt Ruby and Uncle Tom, went camping together in college and had such fan-freaking-tastic times they vowed to camp together every year. That lasted through my entire childhood. Lucky me.

The wood paneling and animal heads on the walls fit beautifully with the stone fireplace, leather furniture, and amazing views of the valley and river outside. I conclude my help must be needed elsewhere as I'm not sure I could have done a better job decorating what I've seen so far.

I wish my mom would get off her phone and say something, but she's acting like we're not even here. I catch a glimpse of her screen and see that she's using emojis like a third grader hopped up on apple juice.

Brogan sits down on the rocking chair next to me. "I hear you're an interior designer."

"Yup." No sense in misleading him into thinking I'm interested in chatting.

"I'm not surprised."

What is that supposed to mean? I don't ask though. I just stare at him with my award-winning RBF (resting bitch face). Seriously, I could turn pro if there were such a thing.

"You definitely seem suited to it."

I pick up my own phone to check my messages. I am not

going to take the bait he's so obviously dangling.

"When we were kids, I used to think you'd either be a librarian or a lion tamer."

I put my phone down and demand, "Why?"

"You were prissy and mean," he says bluntly. "Are you still?"

I've never been prissy. I had to deal with two boys bent on terrorizing me for the entirety of our family's combined vacations, which always involved camping.

I never knew what new torture the Cavanaugh brothers were planning for me next and it made me skittish. "I'm meaner than ever, so you'd be well advised to keep your distance," I warn.

The bonus is that if he stays away from me, I won't be tempted to sniff him. At the moment I'm hard pressed not to lean in and try to discern if that's orange or lemon blending with a decided clove essence.

"Lucky for me I like mean girls," Brogan teases. What's with this guy? Is he being purposefully obtuse?

"You're going to love me then," I say by way of a threat, not invitation.

He seems oblivious to my anger. "We should go swimming in the creek while you're here."

"So, you can try and drown me again? No, thanks." But even as I say it, some traitorous part of me wonders what Brogan Cavanaugh looks like in a swimming suit now that he's all grown up. Against my better judgment, I briefly ponder what he'd look like without one. My stomach plunges like I've turned upside down on a rollercoaster without a seatbelt on. Beads of sweat form on my upper lip and I'm glad to be sitting down.

"I promise I won't try to drown you."

I remind myself to focus and put some clothes on that image of him seared into my imagination. "I can't attest to having the same intentions, so it's in your own best interest to steer clear of me."

Before he can answer, Aunt Ruby sails into the room looking crisp and fresh in a white linen sundress. "Libby, Addison! Come here and let me squeeze you." She hugs us tightly before turning to her son. "Are you all settled up at the cabin?" she asks.

Brogan stands and kisses her on the cheek. "Yes, ma'am. I noticed you spruced the place up for me. Thank you."

She laughs brightly. "If you mean the fresh bar of soap I asked housekeeping to drop off then, yes, I spruced it up."

He looks surprised. "They did a little more than that," he tells her. "There are fresh flowers, a new duvet, and a stack of towels."

"They must have sent Kate up there. She's new and doesn't know we don't take pains with the cabin."

"And here I thought you were rolling out the red carpet for your oldest son," he teases her.

"Dream on, honey."

Turning to us, she says, "Lib, you're staying with me. Addie, I've put you in one of our suites. I want you to get the full experience of the Willamette Valley Lodge while you're here."

While I appreciate it, I once again wish we'd have stayed here once in a while. I know Aunt Ruby and Uncle Tom lived here so it wouldn't have been a vacation for them, but man, I would have loved it.

Genuinely happy to see my mom's old friend, I reply, "Thanks, Aunt Ruby. I'm looking forward to hearing what I can help you with." That's a lie, but there's no sense being rude. I'm already in Oregon.

"We'll have plenty of time for that later," she says. "Brogan, I'll take Libby up to the family quarters. Would you mind showing Addie to the River Suite?" He smiles like he just discovered he was holding the winning Powerball ticket. The enthusiasm on his face sends a heavy warmth and a burst of sparks rushing through my body. Seriously, it leaves me kind of breathless.

"I don't need a guide," I tell him. "Just point me in the right direction."

Brogan grabs my suitcase. "Nonsense. We're a classy operation, and we don't let our guests carry their own bags."

"My suitcase has wheels, idiot," I snarl.

"I wouldn't want you to break a nail."

I'd like to break a nail by picking up my suitcase and hitting him over the head with it. Instead, I ignore him. I assume I'll be doing that a lot while I'm here.

"You can freshen up, Addie, and maybe even have a little rest. We'll meet you at the River's Edge at six for dinner. We have Coho salmon and steelhead tonight," Aunt Ruby tells me.

"I'm starving. I can't wait."

"I'll have room service bring you a little something to hold you over." A snack and nap feel like just the ticket right now. All I have to do is shake Brogan and do my best to keep away from him and I might actually have a nice trip.

What are the odds?

Chapter Six

The Mothers

Ruby leads the way into the family quarters in the lodge's east wing. "Addie is going to keep Brogan on his toes," she announces with more than a hint of glee.

"You think?" Libby releases a nervous laugh as she collapses on the couch. "She doesn't seem that happy to see him."

Ruby's eyes glow with delight as she makes herself comfortable on a soft leather club chair situated next to her friend. "I think my son is in for a wild ride, and we're going to have front row seats. As long as Addie doesn't make a run for it."

"She won't. Do you remember that time when she was two and Brogan was five and he took her lollipop away from her?" Ruby claps her hands together excitedly. "Addie hit him over the head with her talking tea pot!"

"Yup," Libby confirms. "Somewhere along the line, my daughter lost her backbone as far as Brogan is concerned. But I'm pretty sure those days are over."

"Oh, Libs, I can't wait! Let me pour glasses of wine and we can drink to that."

The ladies don't stop there. They toast the school that

brought them together and the husbands they built their lives with. Finally, they raise their glasses to the great unknown and to the old adage both of their mothers taught them to subscribe to, "Good things happen to those who wait."

Brogan

Addison Cooper is one hundred percent not happy I'm here, which makes her that much more intriguing. Who knew the awkward little girl with knobby knees and braids would turn into such a looker? The signs were there when we were teenagers, but she's exceeded all expectations.

I pull her suitcase down the hallway past the gift shop and coffee bar to the elevators. "How long are you planning to stay?" I ask, trying to find a topic that won't annoy her.

"Too long," she snaps. So much for not irritating her.

When the elevator arrives, I wait for her to get on like any gentleman would. She must be at least five-nine without those ridiculous heels. Even with them, she's still shorter than I am, but only by a couple inches.

We wait in silence while we ascend to the fourth floor. The lodge used to host over a hundred and twenty rooms, but fifteen years ago, my parents doubled the number of suites which took the total down to ninety. Their thinking was that even if families were here to enjoy outdoor activities during the day, they still wanted luxury at night. The gamble paid off. There are rarely any vacancies.

"The River Suite is one of our nicest. It's where most newlyweds stay when they have their weddings here," I tell her.

No reply.

"The views are spectacular. Obviously, you get a river view, hence the name. But the bedroom faces the woods, as well."

Nothing.

"My parents used to hire a circus troupe to swing by the windows on a trapeze to entertain the guests."

An arched eyebrow. Finally.

"The sword swallower was a real hit until he slammed into the side of the lodge and took out his own tonsils. That's when they had to stop. Liability issues, you know."

Addie seems to be on the verge of laughing but she catches herself. Ah, Miss Cooper has a sense of humor. Now, that's something I can work with.

"What are the chances you'll stop talking?" she asks, trying valiantly to keep the amusement out of her voice.

"Why would you want me to stop talking?" I love that she's still holding a grudge from when we were kids. It means she's not a pushover. Seeing Addie again is reminding me of my carefree childhood years, a time I miss more than I can express.

Potential melancholy is avoided when she announces, "Brogan, I'm here to help your mother. If not for some decorating emergency she's having, I'd be in the Cayman Islands right now drinking a piña colada on the beach. Can you guess where I'd rather be?"

"What decorating emergency?" I ask, wondering if such a thing actually exists.

"All I know is your mom has some big plans she wants executed by Christmas which means my vacation got cancelled and I'm in Oregon instead of paradise." She adds, "An occurrence

I'd hoped to never suffer through again in this lifetime."

"Oregon *is* paradise. What do you have against it?" I can't stand here and let her insult my state.

"Oregon is gorgeous," she confirms. "I have nothing against the state per se, just the people who live here. One in particular." She glares at me like she's attempting a Vulcan mind meld.

On the off chance she can do it, I avert my gaze and say, "Lady, you've got to get that stick out of your butt and relax a little bit." That obviously wasn't a very nice thing to say to an old family friend, but she's wound tighter than a two-dollar watch.

"Charming."

We finally arrive at the River Suite and Addison runs her key card over the door. When the green light flashes to show it's unlocked, she doesn't even bother to face me as she says, "You can go now."

No way I'm going to let her dismiss me like she's a queen and I'm her servant. I push the door open from behind her and walk in. After parking her suitcase next to the luggage rack, I start the tour. "Your bathroom has a jacuzzi tub. Open the shutters if you want a view of the river."

I head to the bedroom next. "The mattress is a Duxiana. I guarantee it will be the best night's sleep you've ever had." Sitting down on the edge of the white duvet, I continue, "You can see the sunset over the water from here, which is quite impressive."

"Get off my bed," she growls. She sounds like a wild cat protecting her domain.

Instead of following orders, I lean back on my elbows and pick up the television remote before turning it on. "Channel twelve has the menu for dining and spa services. You can book any meal or appointment you want from here."

"Please get off my bed." Her request sounds like a threat, kind of like an axe murderer saying, *please come over here so I can chop your head off.*

I don't immediately respond as I don't want her to think that ordering me around is the way to go. When I finally get up, I walk back into the living room and announce, "There's a private patio outside the french doors …"

"For the love of god, Brogan, will you please just go? I want to unpack and take a shower before dinner."

A knock at the door keeps me from replying right away. Instead, I answer it and let room service in.

"Mr. Cavanaugh," the server says. "I didn't know you were staying here."

"He's not," Addison tells him.

I offer her a look that suggests I'd be more than happy to rectify that situation before telling the waiter, "You can set everything up on the patio table, Frank. I want my friend to appreciate the view."

While the cart is wheeled through the doors, Addie turns to me. "Leave. Now."

"It's been a pleasure showing you around. I guess I'll see you at dinner," I tell her before following orders. I'm not sure I'm going to join them for supper. I want to keep little miss sunshine on her toes and not let her think she's got the upper hand here. Although clearly, she does. If not, I'd go straight up to the fishing cabin and forget she's even here. But heaven knows that's not likely to happen.

Addison Cooper has walked back into my world. She's prickly as a warthog, and skittish as a wild mare, but still, she gave herself away when she almost laughed at my joke a few minutes ago. The warmth in her eyes was very compelling. I can't help but want to push through her frosty exterior, and see what more there is to her. I want to make her laugh.

Chapter Seven

The Mothers

"Your place is beautiful as ever," Libby says, perusing a sideboard full of her friend's knickknacks.

"Tom and I had a lot of fun decorating it over the years. We bought those clay animal miniatures in Vietnam when we went for our thirtieth anniversary." A sadness in Ruby's voice permeates the atmosphere.

"We were both lucky finding the loves of our lives so young." Libby reaches over to take her friend's hand. "Tom was taken from you too soon."

"There are no guarantees in life." Ruby exhales deeply, as if willing the sadness to leave her body, before saying, "Brogan hasn't brought a girl home since Emma."

"What happened to her anyway? It's like she just slipped out of the picture without any warning."

"I don't know. My son has always been incredibly quiet on the subject. The only thing he told us was that Emma wanted to take a job in Chicago and they decided it was best to part ways at that point." Ruby takes a sip of her wine before continuing, "Something big had to have happened for him to have become so tight-lipped and borderline reclusive."

"Addie's pretty quiet on the subject of her social life, too. She's going to be furious when she finds out what we're up to."

"To quote Doris Day," Ruby says, "que sera, sera. Whatever will be, will be. If those kids of ours had taken care of business on their own, we wouldn't have had to get involved. As far as I'm concerned, they've brought it upon themselves."

Addison

My first memory of Brogan was when I was seven years old and he was ten. He picked his nose and wiped his booger on my hamburger bun before handing me the paper plate holding my dinner. I told on him, but he denied it. Since none of the adults saw him do it, he wasn't punished, which really made me angry. At him and them.

Even though I got a new burger, I was put on alert. This boy was not my friend and under no circumstances should I trust him.

Every year after that, when our families camped together, he'd ask me if I wanted my hambooger with or without the extras. I took to standing next to whomever was doing the grilling so I could monitor the preparation of my meal and make sure nothing untoward was added.

As far as memory serves, James wasn't as mean as his brother until he realized how happy it made Brogan when he pulled a prank on me. From that point on, I slept with one eye open.

Contrary to popular belief, I do not hate the outdoors. I adore them. When properly equipped with bug repellent, good food, and comfortable seating, I love dining al fresco. I love riding horses. I just don't understand the desire to sleep outside.

My friends in New York City agree with me. Summering in the Hamptons or on the Jersey Shore is considered enough love of nature to satisfy. I have yet to hear any of them express a desire to sleep on the beach and get consumed by sand crabs. In my opinion, this makes them sane, not haters of Mother Nature.

People from this state are a different breed though. They enjoy sleeping under the stars in Bigfoot territory waiting for the aliens to abduct them. They relish such outings as though their DNA requires it to keep their hearts pumping.

"Does Your Mother Know" blares from my cell phone, breaking my inner critique of the natives. I consider ignoring it, but right before it goes to voicemail, I answer. "Why didn't you tell me Brogan was going to be here?"

"Addison," my mom's tone is stern, "you're a thirty-two-year-old woman. Why don't you consider acting like one?"

She's kind of right. It does seem silly to still be mad about things that happened so long ago. It's just that those things ruined more family vacations than I care to think about.

"Fine," I offer less combatively. "Why are you calling?"

"Ruby was wondering if you'd like to have a massage. She says she can send someone up in fifteen minutes and you'd still have time to shower before dinner."

A burst of real happiness shoots through me. "I'd love that."

"I'll tell her. In the meantime, take some deep breaths and try to calm yourself. I'm sorry you're not in the Cayman Islands, but I suggest making the best of being here. Do you think you can do that?"

My mom makes me sound like a petulant child, and in some respects she might be right, but I'll never tell her that. Instead, I concede, "Maybe."

Sniffing my blouse, I can still smell the lingering traces of marijuana from the two man-buns at the airport. I might have to burn it on principle. I don't care how legal pot is in different parts of the country, until they create a strain of weed that smells like chocolate chip cookies or star jasmine, it should remain a jailing offense.

I hurry into the shower to wash off the day. It's only common courtesy to be clean before having a stranger rub your naked body.

As the rainfall showerhead beats down on me, I visualize all my tension swirling down the drain. I make a mental note to have one of these installed in my apartment when I get home. One point for Oregon.

Once clean, I pick at the cheese platter Aunt Ruby sent up. I briefly consider calling Elle before the masseuse arrives, but it's two hours later there and I'm sure she's out having the time of her life. I gave her my room at the Bainbridge Caribbean along with whatever niceties Roediger had planned for me. Yeah, I'm that good of a friend.

Roediger was lovely when I told him I couldn't make the grand opening and was encouraging of my sending Elle in my stead. He also told me that I'd be his guest whenever I was able to make it back to Grand Cayman. Heaven knows when that's going to be.

My masseuse turns out to be a big strapping masseur named Todd. I'm a little uncomfortable having a strange man rub me until he opens his mouth and says, "Didn't I see you with Brogan Cavanaugh in the lobby? That man is yummy."

Gay men can rub me, no problem. "Brogan Cavanaugh may be good looking, but that's the only thing he's got going for him. If you ask me, he's a boil on the backside of humanity."

"Girl, get up on this massage table and dish! I want to know more." He hurriedly adds, "Of course, it's against hotel policy to gossip with the guests so I shouldn't have said anything, I'm sorry."

"Sorry nothing. You beat the tension out of my back, and I'll tell you all about the time Brogan filled my sleeping bag with slugs."

I get so carried away I also tell him about the time he put mud in my hiking boots, snuck fish guts into my backpack, and poured tree sap on my hairbrush. I reminisce so much that I'm just as tense after my massage as I was when it began. And now I get to go have dinner with him. Super.

Chapter Eight

The Moms

"Do you remember our first day at OSU?" Ruby asks her friend as she places some snacks on the table in front of them.

While perusing the charcuterie platter, Libby says, "How could I forget? It's not often a buttoned-up girl from the East Coast walks into a room to find that her new roommate tie-dyed the matching navy-blue duvets and curtains her mom sent. The room reeked of bleach while screaming, 'hippy-chick.'"

"The look on your mom's face was priceless!" Ruby laughs. "I thought she was going to drag you out of there and demand you get a new roommate."

"She learned to love you as much as I do," Libby says with a smile.

"She loved that I set you up with another East Coast preppy that you later married.'"

Libby nods her silver bob in agreement. "That didn't hurt. But the truth is, I think we rubbed off on each other. You softened my edges and taught me to love camping."

Ruby interrupts, "And you made me burn all of my cutoffs and talked me into getting a business degree instead of becoming a professional belly dancer." She raises her wineglass in salute and adds, "Thank you for that, by the way."

Brogan

The front door to the cabin is wide open. I know I shut it before I went up to the lodge, so that either means the deer have figured out how to turn the knob or Billy is around. He hates closed doors, claiming they make him nervous.

I step across the threshold and call out, "Billy, you in here?" I don't want to startle him lest he throw his pocketknife at me again. Thank goodness he wasn't really trying to hurt me that time or I'd be down an eye.

"Who's that?" a gruff voice calls from the bedroom.

"It's me, Brogan," I reply.

Billy Grimps comes shuffling out of the bedroom. He normally wears the same pair of khaki-colored cargo pants and a t-shirt, but today he looks borderline presentable in a cleanish looking pair of jeans and a loose, cotton button-down shirt.

"Hey, boy," he says. "You planning on staying up here for a while?"

"I thought I'd hang out for a month or two. Is that going to cramp your style?"

"Nah. I wondered why the cleaning gal came in and made things so pretty. Looks like your mom was getting ready for you."

"I can have them bring out a rollaway bed for you, if you want," I offer.

"I mostly sleep outside this time of year. I only come in when it rains hard."

"Well, if that happens, you can take the couch, or we'll call housekeeping and get you that bed." I'm not sure how it happened, but ever since I can remember, we've checked in with Billy to make sure he's not planning to stay in our cabin, almost like we're asking his permission to use it.

"You want some fish?" he asks. "I caught a mess of bluegill and crappies I was gonna fry up for supper."

As my mom has not officially invited me to dinner and because I want to keep Addison off balance, I decide to eat here tonight. "I'll run out and get the beer. You want anything else while I'm at the market?" I ask.

"Yeah, get me some of that bran cereal, would you? I'm a little stopped up lately."

"Bran cereal and beer. That's some grocery list. You want anything sweet for later?"

"I picked a bucket of blackberries yesterday. There's a bunch left if you want to get some ice cream."

"I'll do that." On my way to the store, I think about Addie. That woman is in desperate need of a tranquilizer. While James and I *were* pretty rough on her as kids, I haven't seen her, let alone pulled a prank on her, in over fifteen years. You'd think she would have lightened up a little bit.

Inside the Quick Stop, Cheryl Wilkens calls out, "Look who the cat dragged in. Folks around here have started wondering if you think you're too fancy for the likes of Spartan."

Cheryl and I went from grade school all the way through high school together. Even though we took different paths in life, we have the commonality of a shared childhood. Around this area that means we're as good as family. "You know me, Cheryl; I'm as fancy as they get."

"I told some tourist lady the other day that Brogan Cavanaugh grew up in Spartan and she didn't believe me. I had to run across the street to my place and grab an old yearbook to prove it to her."

I can't help but laugh. This town is just under three thousand people and, as a rule, they don't particularly embrace progress. By and large, what was good enough for their parents, is good enough for them.

When I was a kid, I couldn't wait to get out of here and live in the real world, but as an adult, I realize my hometown possesses a contentment that no amount of money can buy.

"Have you got any Umpqua vanilla bean ice cream? Billy Grimps asked for it."

She shakes her head. "Is that man still up on your property? I keep hoping he'll find a real house to live in."

"He uses the fishing cabin any time he wants. Although, I'm thinking we should update it a little for him." I tell her, "He's making me a fish dinner tonight."

"Speaking of fishing…" She crouches down under the counter and comes up holding a paper cup covered with tin foil and a rubber band. "My dad was going to give these to Billy next time he saw him."

"What is it?" I ask, reaching out to take the Dixie cup.

"Tomato worms. He left a couple plum tomatoes in there to keep them happy. Tell Billy the bluegill love them."

"Will do." I ask, "How are you and Damian doing these days?" Damian was a good friend in high school, but we've drifted apart as the years passed.

"Better now that he's moved out."

"I'm sorry to hear that," I tell her. Couples come and go, but I thought Damian and Cheryl would be together until the end.

"Yeah, well, there are no hard feelings anymore. He seems to think we got together too young and he wants to see what else is out there. Good luck to him," she says with only a hint of bitterness. "What about you, Brogan? Any lucky woman catch your eye?"

"I've managed to stay happily single."

"You let me know when you're ready for me to set you up with my cousin. She's had her eye on you for a while now."

"I don't know, Cheryl," I flirt light-heartedly. "This is the first since we've known each other that we've both been without a significant other, maybe it's our time," I wink at her playfully.

"I know too much." She contorts her face jokingly in a look of horror. I hope she's joking anyway. "In all honesty, I'm taking a nice long man-break. The kids are more or less self-sufficient now and I'm finally going to read all those books I've wanted to read but never had time for."

"Starting with mine, I hope."

"Nope," she deadpans. "I've got my eye on some good old-fashioned trash. I might get around to yours sometime next year."

"Flattering."

"Go get your groceries, fancy man, and don't forget the worms for Billy."

Another good thing about coming home is that people knew me before I was famous. To them, my biggest accomplishment is breaking the rock crossing record at Twitter Creek when I was fourteen.

After getting everything on my list and a few more items that look too good to pass up, I go back to the counter to check out. I'm ready to leave when Cheryl says, "Emma came in the other day."

The only way to respond is to act like I didn't hear her. Emma Jackson is not someone I talk about with anyone. "You have yourself a good day, Cheryl."

I walk out of the store feeling a good deal less happy than I was when I went in.

Chapter Nine

The Mothers

Libby is sitting on the veranda drinking her second cup of coffee when her friend joins her. She inspects Ruby closely from the slump to her normally ramrod straight posture all the way to the puffiness of her eyes. "Rough night?" she asks with more than a tinge of concern.

"All the nights are rough," Ruby answers with aching honesty. "I'm used to Tom and me going our own ways during the day, but nighttime was when we connected. Just knowing he was lying next me was like a battery that charged my soul. I could do anything as long as we were together."

Libby reaches to take her hand. With a loving squeeze she says, "I can't even imagine."

"I'll see something that catches my funny bone and think, *I can't wait to tell Tom.* Or I'll wonder how his day is going and then I'll remember." Her shoulders sag with the weight of her new reality.

"You were a couple for over forty years. It's got to be hard to remember who you were before that."

"It happened way too soon, Libs. It's part of the reason I'm so determined to get the boys settled. Life can be far shorter than we ever imagined, and I want them to feel that kind of love for as many years as possible."

"I'd like the same thing for Addison. Careers are wonderful and important, but they don't take the place of a life partner. I'm pretty sure Addie thinks I've wasted my life because I never worked outside the home."

Ruby scoffs, "You've raised more money for pediatric cancer than anyone I know. Before that it was Alzheimer's, and before that it was something else. You've more than had a career, you just never got paid for it."

"Well, I'm ready to become a full-time grandmother while I'm young enough to get down on the ground and play with babies. It'll be all the more fun if my grandbabies' other grandma is you."

Addison

I roll over and take time to stretch every finger and toe. I had a fantastic dream and I want to linger in its wake before consciousness chases it away.

I dreamed I was dancing with Roediger Bainbridge in a statuary garden I toured at Versailles a couple of years ago. A string quartet was playing, and the breeze smelled like gardenia blossom. I wore a beautiful gown reminiscent of another time and Roediger looked like James Bond in his tuxedo. As I savor every detail, I suddenly remember more.

Roediger gazed deeply into my eyes with such smoldering intent I knew it was only a matter of seconds before we were lip locked. As he leaned in, I closed my eyes to relish the anticipation of the moment. That's when the first egg hit.

Brogan Cavanaugh was leaning against a grecian goddess statue holding a basket of eggs that he was leisurely throwing at us.

"What are you doing?" I screamed.

"Making breakfast," he answered. "Things were looking so hot over there I thought I'd fry up a couple of eggs."

"Why, you son of a …" I started to say.

He dropped his basket and practically sprinted at me, pulling me into his arms before I could knee him in the groin, crippling his ability to father children. He kissed me like a sex-starved pirate in one of those trashy romances. It was so delicious my traitorous body practically melted as sheer longing consumed me. My limbs went limp like cooked noodles, and a need greater than I've ever experienced shot straight to some pretty interesting places.

Damn, I'm not all hot and bothered because of Roediger. Brogan Cavanaugh did this to me! The thought jolts me into consciousness and immediately sours my mood. I'm going to have to redouble my efforts to maintain distance from my childhood tormentor. He already has a history starring in my nightmares, I'm not about to let him invade my dreams.

Aunt Ruby wouldn't tell me why she needed my help last night at dinner, claiming I needed a good night sleep before we talked business. I confess to being more than a little curious. So far, the Willamette Valley Lodge is perfectly gorgeous with nary a decorating crisis in sight.

After getting dressed, I decide to do a little exploring on my own. Down in the great room, I discover a coffee and pastry bar for guests who don't want a full breakfast in the restaurant. There must be nearly a hundred people making use of it.

There are probably more than a hundred being served in the restaurant. If this is diminished business, I can't imagine what the place looks like when it's fully booked. The hostess seats me at a recently vacated table by the window with an extraordinary view of the valley and river below.

"Hi there, my name is Carly and I'll be your server this morning. Can I start you out with some coffee?"

I look up to see the waitress is a pretty woman about my age. "Black tea, please."

"Sure thing." Then she informs me, "Our special this morning is Marionberry crepes."

I hand her my menu. "That's what I'll have." I'm a firm believer in getting a restaurant's specials. It's been my experience they try harder with them than with the standard fare they serve day in and day out.

After she walks away, I scan the crowded room and conclude most of the diners are families, not just couples. There are a lot of kids with their parents and grandparents. How nice for them that they're sitting in a luxurious lodge being served rather than eating burned pancakes over an open fire.

The reason I went into interior decorating was my love for making things beautiful. I specialize in decorating hotels and resorts because I adore staying in them. I design rooms that I want to sleep in and spaces that make people feel special. There's nothing like a bit of luxury to do that.

When Carly comes back with my tea, I ask, "How long have you worked here?"

"A little over two years. I moved home to help my folks. I thought I'd only be here a short time while I looked for another job, but it turns out the hours and pay can't be beat."

"Are you always this busy?" I want to know.

"Our guests like to eat early so they can get out and start enjoying the amenities."

"I meant is the lodge always this full?" I clarify.

"We're in peak summer months right now, so we're probably near capacity." She looks like she's really thinking before saying, "There are a couple of slower weeks before the holidays kick off and another short lull right after them. Other than that, we're pretty packed."

My mom made it sound like business was lagging and that I was an integral part of helping her friend keep the doors open. That's obviously not true. Not only is the lodge beautifully decorated, but business is booming. Questions race through my head like a swarm of caffeinated bees.

From my vantage point, I watch as a group of young children climb onto a cluster of boulder-sized rocks near the river. They jump off with their arms stretched wide like they're trying to catch the wind and fly. A line of horses trots behind them carrying guests of varying ages. Then there are the paddle boarders gently floating on the river. It's an idyllic summer scene.

When my crepes arrive, I practically drool at the heavenly aroma. The first bite has me groaning out loud. Marionberries are a type of blackberry that were cultivated by Oregon State University in the nineteen forties and fifties. They're sweet, tart, and huge. I used to eat them by the bucketful when we camped near any bushes. I forgot about that until now and the memory softens my irritation a bit.

I usually do my best to show some restraint when dining out, knowing full well that restaurant portions are almost alway double what a meal should be, but this morning I practically lick my plate clean. I anticipate that irritation alone will help me burn the extra calories.

When I ask for the check, I discover Aunt Ruby is comping my meals, so I leave Carly a hefty tip before venturing outside to explore more of the Willamette Valley Lodge. I decide to make the most of my time here and so long as I can avoid Brogan that shouldn't be too hard to do.

Chapter Ten

The Mothers

"Are you ready to hear about my plan?" Ruby asks while lacing up her New Balance walking shoes.

Libby pulls her hair back into a ponytail and eagerly replies, "Lay it on me."

"You know those cabins where we used to house summer employees?" she asks with a devilish gleam radiating from her eyes.

"Yes ..."

"I want Addison to decorate them so we can rent them out." Ruby bends over to double knot her shoes, leaving Libby open mouthed wondering at her friend's sanity. Ruby continues, "I thought we'd walk up there and take a look."

"Oh, Rubes, I don't know. You know where Addie stands on camping. I'm not at all sure this is an area she'll be proficient in."

"That girl camped every year of her life until she was seventeen. She'll be great. Plus, the cabin where Brogan is staying is near the cabin I'm going to have Addie start on. I figure she and my son are bound to run into each other a lot when she's working up there."

Libby shakes her head uncertainly. "It's either going to work like gangbusters or it's going to fail so spectacularly our children will never speak to us again."

"That's a chance I'm willing to take, how about you?" But she doesn't wait for Libby to answer; she reaches out and grabs a hold of her friend's arm and pulls. "Come on, let's go exploring."

Brogan

After passing out like the dead last night, I wake at seven to the sound of chirping sparrows outside the bedroom window. I love the sound of surf, but there's something about birdsong that triggers the best rest. I rarely sleep this late at home when I get to bed by eleven.

Billy's dinner was outstanding as usual. He keeps it simple by frying the fish in vegetable shortening and only using salt and wild herbs to season it. Last night he sautéed a bunch of fresh dandelions greens to go with it.

The smell of coffee hits my nose and I realize my part-time roommate must have come in and made a pot. I head out to the makeshift kitchen where there's a refrigerator but no oven or microwave. Just a deep sink, a small wooden countertop, and a camping stove.

"Hey, Billy." He's pouring a cup of coffee into a tin mug.

"Morning," he says.

"Where'd you stay last night?" He doesn't usually volunteer much in the way of conversation unless prodded.

"I have a lean-to up by Jefferson Falls. It's nice and private. Not near any of those hiking paths you folks have up there."

"Just you and Bigfoot, huh?"

"He's better company than most." I'm not sure if Billy has ever met Bigfoot in person, but he claims to have had several sightings. Folks in this area are split on whether they think there really is a giant hairy creature living in Oregon. The closer you get to the mountains though, the more believers you find.

Billy sips from his coffee cup. "You want to go fishing later? I thought I'd try to get some trout." Most people fish at dawn, but Billy doesn't think that's sporting. He says the fish deserve to wake up and have a fighting chance.

"Sounds good. Let me check in with my mom first. I want to make sure she doesn't need me for anything." *After all, she is the reason I came home.*

"Ask her if she wants some for the restaurant. If I have a good haul, I'll drop some by."

"Will do. What are you up to this morning?"

"Looking for cougar activity. They've been spotted in the area. Thought I'd track 'em and see if I could find their dens. Those mamas can be pretty vicious when they have babes to protect."

"You'll tell Dale up at the lodge if you find any, right?"

"Course."

"I'm gonna head up to the falls and take a quick splash before going to see my mom. I'll meet you back here at noon if I'm going to fish with you."

If you didn't know Billy Grimps personally, you might wonder about him. He has a mountain man kind of vibe, meaning he's not always clean and he definitely marches to his own tune. But he's honest folk and in my book that's all that really matters.

After throwing on some pants, I grab a goji bar out of my backpack and head out for a swim. Walking through these woods as a kid, I swear I caught glimpses of Native Americans in full costume. I even fancied I occasionally caught sight of a T-Rex looming over the trees.

Time doesn't seem to exist here and the longer you spend, the more the timeline blurs. I wouldn't be surprised if Billy still thinks he's my age.

A doe crosses the path in front of me, seemingly unconcerned that she's not alone; hawks soar in the sky above; and squirrels and other assorted woodland creatures busily go about their day. The closer I get to the falls, the more I'm convinced it's time for me to move home.

I don't see Billy's campsite up at Jefferson Falls, but if he says this is where he's staying, then this is where he's staying. Billy has become a creature of the forest, and as such he blends in, only showing his face when he wants to.

Jefferson Falls pours into Copper Creek, which is my favorite place to swim. The water is so clear you never lose sight of your feet. There are also plenty of large rocks situated like small islands in the water which are perfect for sitting on and contemplating the beauty around you. I like to come up here because it's not as populated as the bigger falls in the area.

After stripping out of my clothes I jump straight in, knowing full well the degree of chilliness to expect. It immediately loosens the cares from my body and carries them down stream. I can see why Billy chose this lifestyle. There are worse things than being alone in the woods, and not many that are better.

I lie on my back and stare up at the treetops framing the

ethereal blue sky and marshmallow puffs of clouds. With my ears underwater, I've missed hearing someone approach, but I feel eyes on me. I look up to see who has invaded my space, and a smile washes over my face when I catch a glimpse of the person enjoying the view.

There's not much I can do to hide my natural state, so I call out, "I see you've come to join me for a swim after all."

Chapter Eleven

The Mothers

"I just got off the phone with Bob," Libby tells her friend as they sit down in the restaurant for lunch. "They closed the deal early and he wants me to join him in Amsterdam for my birthday."

"NO!" Ruby yells so loudly that patrons at nearby tables turn to look at the source of the commotion. "Tell me you're not going."

"I'm going," Libby says with an economy of words a holy man who's taken a vow of silence would appreciate.

"Why? I thought we were a team here?"

"Ruby, once my daughter knows what you want decorated, she's liable to start walking to the airport. She's more likely to see the project through if I'm not here. If I'm gone, she'll be too embarrassed to walk out on you."

"I'll help you pack."

"I'll be back after Amsterdam. I'm not abandoning you for the entire time."

After unfolding the linen napkin and placing it on her lap Ruby adds, "No stopping off at home first. Come straight back here."

"Absolutely," Libby responds. "After all, by then Addie will know why she's here and she'll be in too deep to just walk away."

Addison

"Take your clothes off and jump in," he invites with a flirtatious intonation that causes me to stagger backwards.

The glorious bronzed god in front of me is none other than Brogan Cavanaugh. And he's naked. Ho-lee heck. I should dispel him of the notion that I'm here to join him, but darn if I can force a sound out of the constricting column of my throat.

"Come on, I won't bite."

My traitor of a brain says, "What if I want you to?" Thank goodness I don't say that out loud.

Brogan stands up in the water and walks toward me lithe as a jungle cat. I can either run, which is the logical thing to do, or I can stay put and see what happens. As much as I want to flee, my legs don't seem to get the message.

The closer he gets, the more my stomach feels like it's ground zero to an attack of warring butterfly armies. For some reason, I visualize them wearing little helmets and carrying spears.

Brogan finally seems to realize he's only wearing his birthday suit and turns around to grab his pants, "What a butt!" the devil on my shoulder exclaims. I wait for the angel on my other shoulder to talk some sense, but she doesn't. Instead, she agrees, "Yummy!"

"I'm surprised to see you out here," Brogan calls out. He has one pant leg on and the other still dangling in the air.

"Why wouldn't you expect to see me here?"

He pulls up his khakis and looks around. "I know how much you hated camping and thought maybe that extended to all of nature," he says teasingly.

"I go outside every day in New York," I tell him. I'm not about to let him get my goat.

"Yeah, but outside in New York City isn't really nature. Traffic backed up for miles, horns honking, bustling sidewalks, that's not the great outdoors."

"Have you heard of Central Park?" I ask doing nothing to hide the annoyance in my voice.

"Do you spend any time there?"

I like to walk from the zoo to the model boat pond on Fifth Avenue. Then I head up to Madison Avenue and pick up a currant scone at my favorite breakfast place before walking back across the park to my apartment. While I usually only do this once a week, I don't tell him that. "I'm there every day," I lie.

"You and thousands of other people," he replies while looking around to illustrate the pristine privacy of our current location. Just him and me. In the woods. Alone.

"Well, being that my job is in New York City, I suppose I'll just have to make do."

"My mom mentioned that you travel all over the world to design resorts and hotels. That doesn't sound like New York City to me. My agent and publisher live in Brooklyn, but I don't."

"Well, bully for you." This man is more annoying than an itch you can't reach in the middle of your back.

"I'm just saying, you should be able to do what you do and live anywhere."

"Then lucky for me I'm exactly where I want to be."

We're locked in a death stare that neither one of us seems to want to break. *People* magazine wrote an article on Brogan a few years ago that I read in the dentist's office—heaven knows I wouldn't have paid actual money to learn about his life otherwise. The article referred to him as a man of mystery. While happy to discuss his books and writing process, he does not talk about his personal life. When asked about his engagement to long-time girlfriend Emma Jackson, Brogan simply said that if and when a wedding occurred, he wouldn't be the one to share it with the press.

According to my mom, his fiancée is no longer around. I can absolutely see why she left. No one likes a bossy, know-it-all, naked god of a man. Whoops. Even when angry at him, my body seems to be having a hard time remembering not to be attracted to him.

"Can you please point me back in the direction of the lodge?" I finally ask, breaking the thick wall-like tension between us.

"You're here because you're lost?" He seems genuinely surprised.

"You didn't think I came looking for you, did you?"

"That's exactly what I thought," he says. Damn, now that he knows I need help, I've given him the upper hand. Note to self: Try not to make him any cockier by drooling.

"I'd be happy to take you back to the lodge, but you're going to have to wait until I'm done with my swim." He moves to take his pants off again.

My heart starts to hammer so intensely it feels like it's trying to make a break for it. "I'll find my own way," I say as I turn to walk away.

"Watch out for cougars," he warns.

I can't tell if he's being serious or if he just wants to scare me. "Cougars?"

"Yup, my friend Billy mentioned there have been some sightings. He's looking for dens so we can make sure to post signs warning guests. But if you feel comfortable enough on your own, I'll see you later." He and his perfect butt—yes, I'm staring—walk into the stream, dismissing me entirely. Which I'm glad about. I'm feeling a little unsteady on my legs and I don't need an audience if I go crashing to the ground.

Once I find a rock to sit on, I consider my options. Either I chance a cougar confrontation, or I sit here and watch my nemesis taunt me with his gorgeous body. There's only one thing to do, I turn my back on Brogan and wait for him to finish his swim.

Unfortunately, the devil on my shoulder starts to whisper the naughtiest things in my ear and I'm hard-pressed to tune her out.

Chapter Twelve

The Mothers

"I'm going to invite James to supper tonight. That way you'll have a chance to see him before you desert me."

Libby ignores the veiled accusation in Ruby's tone. "How nice. I look forward to catching up with him. How's his farm doing, anyway?"

"He just bought fifty acres adjacent to his property with his sights set on expanding. He's also got the best farm stand in the area."

"And he doesn't have a special lady in his life?" Libby asks.

"I'm pretty sure his horse, Dakota, is the only female at present. He's too busy, especially this time of year, to have any time for a social life."

Libby nods her head understandingly. She and Ruby both worked on a farm during the summer of their junior year in college. They'd moved off campus into an apartment and the only way their parents would let them do that was if they paid for half of their rent. "I assume you'll start looking for James's other half once you take care of Brogan."

"Start nothing. I know who she is, but this one is going to be a hard pill for my son to swallow."

"Why don't you just find him someone nice and sweet who he'll immediately be interested in?"

Ruby shakes her head. "My boys don't need nice and sweet. They need strong and opinionated. They need women who will challenge them."

"Well, you've got your wish with Addie. There's no one more pig-headed than my little girl."

"I'm counting on her being just like her mother." Ruby ducks just as the empty water bottle sails across the space her head just vacated.

Brogan

Addison Cooper is sitting on that rock so tall and straight she looks like she has a metal rod up her spine. God, she's fun to torment. I actually like New York City, a lot, and think Central Park is a great place. But Addie seems to think she knows who I am and I'm enjoying toying with her.

I don't hurry my swim for her benefit. I decide to have some fun with her and yell out, "Oh no, I'm stuck! Is that a …" Then I make a gurgling sound as I go under the water.

I wait for what feels like ages before quietly resurfacing to see if she's coming to my aid. She hasn't moved an inch. So, I yell, "Addison, help"—gurgle, splash, gurgle—as I go under water again. I count a full minute before coming up for air. She hasn't budged.

I stand up and holler, "Were you just going to let me drown out here?"

Without facing me, she answers, "That was the plan."

"What's your problem, woman?"

She spins around so fast she falls off her rock. It takes her a moment to jump to her feet before replying, "You're my problem! Have you forgotten the time you stood on James's shoulders underwater to lure me out claiming the creek was shallow? I was only seven and I could barely swim!"

"Yeah, but we saved you."

"I shouldn't have needed saving. That was a horrible trick and it took me a long time after that before I felt comfortable in the water again."

After a massive wave of guilt washes over me, I tell her, "I'm sorry. You're right, we did some pretty crappy things to you, but you have to admit you were the perfect target." *How could I not have realized we might have done some long-term damage?*

"The perfect target? Excuse me? I was a little girl. What about that read *target* to you?"

"Addison," I walk toward my pants that are sitting on the bank. "You were bossy, prissy, and intensely annoying with all of your complaining." Clearly I never wrote a bestseller on how to woo a woman. 'Cause let me say, this is probably not the way to go about it.

"You're saying it's all my fault that you and your rodent of a brother were so horrible to me?"

"No, I'm saying I'm sorry and doing a poor job of it. But please keep in mind I was ten, that's what ten year-old-boys do." I walk by her and add, "Come on, I'll take you back to the lodge."

"What about the times you were eleven, twelve, thirteen ..."

Before she can list every age I've ever been when I pranked her, I interrupt, "Boys do stupid things at all ages. We don't mature as quickly as girls." I lead the way toward the path.

She doesn't look very trusting when I glance over my shoulder to see if she's behind me, but she is following, albeit at a distance. We're walking for ten minutes in total silence before she says, "This doesn't look familiar."

"That's because I need to stop off at the fishing cabin first to get dressed."

"You said you were taking me back to the lodge," she accuses as though I was luring her to a den of iniquity with wicked intent. Which I'd be game for, but she's made it pretty clear she's not interested.

"My mom would pitch a fit if I went down there like this." I walk past her into my ramshackle lodgings. She doesn't follow.

It's been a long time since I've felt as drawn to a woman as I do to Addison Cooper. I'm guessing part of the appeal is her belligerent attitude and the challenge that presents, and part is probably due to the fact that she isn't falling at my feet. Emma always seemed happy to let me make the decisions, but of course that wasn't the model of a good relationship. There certainly wasn't a happy ending, for me anyway.

I decide to make Addison wait a bit longer and hop into the outdoor shower to rinse off. When I stroll by her wearing only a towel and flip flops, she demands to know, "Where are you going now?"

"I'm going to take a quick shower." I repeat my earlier offer, "You're more than welcome to go inside and heat up a cup of coffee while you wait."

"I'd rather lick the pavement in Time Square."

God, I'd love to take her in my arms and give that tart mouth of hers something else to do, other than hurl insults at me. Instead, I just shrug. "Watch out for cougars." Most cats go out of their way to avoid people, but Addie doesn't know that. Therein lies the fun.

"I don't think there are cougars in Oregon," she announces like she's an expert on the subject. "You're making that up to mess with me."

"Ask anyone," I say while walking away. I've lived in Oregon my whole life and have never known anyone who's lost more than a baby goat or chicken to wildcats, but there's always the potential for more, so even though Oregonians aren't usually afraid of them, we're still cautious.

I take my time showering. There's no water heater out here, so it's a cold shower, which is exactly what I need after spending time with the snippy Miss Cooper. That woman could make a man of the cloth rethink his vow of chastity.

I'm either going to have to convince her that I'm worth her time, or I'm going to have to infuriate her enough to appeal to her passionate nature. The fine line between love and hate often blurs during moments of passion. But even more than that, I'd love to make the woman genuinely laugh.

As I contemplate how best to deal with Addison, I also consider checking in with a local real estate agent and looking for my own place in Spartan. I could probably sell my beach house in a day, especially if I list it during the summer. The only thing that has kept me from moving home sooner is the lack of social life. Most people around these parts are married, and while

I'm in no hurry to join their ranks, I'd certainly like the option of dating.

Although at the moment, I'm not thinking about the single women of Spartan. I've got Addie Cooper on the brain in the worst way.

Chapter Thirteen

The Mothers

"What do you say we start going on our annual camping trips again?" Libby asks as she and Ruby walk the path leading back to the lodge. "Our last one had to be nearly five years ago."

"I'd feel like a third wheel, with you and Bob."

"Then we won't take Bob. We'll have a Wild Women Nature Week. What do you think?" Libby stops walking so she can focus on breathing in the fresh scent of the forest.

"Just say the word and I'll be ready."

"Let's do it when I come back from Amsterdam." Libby turns around and leans into a tree while staring up at the tops of the trees. "By that time, Addie will either have gone home never to speak to me again, or she'll be happily diverted decorating cabins in the woods. I'll be as free as that eagle." She points upward for her friend to see the majestic bird.

"Hopefully, she and Brogan will be well on their way to realizing how right they are for each other," Ruby declares.

"From your mouth to God's ear, my friend."

Addison

My decorator brain kicks into overdrive once I step foot into the Cavanaughs' fishing cabin. While it barely feels habitable, I immediately start to visualize its potential. The river rock on the fireplace needs a good cleaning, but if you added a mantel and a rustic nature painting above it, it could be beautiful.

A couple of cane-seated Kennedy rockers would provide the perfect spot to sit and enjoy the fire. The living area is tiny, but an overstuffed loveseat and reading chair would make it very inviting.

The corner of the cabin where the kitchen is located needs to be completely gutted. As it stands, it's nothing more than a glorified campsite. I peek in the bedroom hoping not to get caught by the current resident. It's not horrible. Stark and simplistic, yes, but not without hope.

Brogan is taking forever. I found out earlier that I have no cell phone reception in the woods so I can't check my messages while waiting for him. I hope there's a book or magazine to flip through while his royal highness finishes up.

Rounding the corner to the living area, I run smack into an old man carrying a bucket. "Howdy," he says.

"Ha ... hello," I stutter after the initial shock of him passes. My gaze shifts around the room looking for some kind of weapon should I need one.

"Brogan around?" he asks.

"He's in the shower. Sorry, who are you?"

He sticks his free hand out and offers, "Billy Grimps."

I take his appendage briefly wondering at its cleanliness. This man looks like he might possess a soap allergy although no offensive odor has made its way to my nose yet. "Addison Cooper."

He nods his head once. "Tell Brogan fishing is off for this afternoon. I found two cougar dens and want to get some signs up warning folks to steer clear of them."

Darn it, cougars really do exist here. I'm definitely not going to be wandering around on my own. "I would think people should avoid the trails entirely, don't you?"

"Nah. Cougars aren't interested in folks. But if you get too close to their young, they'll make an exception."

"What do I do if I run across one, lay down and play dead?" I think I saw that on a *National Geographic* special when I was a kid. Either that or it's the only thing I can imagine doing if confronted by a wild animal.

"Not unless you want to be dinner. Just stare 'em straight in the eye and stand as tall as you can. Then lift your arms up and make a lot of noise. Most of 'em will run away if you do that."

"What do the others do, the ones that don't run away?" I ask in alarm.

"They'll attack, but that don't happen often."

Say what you want about New York City, but there's a zero percent chance of a cougar attack in the streets or in Central Park, for that matter. "Do you live around here?" I ask Billy.

"I've got a campsite set up by Jefferson Falls."

So, what, he's a homeless man patrolling the grounds for wildlife? I start to walk toward the door, hoping he'll take the hint and leave. He doesn't. Instead, he heads into the kitchen and bangs around for a bit. When he finally comes out, he hands me a tin mug. "Nothing like a cup of tea to soothe your emotions."

I take the cup, oddly touched by the gesture. I must look as anxious as I feel. Of course, he could have made me a steaming cup of hemlock for all I know. I can see the headlines now, "Woman Disappears in Oregon Wilderness, Local Homeless Man Suspected."

"It's wild raspberry," Billy says. "I picked the leaves myself."

I lift the cup to my nose, and it does smell like raspberries. "Thank you," I finally offer. "I do love a cup of hot tea."

A quick smile crosses his lips as he moves toward the door. Before he gets there, it slams open and another man walks in. Dear God, the potential headlines are feeling more real by the second. The man who joins us is young and tall and as soon as he gets far enough inside that he's no longer backlit by the sunshine, I see that he looks a lot like Brogan.

I immediately surmise the newcomer is James Cavanaugh. I'm so relieved, I nearly sprint into his arms to hug him. Luckily, I compose myself before that happens.

James smiles at me. "Addison Cooper?"

My brief nod is all he needs to stride toward me and wrap his arms around me. Once he's accomplished his goal, he steps back. "I wouldn't have known it was you if my mom hadn't mentioned you were in town. You look great!"

Does he mean he wouldn't have known it was me because he hasn't seen me in so long, or he wouldn't have known it was me because I look great? While I try to figure out whether to be offended, he asks, "Where's my brother?"

"In the shower," Billy answers before I can.

James turns his attention to the older man. "Hey, Bill, how's it shakin'?"

In lieu of a verbal response, Billy shoots James a double thumbs up.

"You want some work out at the farm?" James asks.

"What do you need done?" Billy wants to know. "I'm not gonna weed or nothin'."

"I was thinking you could come out and supervise the kids I hired to pick berries. I'd pay you in cash and all the berries you can eat."

"What kind of berries?" *You'd think money would be enough of a motivator for a person who doesn't have a home.*

"This time of year, it's mostly blueberries and blackberries," James tells him.

"Yeah, okay," Billy says. "But I have to be finished at two. I've got a lot of stuff to do up here." *What, rearrange his rock collection?* For the life of me I can't figure out the relationship between Billy and the Cavanaugh family.

At that moment, Brogan strolls through the front door with a towel slung low on his hips. Beads of water glisten on his sun-kissed body and I have the strangest desire to lick the droplets off of him like a parched desert dweller. *Where did that come from?*

He sees his brother and Billy before turning to me, "Entertaining?"

"Obviously," I reply drolly.

James looks Brogan up and down before demanding, "You want to tell me what you're doing up here with little Addie Cooper dressed like that?" His tone suggests something of a lascivious nature has either occurred or is scheduled to.

I decide to field the question. "I got lost and Brogan is going to show me the way back to the lodge."

"She caught me skinny dipping up at Jefferson Falls," Brogan unnecessarily adds while giving me a slow wink. If I were closer I'd poke him in the eye.

James turns to me. "You want me to show you the way back?"

"I'm taking her," Brogan says.

What I wouldn't give at this moment for a map and ignorance of the local cougar population. I decide to leave the brothers to fight over me and walk out the front door. Within moments, Billy joins me. "Come on," he says. "I'll show you where the lodge is."

I'm not sure why I suddenly feel comfortable with him, but I do. If nothing else, his company is far preferable to the tormentors of my youth.

"Thanks, Billy," I say to his back. The guy might be nearly seventy, but he moves like he's twenty. He's probably twenty yards ahead of me before I catch up to him. Brogan and James haven't followed us out of the cabin which makes me wonder if they even know we're gone.

Chapter Fourteen

The Mothers

> *Ruby: You ready to head downstairs? I told Addie we'd meet her in the lobby at eleven.*
> *Libby: You go on. I have a couple of calls to make. I'll text you to find out where you are when I'm done.*
> *Ruby: You're afraid of her, aren't you?*
> *Libby: I just think you'll have more luck if you broach the subject by yourself. Once she's committed to you, she won't back out.* 🤞 😊
> *Ruby: If you say so.*

Brogan

"Where did she go?" I ask my brother after getting dressed.

"She must have left with Billy." He opens the front door. "I thought she was waiting out front, but they're both gone."

"She's something else, huh?"

"What's she doing here anyway?"

"She said something about helping Mom with a decorating emergency."

"What decorating emergency?" James wants to know.

"You got me. The whole lodge was just redone two years ago. Why are you here?" I ask him, changing the subject. "I thought you'd be up to your eyeballs with harvesting."

James nods his head. "I am, but my delivery guy got held up at the dentist's office, so I'm making the morning run. I brought up the restaurant's order and then decided to come up and welcome you home."

"I haven't spent much time with Mom, but I haven't noticed anything off about her yet."

"I haven't seen her in a week, but I'm telling you she's been acting strange."

"I wouldn't have come rushing home if I didn't agree with you," I tell him. "She's been downright ambivalent toward me when I call. She didn't even invite me to eat with her and the Coopers last night."

"I think Aunt Libby came out because she sensed the same thing we have," he tells me in a voice full of concern.

"Why bring Addison though?"

James shrugs. "Got me. But she sure does enhance the scenery, so I'm not complaining."

"I'm thinking about looking around for a house in Spartan," I say.

"Because you're worried about Mom?"

That's exactly why, but I don't want to worry him until I know what's up. "No, it just feels like it's time to come home."

"It'll be nice to have you around, bro. I've missed you."

"You mind dropping me at the lodge on your way out?"

"Not at all. I left my truck behind the restaurant. I borrowed a golf cart to come up."

We don't pass Addison and Billy on the way, so they either ran or they took an alternate route. There's a reason we tell guests to stay on the marked trails. The last time I took the back path I got a nasty case of poison oak.

We pull into the parking lot in time to see our mom tuck a slip of paper under James's windshield wiper. She doesn't look a day over fifty, though she's lost a lot of her inner light since Dad died. She looks shorter and thinner, more vulnerable. Worry rises within me, and I fancy I can almost feel my dad standing next to me. I silently make him a promise that I'll look after her in his stead.

"Heya, Mom, what's up?" James asks her.

"I was just leaving you a note asking you to supper tonight. Does seven at the River's Edge work for you?"

"I should be able to make it by then. Will Addie and Aunt Libby be there?" He sounds super eager, and I'm guessing Aunt Libby isn't the draw.

"Of course," she answers with a bright smile.

"I assume you want me there as well," I interject hastily. She's acting like I'm not even here.

"You can come if you want," she replies. Wait a second, is she trying to set James up with Addison Cooper? Yeah, no. That's not going to work for me.

"Of course, I'll be there," I tell her quickly. Even though I'm not in the market for a relationship, I feel pretty strongly that I don't want my brother doing any romancing in my stead.

Addie and Billy walk up the gravel path next to the parking lot. They appear deep in conversation, and Addie even lets out a delighted sounding laugh.

"How did you get on this trail from the cabin?" I call out, confused at seeing them there.

"I cut a connecting path back up by the kissing tree. Figured folks might like more options."

"That's nice of you, Billy. I'll make sure to add it to the trail map," my mom says.

"Yes, ma'am." He shyly lowers his eyes.

"Do you need anything, Billy?" she asks. "The kitchen says you haven't been down for food in ages."

"It's summertime, I got plenty to eat off the land. Might come looking once the weather turns though."

"Good," my mom tells him.

Addison smiles kindly at Billy, "Thank you for showing me the way back to the lodge." He bows to her slightly before turning around and heading back into the woods.

Ignoring me and James, Addie tells Mom, "I hope I'm not late for our meeting."

"Not at all, dear. I was just on my way to the great room." She reaches out to take Addie's arm before strolling away from us.

I'm starting to take offense at the way my mom is dismissing me. First, she says I can't stay in the family quarters with her, then she neglects to invite me to dinner both last night and tonight, and now she walks away from me like I'm not even here.

"I really am worried about Mom," I tell my brother.

He releases a loud snort. "Why, because she's not acting like your being here is akin to the Second Coming?" He makes me sound like a real ass when he puts it like that. But, the truth is, that's exactly why I'm concerned. Ruby Cavanaugh loves both of her sons equally, but ever since I moved out of Spartan she's made a point of fawning over me when I'm home. It feels like that ship has sailed.

"I'll see you tonight, James," I tell my brother before hurrying to follow behind my mom and Addison. I don't care if I'm not invited to their little meeting, I'm going to join them and find out once and for all why Addie is in Oregon.

Chapter Fifteen

The Mothers

Ruby: I'm about to tell Addie why she's here. She's just washing up after hiking in the woods.
Libby: 😳 My daughter doesn't hike.
Ruby: She did this morning. Whoops, Brogan just came into the room. I've got him right where I want him, Libs. Now, to hook Addie. 🐗
Libby: Sending prayers from upstairs. 🙏 🙏 🙏 Let me know when you've got her, and I'll come down and join you.

Addison

Billy Grimps is a genuinely nice man. Apparently, he went fishing with us once when I was little. The only thing I remember about that day was that I caught a huge steelhead and needed help reeling it in. Billy was that help.

I'm curious to know more about him, like why does a homeless man live in the woods on the lodge property? Not to mention, why does he walk into the Cavanaughs' fishing cabin

83

like he owns it, and why is he welcome to get food from the restaurant whenever he wants?

Looking in the mirror, I notice a few small bits of nature caught in my hair and some dirt smudged across my cheek. Even so, I look rested and rejuvenated. The little furrow that started developing between my eyebrows seems to have relaxed.

I don't bother retouching my makeup. I just quickly wash the dirt off my face and pick the twigs out of my hair before finger combing it back into a high ponytail. Then I head to the great room to find Aunt Libby.

I spot Brogan first. That man is like a fungus. He will not go away.

Aunt Libby is ignoring him and is texting someone on her phone. She looks up when I get to her side. "Can I order you something to eat while we talk, dear?"

"No, thanks," I tell her. "I'm just curious to find out why I'm here."

"Me, too," Brogan mumbles. He's sitting on a chair next to the sofa his mom is perched on.

I ignore him and sit down next to Aunt Ruby. "The lodge not only seems full, but it's beautifully decorated. What could you possibly need my help with?"

She's quiet for a moment like she's trying to line up her thoughts. Either that or she's afraid to tell me why I'm really there. The latter option causes my stomach to churn.

"The lodge *is* in great shape. It's just that more and more people have been calling, interested in something called *glamping*. Have you ever heard of it?" she asks.

"It's glamour camping," I tell her. Truthfully, it's the only kind of camping I could see myself getting behind.

She continues, "It seems to be all the rage among young professionals these days. There's a place up by Sisters that offers it and from what I've heard, they're booked nearly a year in advance."

"You want to offer glamping here at the Willamette Valley Lodge?" I ask. My chest suddenly feels as heavy as if an elephant plopped down on it.

"I do."

"Why? I mean, if you're already successful at what you do, why add more?"

"We have the space, we have all of the amenities, why not stay current and beef up our menu?" she replies. "Plus, it would allow us to employ more local people."

"My mom made it sound like you were in the midst of a real crisis. She said that you needed my help to complete a project by Christmas." *Where is Mom anyway?* She should be sitting right here where I can shoot her the hairy eyeball. I start to fantasize about getting on the next plane to Grand Cayman, right after giving Libby Cooper a piece of my mind.

"She did?" Aunt Ruby asks before announcing, "I mean, of course she did. It is somewhat of a crisis. I'm just not at liberty to say what that is yet."

Something is definitely up.

Brogan interrupts, "Where are you thinking about setting up a glamping site?"

"We have those old cabins up near the fishing cabin. I thought that would be the ideal place," she tells him.

He visibly jolts. "No one has stayed in those in years. At this point they're probably more shack than cabin."

"That's why I want to do something with them now. I thought Addie could check them out and get a feel for what we'd need to do to make them worthy of the glamping title."

She's got to be kidding! Before I can express my shock, Brogan lets out a great big boisterous that's-the-most-ridiculous-thing-I've-ever-heard-of laugh. He sounds borderline hysterical.

"What are you laughing at?" I demand.

"I just can't see you being interested in a project like this, that's all."

"I've decorated resorts that specialize in all kinds of different things."

"Don't be rude, Brogan," Aunt Ruby admonishes her son. "Addison is an accomplished young woman known the world over for her innovative designs."

"I'm sure," he says. "But she's known for fancy five-star designs, not something like this."

"Are you saying I can't do it?" More than anything, this gets my dander up. I am first and foremost a professional. "How about a little wager?" I ask him.

"I'm game if you are. I bet you can't spend a week up there without running home to New York."

I never said anything about staying up there. But instead of pointing that out, I knowingly and ill-advisedly declare, "I could do that in my sleep. In fact,"—and here's where I totally lose my mind—"I raise your week to a month. What do you think about that?" There go my hardwood floors. Although my company will love it when I tell them I have a new client.

"If you can do that, I'll name the leading lady in my next book after you."

"I just bet you would, too. You'd probably kill her off in some horribly grizzly way like you did with Rebecca Saint in *Dark Alley*." The smile that overtakes Brogan's face is so radiant it's glorious to behold. Dammit, I shouldn't have said that.

"You've read my books," he accuses.

"Someone left it on an airplane. I was bored to death and had nothing else to do."

He lists my options, "You could have slept or watched a movie or worked on your laptop …"

"I should have done all of those things," I tell him primly.

"Yet you had to finish the book to know what happened to Rebecca Saint," he gloats.

I choose to ignore him and get back to the real argument. "If I win, I don't want to be in your stupid book, I want you to hire me to decorate your house and give me carte blanche to do whatever I want to it. I get to pick out all the colors, all the furniture, everything. And you pay for it, no questions asked." Another client to justify my time here.

He looks rightly horrified. In my current mood I'd have everything painted hot pink and purple plaid before installing the thickest, most plush seventies throwback gold shag carpeting I could find. Then, I'd put clear plastic on all the furniture so he couldn't sit on anything without sticking to it. I'm thinking lava lamps for lighting. Hundreds of them.

"What do I get if I win?" he wants to know.

"Whatever you want," I tell him. I belatedly realize what a foolhardy thing that was to say. It's a good thing I have no intention of losing this bet, even though I've just committed my entire month off to it. Gah!

Aunt Ruby interjects, "You two are being ridiculous. This is only a job. Addie doesn't even have to take it if she doesn't want to."

I'm so annoyed at Brogan that I don't grab onto the lifeline she's offering. Instead, I declare, "Oh, I want it." I turn to her son and continue, "You'd better be prepared to spend a fortune; I'm going to make you rue the day you second-guessed me."

"I'll send housekeeping up to get one of the cabins ready for you," Aunt Ruby nervously offers. She rushes off, leaving me practically foaming at the mouth.

Brogan, on the other hand, appears borderline gleeful. "I hope those cougar dens aren't nearby."

My blood turns icy cold as a deep chill runs through me. I totally forgot about the cougars. "I'll be just fine," I bald-faced lie. Just me and wild cats locked away in a remote cabin with no cell phone reception. What could possibly go wrong?

Why, oh why, oh why did I let my anger at Brogan goad me into this insane wager?

Chapter Sixteen

The Mothers

"Oh. My. God. You should have seen them!" Ruby shouts out before setting one foot through her front door.

"Was there bloodshed?" Libby asks nervously.

"Brogan bet Addie she couldn't stay in one of those cabins for a week. She raised the bet to a month."

Making the sign of the cross, Libby replies, "She didn't even want to come here for ten days. And that's when she thought we were staying in the lodge."

"Don't you see how perfectly this is working out?" Ruby claps her hands together like she's just witnessed Queen perform live at the Royal Albert Hall.

"No, no, no, Rubes. Addie needs all the bells and whistles to fall in love. I'm talking champagne, dancing, and luxury."

"You and Bob fell in love while roughing it during a camping trip," Ruby reminds her friend.

"Addie and Brogan aren't me and Bob."

"Mother nature brings all kinds of people together, Lib. You've got to believe me. This is going to be epic."

Brogan

Addison has no idea what she's getting into. Nobody has stayed in those cabins for as long as I can remember. I wouldn't do it. In fact, the fishing cabin is downright indulgence compared to where she's going to be living.

I have no idea how my mom is going to get one of those places cleaned up in time for her to move out there by tonight. Five housekeepers working for the next five hours couldn't do it. I'm pretty confident I will have won this bet by tomorrow, and while that should make me happy, I find I'm looking forward to getting to know Addie in an environment devoid of modern-day distractions.

While my mom is busy getting Addison's accommodations ready, I decide to head down to the stable and see if there are any available horses. A hard ride across the valley sounds like the perfect way to spend my day.

I stop and tell Chris at the front desk what I'm up to in case my mom comes looking for me. She offers, "How about if I have the kitchen send a lunch down for you?"

"Thanks, Chris, that sounds great." Chris has been here since I was a kid. She's like one of the family. Her daughter Megan is one of the zip-line instructors and her husband Dale oversees landscape maintenance.

On the walk down to the stables I'm accosted by a slew of memories. My favorite was the time James and I took our horses out for a clandestine overnight excursion. We were grounded for two weeks when our folks found us.

They searched for hours before discovering us at Cheater's

Ridge—so named for the poker games various farmhands used to play up there in the early part of the last century. Legend has it, a newcomer was accused of cheating and stealing fifty bucks from the other players. When the old timers discovered he marked the cards, they picked him up and threw him off the ridge into the rocky gorge below.

James and I had become obsessed with old UFO movies when we were kids and decided the best way to contact aliens would be to camp on the highest point of our property. Even though we didn't meet any E.T.s that night, we still had a great time.

I walk into the twenty-horse stable—there were only ten when we were kids—and search out Jeet Fritz. He's been the stableman here for the last twenty years. When he sees me, Jeet punches me on the shoulder and says, "Brogan, my man, long time, no see. You here for a ride?"

"That would depend on whether you have a decent mount for me."

He grins and points to an old mare. "Daisy May is free."

"I could walk faster than Daisy May. Who else do you have?"

"We've got Thunder Foot, but it's been a while since you've been out. Not sure he's the best choice."

"Great, I can either drive Miss Daisy in the slow lane or risk life and limb on Thunder Foot. Let me just go over and talk to him. You know, see if we can come to terms before I commit."

Jeet chuckles. "Good luck, although the last couple of times I took him out, he seemed a little more sedate."

I'm not taking his word for it. I walk to the end of the stable to Thunder Foot's stall and find the black stallion busy eating oats out of his trough. It looks like one of the barn cats decided to use his feeder as the nest to house her latest litter. As a result, the horse has a bunch of tiny creatures batting at him while he eats. He doesn't seem to mind.

"Thunder," I greet him in the manner I plan to continue. Cautiously.

He doesn't even give me the courtesy of looking up from his food. I tell him, "I need a ride, but I don't want it to be my last in this life. You got that?"

He snorts like he's saying, "What a bozo."

I pick up an apple out of the barrel next to his stall and palm it. Slowly lifting it to his mouth, I offer, "I'll bring more of these, but you have to behave."

He releases a soft grunt that I choose to believe is acceptance of my terms. "Okay, Jeet," I call out. "I'll take him. Is there a specific time I need to have him back?"

"Nope. We don't let the guests take Thunder out. He was your dad's mount, so you can have him all day if you want." My dad could ride a comet across the sky if he had to. I've never known a better horseman than him.

Jeet puts a brown sack in the satchel of Thunder Foot's saddle and says, "Chris sent down lunch for you. Where are you heading?"

"I don't know yet. I just want to run," I tell him.

"Okay, but you know there are spots out there without cell phone reception. I want to make sure we know where to look for you if you don't come back."

"Thunder and I have an understanding. He gets all the apples he wants, and I come back in one piece."

Jeet shrugs. "That horse is a lot of things, but he's honest. If that's your deal, I'll plan on seeing you later."

I decide to head up to Cheater's Ridge and have my lunch looking down on the valley. The view is unparalleled and always brings me peace. My mount starts out by trying to buck me off. I figure he's just trying to get used to me. He's probably gotten out of the habit of carrying anyone on his back now that Dad is gone.

Three miles later, I'm hanging on for dear life as he jigs and jags in an attempt to get rid of me. I stop at Twitter Creek to let him get a drink, but when I reach into the satchel for his apple, he finally bucks me off. I lie on the ground winded while he ignores me and meanders off to refresh himself in the water.

The last time I rode Thunder Foot I was with Emma. He took an immediate dislike to her and spent the entire time trying to bite her. She never came out with me again. Looks like this stallion has a keener sense of people than I do. Emma turned out not to be the person she portrayed herself to be at all.

I remember what Cheryl said about seeing her down at the market and wonder what she's doing in Spartan. I sure as heck don't want to run into her, which shouldn't be too much of a problem with me staying in the fishing cabin. But the question still niggles, why is she here?

Thunder doesn't want to let me back on, so I grab his reins and we walk companionably the rest of the way to Cheater's Ridge. Sitting down on a big rock staring out at the magnificence below, I wonder if I could get zoning to build up here.

I spend the next hour contemplating what style of house I'd like, and which rooms would overlook which views. The only downside to my living up here is that I might turn into as big of a recluse as Billy Grimps. I have a feeling it would be worth the risk.

Chapter Seventeen

The Mothers

> *Libby: Addie's banging on the door like she's trying to break it down.* 😰😰😨
> *Ruby: Why don't you let her in?*
> *Libby: I'm scared.* 😱
> *Ruby: What happened to your spunk, girl? You're the same woman who made a citizen's arrest when you saw some creep harassing kids at the park. If I remember correctly, you tied him up with Addie's jump rope and sat on him until the police arrived.*
> *Libby: Yes, but I didn't lure him out to the woods under false pretenses.*
> *Ruby: Addie made her deal with Brogan all by herself. You weren't even there.*

Addison

"Open up!" I yell while taking my aggression out on Aunt Ruby's door. I'm not sure if my mom's even in there, but the act of hitting something is highly cathartic.

A good five minutes into my workout, my mom finally answers. She smiles like I just got there and haven't been knee deep in Big Bad Wolf mode. "Hi, honey. I hope I didn't keep you waiting."

"Why are we really here?" I demand, pushing my way past her.

"I told you, Ruby said something about updating the inn."

"She didn't seem to have any idea about needing the changes made by Christmas." Even though my mom's friend tried to play along, there was a solid flash of confusion when I mentioned the deadline.

My mom shrugs. "All I know is what she told me on the phone." She hurriedly changes the subject. "What are your plans for the day?" Before I can answer, she says, "I was thinking about walking down to the river and having a picnic."

"I'm going to stay in my room and turn on the air conditioner full blast before taking a hot bath." I'm guessing the cabin I'll be staying in won't have air conditioning or a bathtub and while I could probably sneak up to the lodge for a bath, I don't know how often I'll be able to.

I don't want Brogan crying foul and trying to collect on our bet. Why did I leave his prize up to him should I lose? He'd probably have me bungee jump off the falls right into a cougar den. The tiny hairs at the base of my neck stand on end at the thought. I'm never going to be able to leave the cabin. I'll be a prisoner there unless somebody else is with me.

"Let me know if you change your mind," my mom says.

"I'll be staying on after you leave," I blurt out.

"What are you talking about?" She doesn't sound as surprised as she could. I wonder if Aunt Ruby already spilled the beans.

"I accidentally bet Brogan I could stay in one of the cabins for a month."

"Addison Marie, are you crazy? Why would you do such a thing?" It might just be me, but she actually looks like she's trying to suppress a smile. I want to call her on it, but it disappears as quickly as it arrived so I can't be sure.

I finally tell her, "He just makes me so mad by acting like he's the only one who can rough it. I wanted to shut him up."

"But a whole month? What about your clients? What about your life in New York?"

My righteous anger turns into raw panic. "I don't know what I was thinking. What have I done? I have to reorganize so many things." My Pilates class for one. I have to cancel my hair appointment and text the building manager to keep watering my plants. I'll have to let the office know, but they'll be delighted because the more I work, the more money they make.

"Don't be silly. You should just back out."

Silly? That word makes me dig my heels in. "I'll figure it out." My voice quivers as tears spring to my eyes.

My mom immediately wraps her arms around me and comforts, "You'll show that overblown man-child who's boss. I believe in you, honey." I might be losing my mind because I swear she giggled in my ear at the end of her words of encouragement.

"Thanks, Mom. I'm going up to my room now. Text me where you'll be and maybe I'll join you later."

That's when a truly terrible thought hits me. Brogan has no cell reception at his fishing cabin. I can only assume I'll be in the same boat. And if there's no cell reception, I'm guessing the internet is out. And with no internet there will be no work, no design software, no way to look at samples, no Netflix. OMG, what in the hell am I going to do up there for a month?

I decide I'd better go online and do some cyber shopping and stock up on things that will keep me entertained. I'll have everything shipped to the inn and pick it up when it arrives. I should also download a bunch of books onto my Kindle. *How am I going to recharge my Kindle?* Mother of God, this is turning into some kind of *Survivor* episode, and I'm way more of an HGTV kind of girl.

I stop in the gift shop on the way to my room and grab a book and a couple of magazines to keep me entertained while I wait for my purchases to arrive. I also pick up an assortment of chocolate bars and some bug spray. From what I remember, the mosquitoes in Oregon are nowhere near as bad as they are in the East, but they're still around this time of year. As for the chocolate, well, that will be my comfort. I'll probably gain ten pounds while I'm here, but that'll be a small price to pay.

I make a mental tally of things I'll have to order and am shocked by how much I'll need. I pull my phone out and call Aunt Ruby. "Can I go up and see the cabin now so I can get an idea of what I need to buy?"

"I'll send up everything with the cleaning crew. Don't you worry about a thing."

She has no idea what my comfort items are, so I tell her, "I'd feel better seeing it sooner rather than later."

"I can't take you now, but Brogan might be able to."

"Why him?" I want to scream, but I manage to resist the

temptation. "Maybe you could just point it out to me on a map and I'll find it on my own."

"Didn't you get lost up there earlier today?" she wants to know.

"I know where I'm going now," I lie. "Billy showed me a few tricks to keep my bearings." I'll need to know how to get myself back and forth for the next month, so I might as well start learning now.

"All right. I'll mark the spot on a trail map and have it sent up to you. I'm sure the path to the cabins is overgrown so you'll need to be careful." As an afterthought, she adds, "You have hiking boots, don't you? And, er, you know what poison oak looks like, right?"

I put hiking boots on my list. Then, I think of the warning from childhood, "leaves of three, let them be." But the truth is, I don't think I've ever actually seen the stuff and I sure as heck don't want to start out this ridiculous bet itching from head to toe.

Damn, dammit. I concede, "Maybe you should have Brogan show me." I don't want that man to think I need him for anything, but I have to see where I'm staying. "Please tell him I'll meet him in the great room in ten minutes."

"I'll do that, dear. Make sure to wear socks when you're hiking up there. You'll want to protect your ankles until I can get the grounds people to clear the area."

I would give both of my baby toes to be home in my apartment, nice and safe in an urban jungle fifteen floors above street level. I'd order Thai food and a bottle of wine. I'd take a bubble bath and watch *Game of Thrones*.

Tears spring to my eye like I've been dropped off on another planet and will never see Earth again. I'm not sure I'm tough enough to see this bet through, but I'm sure as heck going to give it my best shot.

Chapter Eighteen

The Mothers

Ruby bursts through the front door to her quarters and throws her arms around her best friend's neck in a big hug. "Addie is going to check out the cabin!"

Stepping back, Libby asks, "Why is that so exciting?"

"Because I told her I couldn't show it to her right now and that if she wanted to see it, Brogan would have to take her." She pumps her fists in the air before shimmying around in a happy dance. "It's starting, Lib!"

"You showed me that cabin on our walk this morning, and I can assure you my daughter is going to freak out when she sees it."

"Like you did the first time you stayed in a cabin?" Ruby continues to dance around joyously.

"Do you remember the size of those bats?" Libby cringes in horror.

"I remember Bob taking you in his arms and protecting you. I also remember the two of you were inseparable after that trip."

"We were, weren't we?" she smiles dreamily before joining her friend in celebration. "It's on like Donkey Kong, Rubes!"

"I don't think people say that anymore, Lib. They're not cool enough."

Brogan

"Sure, Mom. I'll show Addie where her cabin is."

"No funny business, Brogan. Be nice to her."

I'm not sure what kind of funny business she's referring to, but I'm guessing Addie isn't the only one who remembers our somewhat sordid history. "I will be as sweet as a hot fudge sundae with a cotton candy chaser."

"Good boy. Addison will meet you in the great room in ten minutes," she says before hanging up.

While she might have been there in ten minutes, I end up being late. It takes me forty minutes to tie up a phone call with my agent. When I finally get there, Addie looks equal parts anxious and annoyed. I kind of feel sorry for her, but I also know this experience won't kill her. By facing her demons, she might even learn to love the great outdoors.

"Hi there," I say with what I'm hoping is a contrite look for my tardiness.

"Where have you been?" she demands. "I've been waiting for almost an hour."

Her annoyance pokes me the wrong way. "You know I don't work here, right? I didn't have to come at all."

"Then why did you?" she snaps.

"My mom asked me nicely. I find when people are nice to me, I want to be accommodating." I challenge her with a pointed look.

"Well, you're here now, so let's go."

"Did I hear the magic word?" Okay, so maybe I'm poking the bear, but come on, a little civility never hurt anyone.

Death stare. "Please," she mumbles so quietly I can barely hear it.

"What was that?"

"PLEASE!" she shouts so loudly that other people in the room turn and stare at us.

"I bet you were top of your class at charm school," I say under my breath. Louder, I add, "Let's go." I don't wait to see if she follows behind, I just take long strides toward the door.

Once we're outside, I ask, "Would you like to walk or take a golf cart?"

Her eyes shift longingly toward the golf carts. I know she'd prefer one of them, but she answers, "I have two feet, I can walk." Clearly Addie has never heard the saying, "Pride goeth before a fall." If she had, she sure as heck wouldn't have let her pride force her into a wager she has no chance of winning.

I decide to throw her a bone. "You've hiked a lot today and we still need to come back to the lodge for dinner. Let's take a cart."

Her body sags in relief like she's just gotten that stick removed from her backside. I get behind the steering wheel and watch as she perches next to me in such a way that she could jump out at a moment's notice.

"Relax," I tell her. "It's going to take at least fifteen minutes to get there."

"Fifteen minutes? How far is this place?"

"Not much farther than my cabin, but this is a golf cart, not a

Ferrari," I point out, earning another sour look from my passenger.

The ride is so silent it's almost like being alone. Addie has her phone out and appears to be trying to figure out at what point she'll lose her signal. As we pass the kissing tree, she asks, "Why can't I get cell service out here?"

"We're about ten miles from the nearest tower. Also, the heavy vegetation blocks whatever signal we might have been able to get."

"It doesn't feel safe to be out here without having access to a phone," she says, sounding vulnerable.

"You do realize that in the early years of camping with our parents, they didn't have cell phones. And when they finally got them, they never had service in remote areas."

"Yeah, yeah, yeah," she replies. "They didn't have any of that stuff on *Little House on the Prairie* either, but that's not the time we're living in."

"If it makes you feel any better, my cabin is fewer than five hundred yards from yours and I survive just fine without phone reception."

"Will you be able to hear me scream at that distance?" she asks nervously.

"Five hundred yards is just over a quarter of a mile, so yes. Just do it loudly." I can only imagine how often I'll be running up there because of a twig snap or a bird flying into a window.

I pull off the path at my place and announce, "We'll drive as far as we can, but at some point we may need to walk if the path narrows." She looks terrified. The only cabin I've been into in the last several years is the fishing cabin, so I have no idea how bad things have gotten back here.

Amazingly, I'm able to drive the whole way and wonder if Billy has been out here doing some clearing. The cabin Addie will be staying in doesn't look as decrepit as I thought it would. I get out of the cart first and head to the front door. When I notice she isn't with me, I call out, "You coming?"

Her face has taken on a gray tone. I'm guessing Addie Cooper will do just about anything to prove me wrong about her, so I add, "Do you want to concede defeat already?"

She hops out of the cart and stands so straight you'd think she was a puppet whose strings were pulling her off the ground. "I'm coming." Stomp, stomp, stomp until she's standing next to me. "Do you have the key?" she demands.

"These places don't have locks. They're out in the middle of nowhere."

"All the more reason to have a lock," she says with horror etched across her brow.

"Things out here can't open doors."

"What kind of things?" her voice trembles as she asks.

"Skunks, wild dogs, possums, bats…"

"Don't forget the cougars," she interrupts. Her whole body convulses as she says this.

"And black bears," I add.

"What do you mean, black bears? In all the times I've been to Oregon no one has ever mentioned cougars or black bears to me."

"You can't blame them," I tell her. "You were enough of a handful when you thought it was only the spiders and snakes you had to worry about."

"What snakes?"

"I see they didn't tell you about those either. Don't worry, the only dangerous ones in this part of the state are rattlesnakes, and I haven't seen one in years."

Addie sways on her feet, causing me to reach out for her. I grab her just as she keels over. I really do feel bad now. I was just trying to be upfront about what she might encounter up here, I wasn't trying to scare her. Well, I *was*, but I didn't know she'd faint.

I carry her over to the porch and gently lay her down. If this woman is afraid of the idea of wildlife, how in the world will she react if she actually runs into it?

Chapter Nineteen

The Mothers

"Remember how Tom used to tease Bob that growing up in New York City left him completely ignorant of the great outdoors?" Libby asks her friend while playing Chinese checkers on Ruby's deck overlooking the valley.

Ruby starts to laugh. "He told him that elephants ran wild in Arizona. Bob knew enough not to believe him, but Tom sold it so well that Bob called his mom to see if it was true."

"Helen was mortified!" Libby practically doubles over in merriment. "She threatened to pull Bob out of college and sue that fancy academy he attended for high school. I haven't thought about that in ages."

"I'm still not sure why the Coopers ever let him come to Oregon for college. You'd think they would have made him go to an Ivy League school."

Libby jumps three yellow pegs on the board, winning the game. "They took him to all the schools he wanted to see and then let him decide. Thank goodness OSU has such a great engineering program or our paths might have never crossed."

"Oregon has been good to you," Ruby tells her friend.

"It's been good to all of us. I can't imagine my life without you in it." Libby reaches her hand out to her friend.

Addison

I open my eyes to discover I'm lying across Brogan's lap. What the ... I smack at him and demand, "What am I doing here?"

"You fainted," he tells me.

"You big liar. I've never fainted in my life. You must have drugged me or hit me over the head or something." I touch the back of my head to see if it hurts. It doesn't.

"You're crazy." He laughs before asking, "Do you think you can stand without falling over?"

I push off him and force my legs to steady themselves. Then I look around and remember our conversation about rattlesnakes and bears. Dear sweet baby Jesus in a manger, I probably did pass out. "About those rattlesnakes," I ask, "what do I do if I spot one?"

"Avoid it."

"Of course, I'm going to avoid it. I mean, what do I do if I get bit?"

"That would be the time to yell," he tells me.

"Obviously, that would be the first thing I'd do. I was thinking more along the lines of how to treat it."

"Whatever you do, don't cut the wound and try to suck the poison out. That can actually cause it to spread faster if you don't know what you're doing. That's why I said to yell. You'll want someone to help you get to the lodge where we keep antivenom if it's needed."

This information does absolutely nothing to make me feel better. After all, why would the lodge keep antivenom on hand if snakes weren't an issue? "What about the bears?"

"You want to maintain eye contact with them. Lift your arms up and make as much noise as you can."

"That'll scare them off?"

"Most of the time." Every pore on my body opens and feels like it releases a gallon of water. I'm suddenly drenched in sweat when he adds, "Although sometimes they like to charge to see if you'll turn and run. Don't do that or they'll get you for sure."

He can't be serious.

"They'll stop several feet away when they see you're not scared. Then they usually leave," he concludes.

"You expect me to stand still while a black bear charges me? Shouldn't I climb a tree or something?" I'm ninety percent sure I can't climb a tree, but being potentially attacked by a bear seems like a good time to give it a go.

"Bears climb better and faster than any human can. Keep your feet on the ground and act tough."

I want to quit this stupid challenge right now. What was I thinking, taking this bet? Brogan seems to read my mind because he says, "Hey, if you're too scared, you can throw in the towel before you even start."

Great, now I can't quit. "If you can live out in the woods, then so can I." I turn to walk into the cabin without another word.

Holy Hello Kitty, this place is a dump. There are only a few chairs scattered about and a small wooden side that has toppled over, otherwise it appears totally empty. The dirt is an inch thick on nearly every surface and there are so many cobwebs it looks like someone was decorating for Halloween.

"The chinking looks like it's held up well," Brogan says while examining the walls.

"What's chinking?" Unless it's a magic genie that can snap its finger and turn this place into a suite at the Ritz Carlton, I don't really care, but on the off chance it is, I figure I should ask.

"It's the mud and clay that was packed between the logs of the cabin to make it weathertight."

Thrilling. I might as well be sleeping outside.

"You think you'd know that being an interior decorator," he adds.

"I don't decorate for the Flintstones," I tell him, not doing anything to conceal the annoyance in my tone.

"The Flintstones lived in a rock house. I'm pretty sure they didn't use chinking."

Why are we having this stupid conversation? I ignore Brogan and start to look around the place. The bedroom is smaller than my closet at home which is saying something as New York apartments aren't known for large closets, unless you have a trust fund and a penthouse. I don't have either. "Where's the bathroom?" I call out.

"Out back," comes the answer from the living room.

"Out back, where?" I've run out of cabin.

Brogan peaks his head around the corner. "Follow me."

I'd rather not, but what choice do I have? I'm going to have to use the toilet in the month I'm up here.

He leads me out the front door and around to the back of the cabin. My feet are planted firmly in denial. I don't know where

I think he's taking me, but when we arrive at a tiny grey wooden structure with a half-moon carved into the door, I realize the bitter truth of my circumstances. He expects me to use an outhouse. I stand as still as if I were playing that old childhood game statue maker.

"You want to check it out?" he asks.

I have no words.

He walks over and opens the door before saying, "Make sure the cleaning crew spends some time in here."

I can't even. Brogan tricked me into accepting a bet that will have me using an outhouse for an entire month. I'm about to call him out on it and use the information to break our bet, when he says, "This will actually be nicer than mine when it's cleaned up a bit."

"I didn't see an outhouse at your place," I accuse like he's making that up.

"Were you looking?" Before I can answer, he adds, "Did you see a toilet when you snooped around while I was in the shower?"

"How do you know I snooped around?" I demand with my hands on my hips.

I want to smack the smug look right off his face when he answers, "Please, there's no way you didn't snoop." What in the heck is that supposed to mean?

I choose to ignore him and ask, "Where were you taking a shower if not in a bathroom?" He did walk out the front door in his towel, but I assumed there was some kind of shower house nearby like they have in a lot of campgrounds.

"I have an outdoor shower," he says.

Alarm does not begin to describe the sharp jolt of dread that shoots through me. I cannot stand naked in the middle of the woods and clean myself.

I've seen outdoor showers. Heck, I've designed them, but they've always been used for the sole purpose of rinsing off sand from the beach. They aren't meant for real cleaning.

"You look like you're going to faint again," he says with a huge smile on his face.

"Hardly." I roll my eyes so hard I think I might have detached a retina or something. Full of false bravado, I announce, "I can shower in the great outdoors just as easily as you can."

"I'm sure you can. There's nothing like cold well water to wake you up in the morning." He adds, "You know there's no hot water up here, right?"

"Obviously," I scoff. *Why isn't there hot water up here?*

A flood of childhood memories come back to me like a tsunami wave. Memories that must have been blocked to protect my sanity. Son of a mother dog, I might just lose this bet after all.

Chapter Twenty

The Mothers

"I'm just going to run down to the gift shop for a minute," Libby announces after she and Ruby finish another game of checkers.

"I'm sure I've got whatever you need up here."

"I want to buy a couple postcards. I thought I'd start a memory book for Addie."

"You think it's likely she'll forget this trip?" Ruby asks, surprised.

"No. I just want her to remember how beautiful everything is here. You know, for when she goes home and tries to convince herself that Oregon is as bad as she remembers from childhood."

"I think we're going to have to trust that nature will do its thing and she'll be too full of love hormones to think differently," Ruby says.

"You might be right, but I'm still going to get some postcards."

"Ask Chris to give you a couple brochures while you're down there. They're full of pictures that are great for scrapbooking."

"Good thinking. I wanted to chat with Chris anyway."

Brogan

"Hey, Billy," I greet my sometimes roommate who's just shown up at Addie's cabin. "What are you doing here?"

"Your mom asked me to make sure there was a wide enough path for the cleaning crew to get a pick-up through."

"Are they on their way up?"

"They're just behind me." Billy turns to Addie and says, "This is a pretty nice place, huh?"

"You're joking," she replies under her breath. She must think better of it because louder, she adds, "I'm sure it'll be fine once it's cleaned up a bit."

"I'll check the outhouse for snake nests," Billy tells her matter-of-factly.

If I'd have caught Addie's reaction on video, I could have broken the internet with all the hits it would get on YouTube.

"What. Snake. Nests?" Each word is delivered so precisely she sounds like she's pronouncing them for the first time.

"Don't know if there are any, but it's always good to make sure," he tells her.

"Did you check my outhouse for nests?" I ask him curiously.

"Are you royalty?" he wants to know. "Check your own outhouse."

I can't help but laugh. "I've been using it for a couple days, and I haven't been bit yet, so I'm probably good." Addie leans against the cabin to hold herself up as she digests the news of possible snake nests.

A pickup truck pulls into the clearing carrying a rollaway bed from the hotel and a slew of other supplies. I tell Billy, "I'll be bringing Addison back up after supper tonight. Do you mind hanging out and making sure the place is ready?"

He nods his head once before turning toward Addie. "Don't you worry none. It'll look like new by the time you get back." She does not look convinced.

"Come on," I call out to her. "Let's get you to the lodge so you can pack up before dinner. Your month begins tonight."

"Four weeks from today," she says while thrusting her hand out to shake.

"Four weeks is only twenty-eight days," I inform her. "Being that it's not February, I'll settle for thirty days instead of pushing for thirty-one."

Addie glares at me like I just cooked her pet bunny. "Fine." It's all I can do to keep from laughing out loud, but I don't want to look like a sore winner, so I stifle it.

The drive back is made in total silence. I leave Addie to her thoughts as I sink into the serene sensation the woods always give me. Safety, security, and a sense of belonging to something bigger. I'm a firm believer God created the woods to remind man of the power of his goodness.

I'm so lost in my reverie that we're at the lodge before I know it. I pull up front to let Addie out, when a familiar blonde woman walks up to the driver's side of the golf cart. She stops right next to me and says, "Brogan, how are you?"

I want to ask her how she thinks I am, but I don't. Instead I merely reply, "Emma, what are you doing here?"

"I'm here to spend a few hours at the spa."

"Aren't there spas in Chicago?" I ask.

"I moved back to Oregon a couple of months ago," she says

as if she's surprised I don't already know this.

I begin to have second thoughts about building a house here. If Emma is in Spartan—and why is she here?—there's no way I won't run into her, even if it's only on the rare occasion. "What about your job?" I ask, hoping she's only here temporarily.

"I quit." Emma is a news anchor on television. It's part of the reason we broke up. She took a job in Chicago without consulting with me to see if I wanted to live there, and while that's a pretty sure indication of where I was on her list of priorities, it's also not the only reason we parted ways.

I have all kinds of questions, but there's no way I'm going to engage her in conversation long enough to ask.

Emma's eyes roam over to Addison as she asks, "Is this your girlfriend?" She says the word in such a way that you'd say cesspool or locust invasion.

"Family friend," I answer before Addison says something that makes me look like a total loser. Not that I should care, but everyone likes to look their best when their past comes back to haunt them.

There's no way Addie can miss the tension in the air. She merely smiles at Emma and says, "Addison Cooper." This is not followed by a tirade of how she thinks I'm the devil's own. Thank goodness.

"Emma Jackson," my ex says. "Do you live around here?"

Addie jolts in her seat. "Not even close. I live in New York City."

"Why are you here then?" Emma demands.

Something about her makes Addie bristle because she answers, "How is that any of your business?"

"I was just making small talk," Emma says with her famous fake anchorwoman smile plastered to her face.

"I'm staying out in the woods with Brogan," Addie surprisingly offers.

This has Emma raising her eyebrows clearly wanting to know more, but she doesn't ask.

Instead, she says, "That ought to be cozy."

Addie ignores her and turns to me. "I'm going to head up now."

"I'll see you at dinner," I tell her with a genuine smile on my face. I have no idea why she didn't throw me under the bus and tell Emma what a good for nothing pain in her butt I am. But she didn't, and I'm grateful to her for that.

After she goes, Emma says, "She's more than just a family friend, isn't she?"

"I believe Addie said it best when she said that isn't any of your business."

"Brogan," Emma takes a step closer like she's about to share classified information and doesn't want to be overheard. "I've missed you."

"Huh." I have no idea what I'm supposed to say to that. I finally settle on, "What about Jeremy?"

"Jeremy who?" she asks, playing dumb.

"Your boss in Chicago," I remind her.

If this were a movie, Emma would be up for an Academy Award. "I have no idea how he is. I assume he's alive and well in the Chicago suburbs with his family."

Apparently, Jeremy wasn't interested in leaving them for Emma after all.

I shake my head slowly. "I should probably tell you that it was nice to see you before I drive off, but the truth is, I'd be happy to never lay eyes on you again."

"Brogan," she says as she reaches out to touch my arm. "I'm back in Oregon for good. Surely we can find a way to be friends again." Friendship sounds like the last thing on her mind.

"I have all the friends I need, Emma," I tell her before stepping on the gas. Sadly, I merely creep away as the golf cart doesn't have that much get up and go, but no matter, it's nice to be the one to leave her behind for a change.

Chapter Twenty-One

The Mothers

"Are there any topics I should steer clear of at dinner?" Libby asks her friend while they finish getting ready for the upcoming family meal.

"Don't ask about Emma or organic farming practices."

"Um, okay. I can understand the Emma situation, but what's up with the farming thing?"

Ruby shakes her head before sighing. "I'll explain it in detail later. Right now, suffice it to say, I'm worried the woman I've picked out for my younger son might be too feisty for him."

"Curious. I look forward to hearing more."

Ruby visibly shudders. "James is particularly hard to find a match for. He might go down kicking and screaming, but I promise I'm going to get him settled if it's the last thing I do."

"I'm looking forward to seeing Addie and Brogan together again. Things didn't look so good yesterday when we arrived," Libby suggests.

"I'm glad things didn't go smoothly. That would have meant they're ambivalent toward each other."

"They certainly weren't that."

Addison

Coming to Brogan's defense is not something I set out to do, but that woman Emma positively made my skin crawl.

I'm a firm believer in always looking your best, but there was something about her that seemed over the top. I'm not sure if it was the fact that her hair didn't move in the breeze or that her tan was so fake her skin looked like processed cheese, but something really set me off.

As soon as I get back to my room, I flip open my laptop to start shopping for survival gear while I call Elle. She picks up after only half of a ring. "Addie! How's Oregon?"

"You would not believe the situation I've gotten myself into." I spend the next ten minutes filling her in.

"A month?" She rightly sounds appalled.

"I don't know what happened. One minute I was staying in the lap of luxury and the next I'm declaring that I can last a month in the woods. With no indoor toilet or shower."

"You could tell them you're going into town one day and drive to the airport instead," she suggests.

"I can't let Brogan Cavanaugh think he was right about me. I'd rather die first."

"You might," she suggests none too reassuringly.

"If he can do it, so can I."

"Addison, I'm the one you complained to every summer after coming back from vacationing with his family. I'm also the one who forged a note from your mother when our gym class was learning how to rock climb."

"I was afraid I'd get so scared up there I'd wee on the person under me," I remind her.

"The point is, the wilderness is not for you."

I hate that people know this about me. It makes me feel like such a wimp. "Maybe it's time for a change," I suggest.

"If you say so. Just keep your cell phone handy so you can call for help."

"About that," I say. "There's no cell reception where I'll be staying, so if you don't hear from me, don't worry."

"Oh, my god! What does your mom think of this?"

"She thinks it's as dumb as you do, but I've committed, so I'm going to see this through."

"You ought to be committed," she says before asking, "Do you want to hear about Grand Cayman?"

"Yes. No. Yes." I do but I don't want to know what I'm missing. I ultimately decided on, "Maybe."

"How married are you to the idea of you and Roediger Bainbridge becoming an item?" she asks.

"I wasn't looking at it in terms of marriage," I tell her. "I mean, I'd never see him. We live too far apart." Wait a sec, why is she asking me this? "Is there something you want to tell me?"

"He asked me out to dinner, and I didn't want to say yes until I checked with you."

My heart plummets to my ankles. I don't sound any too enthused when I say, "You should definitely go."

"Are you sure?" she asks before excitedly adding, "Because, Addie, I'm starting to feel like Julia Roberts in *Pretty Woman*. You know, minus the part about being a hooker."

No, I'm not sure and as my lifelong friend she should know better than to ask, but she *is* asking, so she must have really clicked with him. *Damn.* "Of course, I'm sure," I force myself to say. "Go, have fun. Don't worry about me." I'll just be getting eaten by cougars and bears in the woods …

"You're the best!" she exclaims before adding, "Hang on, someone's at the door." I can hear her in the background. "For me? They're lovely!" Then she giggles like a schoolgirl.

When she comes back on the line, I hurry to say, "Have fun tonight. I've got to go."

"Call me when you're in a place with cell service so I know you're still alive."

"Will do." I hang up before jealousy consumes me and I say something I'll regret. Elle is starring in my movie. *I* should be Julia Roberts. Instead I'm Kathy Bates in *Misery*.

I spend the rest of the afternoon buying an insane number of things I'll need to survive in the wild. Then I take an hour-long bath using the jets in the tub to beat away the bands of tension that have been building.

Everyone is already at dinner by the time I show up. I'm late because I packed and repacked my suitcase, double and triple checked all the lists of things I ordered, and possibly succumbed to the tiniest little crying jag.

I half expect Brogan to reprimand me for being late. Instead, he stands to pull out my chair and offers, "You look very nice tonight."

He's right about that. I'm wearing a simple but elegant black dress. I'm much more dressed up than most of the other diners, but nice clothes make me feel powerful, and right now I need all the strength I can get.

James picks up a bottle of cabernet and asks, "May I pour you a glass?"

"Yes, please," I tell him. I'd prefer my own bottle with a straw, but at this point I'll take whatever I can get.

"Are you all ready to go to the cabin tonight?" Aunt Ruby asks.

"I am." I look over at my mom and practically beg, "Why don't you come out and stay with me? We'd have so much fun!"

She nearly chokes on her wine. "That's okay, honey. I've reached the stage in my life where I've come to rely on indoor plumbing."

I want to fight back and remind her the only reason I'm even in Oregon is because of her and the least she could do is suffer alongside me, but I don't. Primarily because I don't want to look bad in front of Aunt Ruby, but also because it's my own fault I'm in the situation I'm in.

"I was hoping you might come out and see my farm some time while you're here," James says before dangling the mother of all carrots. "I have a toilet."

"I'll be there," I tell him. I'm as excited about farming as I am about camping, but at least I appreciate the need for farmers. They keep the country fed. Camping just confounds me.

Aunt Ruby announces, "You're welcome to use my bathroom any time you want. In fact, why don't you plan on showering there at the very least."

"I'm sure she will," Brogan says under his breath.

"Excuse me?" I demand. His tone is far too cocky for my taste.

"Let's be honest, Addie, I don't think you're going to make it a week in the woods, let alone a month and that was before you knew there wasn't a bathroom in your cabin."

How dare he doubt me? My body fills with anger and my head becomes so hot, steam is surely going to start pouring out of my ears. I smile at Aunt Ruby and reply, "Thank you for your lovely offer, but I won't be needing your shower. Apparently your son needs to be proven wrong yet again, and I happen to be in the mood to do that."

She smiles encouragingly. "My money is on you." Then she turns to Brogan and announces, "Five thousand dollars that Addie makes it the whole month without using any hotel amenities."

Wait a second, I didn't say anything about not using hotel amenities. I only declined the offer to use her bathroom. I was absolutely planning on using the shower in the workout facility and I was obviously going to eat the majority of my meals in the restaurant.

I'm about to tell her that when Brogan matches her grin and says, "You've got a deal, but I don't want your money. I want an acre of property overlooking Cheater's Ridge so I can build a house there."

"Done," she reaches over to shake his hand before I can set them straight.

What just happened here? This stupid wager between Brogan and me has taken on a life of its own. That's when James decides to enter the fray. "I've got five thousand on Addie, too."

"You don't have five thousand dollars to spare," Brogan tells him.

"That's true, but I sure could use your money." He nudges me like I'm his partner in crime and not just his new gravy train. So much for my inclination to like him more than his brother.

Dinner starts to feel like it's taking place in the twilight zone. I watch everyone enjoy their meal and animatedly carry on a conversation, but for the life of me I don't know what they're saying. The only sound I hear is the loud whooshing inside my head like rapidly rising flood waters. I click my heels under the table a la Dorothy from the *Wizard of Oz* hoping it will transport me back to my apartment in New York. It doesn't.

Chapter Twenty-Two

The Mothers

Ruby stands up from the dinner table and announces, "Will you all excuse me for a moment? I want to have a word with the chef." She hurries away from the table toward the kitchen where she pulls her phone out of her pocket and sends a text to Libby.

> *Ruby: This is just getting better and better!*
> *Libby: Are you kidding? Addie in the middle of the woods with no way to get clean? That is not a recipe for romance.* 😳
> *Ruby: There's always the falls. It could be like that scene from Dr. Quinn Medicine Woman.*
> *Remember when she and Sully bathed in the falls together?* 😍
> *Libby: I can't say that I do and I'm a little nervous that Dr. Quinn has anything to do with your inspiration for our kids.* 😳
> *Ruby: I know what I'm doing, Libs. Just hang with me, it's about to get exciting!*

Brogan

It's not like I set out to bait Addison, but let's face it, it's darn easy to get her goat. I pretty much figured she'd find a way to spend her entire day at the lodge and only sleep in the cabin. And even then, I didn't think she'd make it a full week. But now that she's promised to not to hide out at the lodge all day? I'm going to need to find an architect to start drawing up plans for my new place.

Before dessert is served, James announces, "I get up at four thirty during the summer months, so it's already past my bedtime." He stands up and makes his way around the table to say goodnight to the ladies. Then he winks at me. "Thanks for the down payment on my new hay baler."

"She hasn't won yet," I remind him.

"She's not a scared little girl anymore," my brother informs me. That knockout of a dress Addie's wearing makes it perfectly clear she's a full-fledged woman, but that doesn't mean she isn't scared. I know for a fact she's petrified.

My mom's been shooting me smug looks all night and she still doesn't appear to be that happy that I'm here. So once James leaves, I hoover down my blackberry cobbler and announce, "I think I'll say goodnight, too."

"What about me?" Addie wants to know.

"What about you?"

"Aren't you going to drive me to my cabin?"

"I wasn't planning on driving. I like walking through the woods at night." It makes me feel like I'm in the pages of a fairy tale from childhood.

"Brogan ..." my mom says in the same tone she used when she'd catch me storing frogs in the bathtub.

"You can walk with me," I tell Addison graciously.

"I can't carry my suitcase two miles into the woods wearing high heels."

"I thought it had wheels," I tease her.

"My son will be happy to drive you up to your cabin, Addison," my mom informs her.

"Thank you, Aunt Ruby." Addie looks pleadingly at her mom. "Are you sure you don't want to spend the first night with me?"

"Honey, there's only one twin bed up there," my mom tells her. "Let's chat in a day or two and you can tell me what you think you'll need for the full glamping experience. We'll start moving stuff up after that."

Addie's acting like she's about to walk off a cliff into a pool of boiling hot lava. In my opinion, staying in a cabin in the woods is one of the most enjoyable parts of life. It's a gift most people never get to enjoy.

"I'll pull the golf cart up front and meet you there in a couple of minutes," I tell her.

As I walk away, I hear her tell my mom, "I ordered some things through the mail that should start arriving soon. Would you mind letting me know when they get here?"

"Don't worry, dear. I'll send them straight up."

I can only imagine what Addison Cooper feels she needs to spend a month in the woods. UPS is going to need a semi-truck to get everything here. She'll have to have an addition built onto her cabin.

Walking through the restaurant, my eyes scan the faces of the other diners. It's full of happy families fulfilled and exhausted by the day's activities. As I near the hostess stand, I spot a lone person sitting by the window. I stop dead in my tracks. What is *she* still doing here?

Emma raises a glass of champagne like she's toasting me. I walk away without acknowledging her in any way. That woman has some nerve showing up here. I don't think for one minute it's pure coincidence that we've run into each other either. She's up to something.

I wait a solid thirty minutes before Addie finally shows up. "What took you so long?" I wonder.

"I was changing," she says. Her hair looks slightly damp as though she decided to take another shower. Addie is lucky she wasn't born a hundred years ago. She'd be the worst pioneer in the history of pioneers.

As we near the woods, the night sounds start to pick up. Hooting owls and wind rustling in the treetops, as well as some undefined crunching sounds at ground level. It could be anything from a raccoon to something much bigger. Addie jumps in her seat every time she hears it.

When I pull off the path by my cabin, she asks, "Why don't you leave a light on so it's easier to find at night?"

"I don't want to risk a fire while I'm gone," I answer simply.

"I don't think lights are a big fire hazard." Even though I can't see her face in the dark I'm one hundred percent sure she's rolling her eyes at me again.

"They are if they're made of fire," I tell her.

Five. Four. Three. Two. "Made of fire?" Her confusion is clear.

"Addison, there's no electricity in the cabins."

Silence.

"Addie?"

Nothing.

"You didn't think there was electricity, did you?"

"Of course, I did!" she finally yells. "I mean, you have a refrigerator. How does that run if not on electricity?"

"Propane." How did she think there was electricity up here when there's not even indoor plumbing?

"Just like the Amish," she mumbles under her breath dejectedly.

"I don't know much about the Amish, but if you say so."

"I watched a show on Netflix," she says almost conversationally.

When I pull up to her cabin, I take pity on her and ask, "Do you want me to go in with you?"

She doesn't even stop to consider her options. "Yes, please." She sounds sincere, and clearly scared to death because she used her manners without being reminded.

I pick up her suitcase out of the back. "Follow me." I forget to remind her about the step up onto the porch and she trips over it and falls into my back.

I wait until she's steady on her feet before opening the door. I don't know where housekeeping put the lanterns, so I turn on the flashlight app on my phone. I spot several kerosene lamps and methodically start lighting them. The main room takes on a romantic glow that I'm sure even Addie can't help but appreciate.

I turn to her and her eyes are so big they look like they're about to pop out of her head. "This place cleaned up pretty well, huh?"

She nods her head almost imperceptibly. "Do you want me to stay the night?" I ask knowing full well that's the only thing I can say that will force her to get her courage up.

"Don't be ridiculous," she replies without much heat.

"Okay, then, I'm off."

"Wait!" she grabs my arm before I'm out of reach.

I turn so she's nearly in my embrace. "Yes …"

"Nothing. I just … I mean … I … how do I turn the lights off?"

"There's a dial on them so you can either dim them or turn them off entirely. I'd leave at least one of them going though. You know in case you have to use the outhouse."

She groans pitiably before I wish her a nice evening and walk out the front door.

Chapter Twenty-Three

The Mothers

"I hope Addie's okay. She looked positively green when she left for the cabin," Libby says nervously while kicking off her shoes and getting comfortable on Ruby's sofa.

"Brogan may have bet against her, but I promise you he won't leave her up there if she's too afraid."

Libby scrunches up her face with uncertainty. "That daughter of mine is proving her common sense doesn't work in the presence of your son."

"More confirmation that they're perfect for each other," Ruby decides.

"I wish I shared your confidence. Brogan has been nothing but gentlemanly as far as I've seen, but he sure seems to enjoy baiting Addie."

"That's the best part! A couple who fights together gets the fun of making up."

"If they don't kill each other first …"

Addison

Holy mother of god. I don't know what to do first. I'd normally lock the door, but as there's no lock, I resort to pushing my suitcase in front of it. It won't be enough to keep anyone out, but it will give me notice in case someone tries to break in. Every B horror flick I saw as a kid rushes through my brain.

If this were such a movie, I'd be sitting on my couch screaming, "What kind of bubble brain are you? Don't go in there!" Yet here I am, letting myself be led to the slaughter.

I pick up a lantern and start to investigate my new lodgings. The cleaning crew really did do a great job. I don't see any cobwebs, so I conclude that means there are no spiders. What I don't know can't hurt me, right?

I spot a refrigerator in the kitchen area and open the door to find it thoughtfully stocked with everything I'll need for basic meal prep for several days. There's a bowl of fruit on the counter along with a bottle of wine that's thoughtfully been opened. Nice touch, although I would have preferred a bottle of sleeping pills. I mentally add that to my list.

Not one to fool around, I uncork the bottle of merlot and pour a plastic cupful to help take the edge off. By the time I down my second, I feel ready to continue the investigation of my new home. The bed is a rollaway from the lodge. From a glamping standpoint, that will have to be one of the first things changed. Every photo of glamour camping I've seen pop up on designer sites for resorts has a king-size bed.

Housekeeping did leave several pillows and an extra blanket, which is nice. There's a stack of plush towels, as well. Sitting on the edge of the bed, I finish my third glass of wine. If you count the glass I had at dinner, I've consumed nearly a bottle by myself, which I know because my head is spinning. I've never been a big drinker, but I'm pretty sure that's about to change.

Before going to sleep, I need to turn off some of the lanterns in the main room, so I don't burn myself down in the middle of the night. The cabin looks a great deal less welcoming in the dark shadows left behind.

If I were at home, I'd turn on the TV and lull myself to sleep with old episodes of *Love It or List It*, but that's not an option here.

Opening my suitcase, I grab a book that I picked up in the gift shop. Taking it back to my little bedroom, I crawl under the covers fully clothed. I toy with the idea of opening a window for the fresh air but ultimately decide it would be too much of a risk. There's no telling what might crawl inside while I slept.

The quiet is hard to adjust to. My nighttime lullaby in New York is the sound of sirens and horns in the streets below. When I'm in the hotels I'm decorating, the constant string of binging elevators as well as other guests roaming the halls soothes me. After several minutes of no new noises, I finally feel comfortable enough to open the cover of my book. *Mail Order Bride* is not my normal kind of reading material, but right now I don't need political intrigue or medical dramas. There's enough excitement on my plate without adding more.

I'm just getting to the point where Felicity Huffleman is about to board the train in Boston for the Oregon Territory when I realize I have to tinkle something fierce. Dammit. Drinking all that wine wasn't the best move.

Faced with walking outside to use the outhouse or being innovative and trying to find something in here, I hurry to the kitchen in hopes of locating a receptacle. Don't judge me, any sane person would do the same.

The only semi-appropriate thing I see is the bowl holding the fruit. I hurriedly dump the bananas and peaches on the countertop and drop squat right there on the kitchen floor. We won't discuss my aim. I'm definitely going to have to work on that this month.

I'm not sure what to do with a bowl of urine. If I throw it outside, I'm liable to be attacked by the wildlife, so I opt to go to bed and deal with it in the morning.

Unconsciousness is about to claim my brain when the sound of creaking boards jolts me awake like I just downed a Red Bull with a double espresso chaser. Holy crap. Something is out there trying to get in. I could shut the bedroom door and move the bed against it, but I fear the smart thing to do is to get up and figure out how to deter a wild animal from breaking in.

According to the advice I've been given, the best way to get rid of most beasts is to make an inhuman amount of noise to scare them away. Before I do that, I press my ear against the front door, listening for the sounds that woke me. There's some scratching and another creak of a board before the noise stops. I'm about to go back to my room hoping that whatever it was decided to leave. That's when I hear a sneeze. A very human-sounding sneeze.

"I have a gun and I'm not afraid to use it!" I yell.

"Girl, you better not have a gun or you're liable to shoot yourself."

"Billy, is that you?" I ask, opening the door a sliver.

He's lying on the porch with a thin blanket over him. "Yes, ma'am," he says.

"What are you doing out here? I thought you were up by the falls."

"I normally am, but you didn't look so good this afternoon. I decided to make sure you got through your first night okay."

I'm so touched by his thoughtfulness my throat constricts with emotion. "Thank you. I can't tell you how much I appreciate that."

He pulls his blanket up under his chin and orders, "Go on back to bed and quit threatening to shoot folks. It's not very neighborly."

"I'll do that, Billy. And thanks again."

He merely grunts in response.

If I told anyone back home that I'm sleeping in a cabin in the middle of the woods with a homeless man acting as my guard against all things that go bump in the night, they'd never believe me. I barely believe it, yet there's a bowl of pee on the kitchen floor to prove the nature of my current circumstances.

Knowing Billy is out front ready to warn me of danger makes me comfortable enough to risk opening the window a bit. I mean, seriously, if he can sleep out in the open, I should be able to handle a little fresh air.

I close my eyes and within minutes start a mental list of everything that needs to be done to turn this place into a Grade A glamping site. If I can accomplish everything in a week—which I know sounds insanely fast, but I'm highly motivated—I may be able to get through the rest of the bet in relative comfort.

Chapter Twenty-Four

The Mothers

"When are you going to tell Addie that you're leaving?" Ruby asks during morning coffee.

After swallowing the bite of chocolate croissant, Libby answers, "I'm not going to tell her."

"You can't just leave and not let her know."

"Really, why's that?"

"Because she'll flip her biscuit when she finds out," Ruby decides.

"So according to you, my options are to tell my daughter that I'm abandoning her and watch as she loses her ever-loving mind or sneak out of here with her none the wiser. Hmm ... whatever should I do?"

Ruby tips her head back and forth thoughtfully. "Point taken."

Brogan

I can't wait to find out how Addison did on her first night by herself in the woods. I'm not quite sure what to expect when I get up there, but I purposely don't take the golf cart in case she tries to make a run for it.

I pound on the door and wait for her to answer. Either she's not in there or she died of fright. My money is on the latter.

I wonder if I should go in and check on her and am considering doing so when I see a large buck standing in the clearing next to the outhouse. He's magnificent to behold and not the least bit afraid of me.

I walk over to him to see how close I can get before he meanders off. "Hey, buddy, are you looking for food for your family?" I ask. Yes, I'm one of those people who engages animals in conversation. I even answer for them sometimes using an array of cartoony-sounding voices.

He bends down and nibbles at the plant beneath his feet, which I take to mean that's exactly what he's doing. As much as I love the ocean, I really miss this close contact with wildlife.

I could probably get near enough to touch him, but I don't. Even though deer are generally placid, there are a number of reasons not to make friends with them, especially the bucks.

"You have yourself a nice day," I tell him.

I'm about to walk back to the cabin when I hear a frantic call. "Brogan, is that you?"

"Addison?"

"I'm in the outhouse." She sounds panicky.

"Why don't you come out of the outhouse?"

"I'm stuck."

"What do you mean you're stuck?" I have a vision of her having fallen through and for the life of me can't imagine how she could have done that.

"I can't get the door open," she says.

"Are you done in there?" I ask as I walk over.

"I've been done for at least an hour." She sounds irritated per usual.

"You've been in there for an hour?"

"Are you going to help me or not?"

Thank goodness I came over to check on her. I was tempted to give her another night, thinking that fear might help to soften her sharp edges.

"Move away from the door," I tell her.

"Where exactly do you want me to go?" she asks sarcastically. "I'm in an outhouse, not a mansion."

It's clear Addie is as sweet as ever. I reach out for the door handle and give it a hard pull. She's right, it's not opening. That's when I notice the hinge on top has lost a screw or two. The lack of support is causing the bottom of the door to dig into the dirt. Once I lift the handle, the entire door moves above ground level, and it opens easily. Any day is a good day when you don't have to knock over an outhouse.

Addison is standing there looking wild with relief. Instead of thanking me, she storms past with her arms out to the sides like she's relishing the open space. Then she turns around in a circle like a little kid pretending to be an airplane before dropping to the ground.

"Are you okay?"

"I'm claustrophobic," she whispers in response.

"Really? Why?" I ask, even though I know there's no rhyme or reason to why people fear things.

"It might have something to do with that time two horrible

boys closed me in the trunk of a car." She glares at me like her eyes are lasers and she's trying to dismember me with them.

I instantly flash back to the occasion she's talking about. James and I used to think the trunk of a car was the perfect place to hide when we played hide and seek around a campsite. Addison obviously saw one of us do it and thought she'd try it herself. I remember slamming the lid down on her.

"I'm really sorry about that, Addie, I was actually trying to be helpful. James would have looked in there otherwise," I say sincerely. "How was I supposed to know my dad took his car keys fishing with him?"

"I was in there for ages!" she screams. "I could have suffocated."

"I'm pretty sure you wouldn't have suffocated," I tell her. I researched that for a book once and learned that some people have survived as long as two weeks in the trunk of a car. Addie was in no jeopardy of dying after only three hours. Of course, no one needs to tell me this isn't the time to share that information with her.

"I was terrified." She sounds like she's reliving the experience in her mind.

"Again, I'm truly sorry. Hopefully by saving you today, I partially made up for it."

She appears to be carefully weighing her response. Instead of accepting my apology, she says, "I need you to show me how to make coffee."

"I'd be happy to, but you know it's not a particularly hard concept."

"It is when there's no coffee pot."

How can Addie not remember how our parents made coffee all those summers our families camped together? I lead the way into the cabin and nearly trip over her open suitcase. "What is your suitcase doing here?"

"Where do you think it should be?"

"In the bedroom maybe?"

She follows me in and pushes it off to the side. "I'll put it in the bedroom once I get a lock on the door."

"You thought putting your suitcase up against the door would keep someone out?" I ask incredulously. Addison Cooper does not particularly seem to be grounded in reality.

"It would have given me enough time to wake up and defend myself," she snaps.

"With what?" I seriously want to know. I mean, there are no weapons to speak of up here.

She walks into her bedroom and comes out with the fire poker and a kitchen knife. "With these."

"Have you ever stabbed anyone before?" I try to get a visual of Addie getting the jump on someone. She's certainly ornery enough, I'm just not sure she has the necessary agility.

"There's always a first time," she says in such a way that suggests she's thinking about making me the recipient of her first assault.

I walk into the kitchen corner and pull a pan out of the cabinet. After filling it with well-water from the sink, I put it on top of the camp stove. "I thought you preferred tea," I say while we wait for the water to boil.

"I do, but I didn't sleep well last night. Coffee will give me more of a kick."

"You know what would really give you a kick?" I don't wait for her to answer. "A swim up at the falls."

"Maybe you can show me how to get up there later," she suggests.

Could she really be game to swim in the great outdoors again? "It would be my pleasure," I tell her. And believe me, the thought of her in a teeny tiny bikini is quite a pleasant thought indeed.

Chapter Twenty-Five

The Mothers

Libby puts her phone down and announces, "The airline just called. They have a seat in first class for me if I leave today."

"You'd better take it. That's a pretty long flight," Ruby says.

"Remember that time we flew to Austria senior year in college?" Libby asks.

"Do I ever. My dad got us tickets for an early graduation gift but neglected to mention they were for middle seats on opposite ends of the plane. What a nightmare that was. I sat between two hefty businessmen who both felt entitled to all the armrests. I gave my dad an earful when I called home. Looking back, I sounded like an ungrateful brat."

"It was a great trip though. Who knew we were such great yodelers?" Libby jokes. "But seriously, I've reached the point where I can no longer do those overseas flights in coach. And as long as Tom keeps racking up those air miles, I might as well use them."

"We should take another trip like that now. What do you say to Venice or Rome?"

"We could send the kids there for their honeymoon and go with them!"

Addison

I have no intention of swimming in the falls with Brogan. Billy said his campsite was up there and I'd like to find out where. He was gone when I woke up this morning, so I didn't have a chance to thank him properly for keeping an eye out on things.

Brogan pours hot water into a tin mug before handing it to me.

"I thought you were making coffee."

He points to the bag floating in the water and says, "Housekeeping seems to have left you quite a supply of coffee bags."

While my coffee steeps, I ask, "What do you do up here to pass the time?"

"I hike, fish, lie in a hammock and read a book ..."

"You have a hammock?" I ask excitedly. Rocking in a gentle breeze in a hammock was one of the few things I enjoyed about camping as a kid. Hanging suspended in a cocoon between two trees was a heavenly break from the stress of spending time with the Cavanaugh brothers.

"You should put that on your list of supplies to turn this into a glamping site," Brogan suggests.

"I definitely will. But, I'm going to have to go up to the lodge to get access to the internet. I don't want you thinking I'm breaking the terms of our bet."

"You don't need to go into the lodge for internet coverage. You can get it as soon as you leave the woods."

"How am I supposed to work outside?" I demand.

"The same way you work inside," he tells me. "Sitting on your butt with a laptop."

"You expect me to sit out in the middle of nowhere to design a glamping site?"

"What better place? Plus, if you're up at the lodge you'd be enjoying amenities without trying."

"How do you figure? I'm hardly going to order a steak and a pedicure while I'm working." *Although, I could ...*

"There will be electricity and air conditioning," he says.

Somehow this bet has evolved from me sleeping in the cabin to becoming a wilderness warrior. "I can't see my computer screen in the sunlight," I inform him, confident that I've won the battle.

"Lucky for you there are covered picnic areas all over the place." He sips his coffee and smiles so brightly my heart skips a beat. Why did Brogan Cavanaugh have to grow into such a gorgeous hunk of a man? Thank heavens he's so irritating or I might actually get ideas about him.

I open the refrigerator and pull out a bowl of blueberries and a yogurt. There's no furniture in the living area yet so I sit down on the floor to eat.

"I'd love some breakfast, thanks for offering," Brogan says while pulling a basket of eggs out of the refrigerator.

"How was I supposed to know you didn't eat breakfast before coming up here?" I say petulantly.

"Good thing I didn't, or you'd still be stuck in the outhouse."

"Glamping sites need real bathrooms," I decide.

"If real bathrooms mattered to a person who wants to camp, they'd stay up at the lodge."

"I don't think you're the target audience for glamour camping." With a snort, I add, "I'm sure you'd be just as happy peeing in the woods and sleeping out under the stars." At least we had tents when we went on our absurd family camping excursions.

I'm being quite a trooper if you ask me, but I put my foot down on sleeping outside without a shelter over my head. That's never going to happen.

After breakfast we head out to find the falls. I don't remember Oregon being humid when I was a kid, but today is positively moist. As a result, so am I.

"Would you mind walking a little slower?" I yell at Brogan's back.

He reduces his speed slightly. "I'm anxious to get into the water. It's a bit steamy out here today." He points to my citron green sundress and says, "I hope you have on your swimming suit under that."

"I'm not going to swim," I tell him.

"Why in the world do you want to go up there if not to cool off?"

"I'm trying to get a feel for the whole area so I can create the best space I can," I tell him. "It's part of my process. I spend a couple days getting to know the region where my project is located before I start to design it."

He stops walking so he can examine me closely. "That's impressive," he finally says.

"Why?" I mean seriously, I'm just doing my job. "Do you think I just lounge around inside without taking into account where I am?"

"Pretty much."

I decide to ignore him and ask, "What about you? Where do you write?"

"In my office at home."

"Do you live around here?" I never thought about where Brogan lived before, but seeing him in this environment it's hard to visualize him anywhere else. He seems to fit.

"I live on the coast. But, now that my mom is going to hand over a chunk of land to me, I'll be building a house right here in Spartan."

"If you win the bet," I remind him.

"*When* I win the bet." There's a gleam in his eye that makes me want to punch him.

"You're a real butthead, you know that?"

He puts his hand up and shrugs innocently. "I like to think I'm a keen observer of life."

"I'm sure you'd like to think a lot of things, but I'm here to prove you wrong."

"Says the woman who got stuck in the outhouse," he laughs.

"That could have happened to anyone."

"Yet, it's never happened to me." Oh. My. God. He's lucky we're not standing near a precipice or he'd be wishing he could fly right now.

I ignore him and try to absorb my surroundings. The woods are very peaceful, dappled sunlight shines through the trees adding to the ethereal quality. It's probably a solid fifteen degrees cooler here than by the river, where there's no shade. It must be ninety degrees in the valley today. I'd look it up on my phone, but alas, that's not an option.

I'm so busy staring at the tops of the trees, I don't realize Brogan has stopped walking until I run into him. Before I can yell at him to move, he puts his hand to his mouth to shush me.

Then he points to an area about twenty feet in front of us.

A mother deer is standing there with two fawns grazing contentedly. It's the sweetest scene ever. I'm about to walk closer to them when Brogan grabs my arm to stop me. That's when we hear growling.

Chapter Twenty-Six

The Mothers

Ruby: Sorry I didn't text you back sooner. Where are you?
Libby: Sitting in the Sky Club enjoying crab cakes. I wanted to ask you about the cougar signs I saw when I left the lodge. Should I be worried?
Ruby: Addie will be fine. We just like to be extra vigilant to let guests know when there have been sightings.
Libby: I'll never forget the time we came upon that cougar family when we were camping. I've never been able to get that vision out of my head.
😳 🧳 🐆
Ruby: Mother Nature can be pretty cruel sometimes. But don't worry, Brogan will keep an eye on Addison. 😍 *Then with any luck we'll soon have a* 💍 *followed by a* 👶*.*

Brogan

Cougars generally hunt from the early evening to early morning hours. I'm surprised to come upon one at this time of day, but I suppose when faced with a prime opportunity, any wildcat would take advantage of an easy meal. And that's what baby deer are, an easy meal.

As I try to decide how best to intervene, Addie pushes past me, and runs straight into the opening. She claws at the air and yells, "Arrrrrrrrrrrrrrrrrrrrrrrrrrrrr!" She sounds like Captain Hook on crack.

What in the hell is she doing? I watch as she dances in a circle carrying on for all she's worth. The deer dash away into the woods, but even then, she doesn't stop.

I walk toward her and calmly ask, "What are you doing?"

She turns to me all wild-eyed. "I'm scaring the cougar away," she says breathlessly while hopping around like she's about to engage the beast in a Kung Fu challenge.

"Addison, you can stop now. I'm pretty sure the cougar followed the deer when you scared them away."

"What? You don't think he got them, do you?" She sounds worried.

"I don't know," I tell her honestly.

"We have to go after them and help!"

She turns to run into the woods, but I grab her arm before she gets away. "You can't run screaming through the woods all day to save the deer."

"I can't just let that beast get them!" she says feistily.

"It's part of the circle of life."

"This is no time to quote The *Lion King*, Brogan. We have to help."

"I was going to," I tell her. "I was trying to come up with a plan when you lost your mind and charged at them."

"What could you have done that I didn't?" she demands.

"I thought we might walk around them and scare the cougar out of the area so the deer could get away."

Tears fill her eyes and threaten to pour out as she realizes the error of her ways. "I was just trying to help. What if they got caught? It would be all my fault, wouldn't it?" *She's really upset with herself.*

I reach out to pull her into my arms. It's a sign of how freaked out she is that she actually lets me. "One of those babies would have been taken for sure if we didn't come upon them when we did."

She really lets loose now and starts to sob. "But they're so little. How can they defend themselves?"

"They're fast runners," I try to console. I don't mention that cougars easily run twice as fast as deer and often climb trees to get the drop on their prey.

"I shouldn't have done what I did," she says while I hold her in my arms. It's like cuddling a porcupine. I'm fully aware things could go wrong at any moment. But still, it's sweet while it lasts.

I gently push Addie back and look into her eyes. "You were very brave."

She gloms onto my praise like a lifeline. "I was, wasn't I?"

"I don't know anyone who would have done what you did," I tell her. The truth is, I don't know anyone that crazy, but I don't go there.

"Do you think it's safe to keep going to the falls?" she asks.

"I do. I think that cougar probably went off to tell all the other cougars not to mess with Addie Cooper."

A flicker of a smile crosses her face which makes her look like a little girl again. I wish I could go back in time and treat her better than I did. Unfortunately, I can't do that. The only thing I can do is try to get her to forget the past and learn to embrace the present.

Taking her hand, I say, "Come on, let's go." I pull her along next to me and she doesn't even try to get away. While hers is much smaller than mine, our hands feel like the perfect fit.

When we enter the clearing by the falls, I stop and take a moment to appreciate the scene before me. The sheer power of the water is something I could sit and contemplate for hours on end. You'd think that with so much of it moving so quickly it would eventually run out, but as far as I know, that's never happened.

"I want to stand underneath it and wash my hair," Addie says in wonder.

"It would knock you right over," I tell her, effectively breaking her trance.

She yanks her hand away from mine. "I didn't say I was going to do it. It just looks refreshing."

"Too bad you didn't bring your swimsuit," I tease while unbuttoning my shirt.

She looks at the water longingly and walks toward the same rock she sat on the last time she was here. The basin is particularly enticing on a hot day like today.

"You can always go in like that or you know, you could take

your clothes off." I add the last part just to get her dander up. God help me, I'm really starting to enjoy spending time with this spunky woman.

I decide to keep my shorts on. It was one thing when I didn't know I had company, but I don't think Addie would appreciate an encore of yesterday. I feel her angry eyes on me as I jump into the water. Her scrutiny is the only reason I don't yell when my body temperature plummets. As I lie on my back to let the current wash over me, I spot Addie walking closer to the falls to get a better look.

I decide to swim in the opposite direction and give her a chance to appreciate her surroundings in private. If you'd told me just a week ago that I'd be in Spartan with Addison Cooper I never would have believed you. Of course, I never would have thought I'd run into Emma again either. What are the chances of both of those things happening at the same time?

Thinking about my ex is not something I enjoy doing, but I can't seem to get her out of my brain now that I've seen her again. Emma moved to the Oregon coast when she got a job as a newscaster in Salem. Having grown up in a small town, she knew she wanted the perks that kind of life could offer while still living close enough to a bigger city to enjoy those benefits as well. She's the kind of person who wants it all. But even with the best of both worlds, she apparently wanted more. That included a promotion to a city with a larger viewing audience and an affair with a boss she undoubtedly thought would leave his family for her.

The breakup with Emma was a real blow to my self-esteem. No one likes to be the one left in a relationship, but it's much worse when you've already been replaced.

Emma had never been to Spartan before we started dating. She claimed she liked it well enough, but she also made it clear that it was way too bumpkin for her to consider ever living here. Why she's here now is anyone's guess. But I will not let her sour me on my hometown, especially being that I've decided to move back.

I don't know how long I swim around, but when I finally head back to the basin where I left Addie, she's nowhere to be found. Where could that woman have gone?

Chapter Twenty-Seven

The Mothers

Libby: I'm about to board the ✈️. Sending you lots of ♡ and ❄️.
Ruby: I'm going to go up and check on Addie later. I'll let you know how she is, but I suspect she's a 😺.
Libby: Smiling cat?
Ruby: Contended kitty. Work with me here.
Libby: How about 😁🏕️.
Ruby: Happy camper, good one! How did we ever live without emojis?
Libby: I have no idea.

Addison:

Holy crap, I charged a cougar in the woods. Who does that? I totally took leave of my senses when I saw those two sweet babies. I couldn't just stand there and watch them get eaten.

While nauseated by the thought of what could have happened, my confidence is buoyed by the fact that I confronted my fears.

I turn to discover Brogan swam off somewhere, so I decide to check out more of the area.

Unfortunately, I become so lost in my thoughts I venture farther than I'd intended and wind up somewhere in the woods where I can barely hear the falls.

The forest would be the perfect place to bury a body. Even though most nature fanatics probably aren't murderers, there must be more than a few among them. You can't watch the news without hearing of dead people popping up everywhere in the wilderness. The tiny hairs on my arms abruptly leap to attention.

I'm about to turn around and head back to the water when I stumble across something on the makeshift path I'm wandering down. It's a shoe. OMG, why is there a shoe out here? Maybe it fell off a body being dragged to its final resting place.

I wish I'd brought my phone. Not that I could call anyone, but I could show the picture to the police to see if the footwear was a match for any missing persons in the area. I want to go back to nice, safe New York City.

I hear a branch snap somewhere near me and I freeze. It could be that cougar again, or worse, the person who was dragging the body that lost the shoe. I start to back away from the sound carefully.

As I look around in a panic for the source of the noise, a flock of birds descends on the tree above me. I nearly jump out of my skin. Two squirrels round the same tree trunk in a game of chase and a chipmunk practically runs across my feet. While Snow White would view this all as an opportunity to bring her forest friends together to clean her house, I'm a nervous wreck.

Where is Brogan when you need him? I'm not sure what to

make of that man. Yes, he's gorgeous, but he's also the reason I'm staying in a cabin in the middle of nowhere. Okay, it's not exactly the middle of nowhere, but it might as well be for the lack of creature comforts. I relieved myself in the fruit bowl, for Pete's sake.

I try to find a loophole in my bet that will get me out of this place, but the only ones that come to mind that would allow me to keep my pride involve being in a full body cast or a coma. Hard pass.

I need to find something to do outside of my dismal little cabin. Now that the lodge is off limits, where can I go to feel like I'm still part of the modern world? I know, I'll drive into town. There were no stipulations barring me from that.

As soon as I get back to my cabin, I'll take the golf cart to the lodge and see if my mom wants to go with me. The trip to Grand Cayman was her gift so I don't have anything for her to open. Maybe I can find a nice charm bracelet with a beaver to represent her love of the beaver state. Sarcasm intended.

Wandering aimlessly through the woods, I wonder what Little Bear would do. I try to channel the hero from one of my favorite childhood programs and decide he would probably blow up a balloon, then wait while it defied the laws of physics and lifted him up into the air to give him a bird's eye view. Then he'd float over the falls and gently touch down to swim with mermaids. Damn Little Bear and his unrealistic adventures.

According to the trail map I picked up at the lodge, the falls are north of the cabins. According to Mr. Phelps from eighth grade science class, moss grows on the north side of trees. I inspect the trees and am not surprised to find that moss grows on every side of the tree in Oregon.

For future jaunts into the woods, which I hope there aren't any, I need to mark my path, so this doesn't happen to me again. I belatedly remember my dad doing that by breaking branches and using rocks.

I keep looking around for signs of danger, but so far so good. That is until I hear loud rustling in the near vicinity. It could be a bear fight or a deranged person dragging a body. What *is* that sound?

Crouching next to a tree, I consider burrowing under a pile of leaves to further conceal myself when I see the source of the commotion. Billy, wearing a pair of antiquated headphones, appears to be dancing or air fighting or succumbing to convulsions, I can't tell which.

I stand up and walk toward him slowly so as not to surprise him. But before I get to him, he turns around and waves. Then he takes his headphones off. "You lost?"

"Absolutely," I tell him.

"Where did you start?" he wants to know.

"The falls. Brogan took me up there so I could get a feel for the area. He's swimming."

"The falls are that way," he points in the opposite direction of where I was heading.

"Really? I figured I had to hike up because the water has to fall from somewhere, right?"

He nods his head. "Sound reasoning if the falls are the highest point in the area, but they're not. Come on," he says, motioning for me to follow him.

I ask, "Is this where your campsite is?"

"Nope," he says.

"Is it close by?"

"Nope."

"What are you doing up here then?" I ask, hoping for more than a one-word answer.

"Dancing," he tells me.

"Billy, why do you live in the woods?" I'm sure Oregon has homeless shelters. At the very least he could squat in one of the deserted cabins near where I'm staying.

Instead of answering my question, he asks, "Where are you from, Addison?"

"I live in New York City."

"What part?" he wants to know.

"You know New York?"

"I grew up there."

I'm so shocked you could knock me over with a feather. "Seriously? Where?"

"East Side," he answers. "How about you?"

"Upper West Side," I tell him. "Ninety-first and Amsterdam."

"The Mirabeau?" he wants to know.

"I live just down the street from there. You really do know New York."

"Yup."

"Why did you leave?" I'm curious how Billy came to be homeless in Oregon if he's from the East Coast.

He's quiet for a long time before he says, "I wasn't in a good place after the war."

"Vietnam?"

He nods his head. "I came home with a lot of demons. Then

my mom got sick and she told me some things that plain shook me up."

I want to know what, but I also suspect Billy is a super private person. I'm guessing that asking too many questions is probably a sure-fire way to get him to clam up. So instead I say, "Oregon is as different from New York City as you can get."

"I'd never been out this way before I moved here. Didn't quite know what to expect."

I have to know. "Why in the world would you move here without having visited first?"

"I didn't know I was moving here. I thought I was coming to meet someone."

"Billy, this is obviously none of my business, but may I ask who you came here to meet?"

"My father." He doesn't offer more so I let it go for now.

"And you decided to stay?"

"It was quiet. I liked that. I'd had enough noise between war and city living. I just wanted to hear quiet."

"We came here every summer when I was a kid," I tell him.

He nods his head. "It's not your kind of place though, huh?"

I shrug. "It might have been, but Brogan and James went out of their way to make sure I hated it."

"Those boys sure did like to get up to some mischief." He stops walking and turns to look at me. "You know you can get even for all their nonsense?"

"I'd like nothing better. But how can I do that?"

"Stick with me," he says.

For the first time since arriving, I start to feel some real excitement about being here.

Chapter Twenty-Eight

The Mothers

Ruby: I left a little something for you in your suitcase. 🎁
Libby: What?
Ruby: Go look.
Libby: I'm unwrapping it now ... Oh Rube, I love it! I forgot about this picture. 📷
Ruby: We had so much fun on that first camping trip we decided to do it every year. The older I get, the more I cherish those years.
Libby: I want to tell Addie to quit working so hard and to make time to enjoy her life. I loved camping so much because it forced me to live in the moment. I didn't have a laundry list of things to do when we were out in nature. I could just be. Addie doesn't realize what a gift that is, but I'm hoping she finds out. 🏕️

Brogan

Where the heck did Addison go? She wandered away from the falls and could be anywhere by now. Also, why would she go exploring after our near miss with a cougar?

I hurry to get out of the water and put my shirt on before heading toward the area where I last saw her. "Addison!" I call out. There's no answer, so I continue my search/shout pattern for a good thirty minutes.

I'm jogging by the time I pass my cabin on the way to hers. If she's not there, I'm going to head to the lodge and gather as many people as I can to help me search.

Addie is sitting on her porch drinking from a tin cup when I arrive. "Where did you go?" I ask by way of greeting.

"Where did *you* go?" she counters. "One minute you were swimming by the falls and the next, you were gone."

"I was giving you some space," I tell her. "I've been worried sick something happened to you."

"As you can see, I'm perfectly fine." She seems way too calm for having just walked through the woods alone, especially considering our earlier excitement.

"How did you get back here?"

"I sprouted wings and flew," she says. "How do you think I got back here?"

"I thought you were terrified to be out in the woods alone," I say.

"If I'm going to be here for a month, Brogan, I'm going to need to get over those fears."

The Addison I left at the falls was practically a basket case.

What happened between then and now to change her tune? "So, you just decided to wander back on your own?"

"I'm not the same little girl I once was."

I'm not sure what to do at this point. She's not inviting me in and nothing about her demeanor suggests I'm a welcome guest. I finally ask, "Do you want to come to my place for dinner tonight? I'm a fantastic cook."

"Thank you, no."

"Why not?"

She informs me, "If I'm going to turn this into a glamping site, I need to experience it for myself. That includes making my own meals." She's brushing me off.

"Did you fall and hit your head out there?" I'm only semi-joking. I don't remember Addie being the most graceful creature when it came to hiking.

She rolls her eyes. "I did not fall and hit my head."

Before I can find a chink in her armor, a golf cart pulls into the clearing. It's my mom.

When she's close enough, I call out, "Hey, Mom. What are you doing up here?"

"I'm here to have a meeting with my interior designer," she replies with a wave.

"Why don't we all go inside?" I suggest.

"We don't need you here, honey," my mom says.

"Why not?" I'm starting to feel very unwanted and I have to admit, I find that worrisome.

"Being that you're wagering against Addie, I think it's best if you scoot along."

She's seriously telling me to leave. "I was just checking to make sure Addie was okay. I saved her when she got stuck in the outhouse this morning. If I hadn't come over she'd still be there."

"Is this true, Addison?"

"It is. But now that I know what the problem was, I can get out by myself."

"You see?" my mom addresses me again. "Addie doesn't need you. Bye now."

I have no idea what's going on. None. Not only was my mom not excited about my coming to visit, she's been disregarding my presence since I got here. "Do you want to have supper tonight, Mom?" I know I sound pathetic, but somebody must want to eat with me.

"Maybe later in the week. I'll be pretty busy with Libby."

"Why didn't my mom come with you?" Addie asks.

"She's spending the day at the spa. She said to tell you not to worry about her. She'll catch up with you in a couple of days."

"I wanted to use our rental car," Addie says. "Can you tell her I'll be up later to get the keys?"

My mom is quick to answer, "You can use one of the Jeeps that belong to the lodge. That way if your mom wants to go out later, she can."

"Where are you planning on going?" I ask Addie.

"I told you, I like to spend time in the town where I'm decorating. I thought I'd head into Spartan and get a feel for it."

"I'd be happy to come along and give you a tour," I offer. How can she possibly resist chivalry like that?

"No thanks, I'm good."

After a bit of hemming and hawing, I finally decide, "I guess I'll take off then." I walk slowly to give them plenty of time to stop me.

When neither of them calls out, I look over my shoulder to see if they're still there, but they've already gone inside.

Maybe I should go back to the coast and return when my mom has time for me, but that would mean not being around Addie. And while Miss Cooper seems to have decided she doesn't want to see me, that oddly makes me more determined to hang around.

I don't care what she says, I'm going to keep checking to see if she needs anything and if the opportunity arises I'll come to her aid again. I'm going to break down those barriers she's building no matter what it takes.

Chapter Twenty-Nine

The Mothers

Ruby: Addie is settling in sooner than we'd hoped!
Libby: How do you mean 🤔
Ruby: I just left her, and she seems in really good spirits. She's even going to go into town to do some shopping today. 🛍️
Libby: Did she ask about me?
Ruby: Of course. I'll keep making excuses for as long as I can, but I'm eventually going to have to come clean.
Libby: Do what you can, my friend. In the meantime, I'm going to enjoy my time away with Bob. 👫
Ruby: I'm one hundred percent on board with that. Every moment you have together is a gift.

Addison

"So, how was your first night?" Aunt Ruby asks me after we walk into the cabin.

"It was pretty weird," I tell her honestly. "I was scared to death when I went to bed because of all the unfamiliar sounds, but it turns out some of them were Billy."

She raises her eyebrows, waiting for more of an explanation. "He thought I might be nervous, so he slept on the porch to make sure I was safe."

"He's a special man," she says with a smile.

"Have you known him long? I want to discover as much as I can about him. I can't imagine having given up a life in New York to be here."

"He's been around ever since I started visiting the lodge with Tom before we got married."

"Has he been homeless the whole time?" I want to know.

"Billy doesn't consider himself homeless," she answers.

"But he is, right?"

She shrugs. "Maybe by society's definition."

What other definition is there? "He works for you sometimes though, right?"

"Not in the traditional sense. Billy likes to barter. For instance, he'll bring fresh fish to the restaurant when he gets a big catch and in return we'll give him whatever he needs, sometimes it's coffee or bread and butter. Sometimes a blanket or soap."

"How does he clothe himself?"

"He must trade with someone else for that. Since Billy isn't much of a man about town, his needs are pretty modest."

Billy and I mostly spent our time talking about things I could do to get even with Brogan for the pranks he pulled on me when I was a kid. He was a fount of ideas and when he left, I felt like we'd become partners in crime.

"He told me he's been here for just over forty years. That's a long time to live in the woods," I say.

"He uses the fishing cabin when it gets really cold and we make sure to stock it with firewood and propane to keep him warm."

"So, he lives on your property and you're fine with that." It seems a weird situation at best.

"As far as I'm concerned, he came with the place. He was living here before Tom and I took over from his parents."

The more we talk about Billy Grimps, the more I want to know. "He seems like a nice man," I finally decide.

"He is. If you're ever in need of anything and Billy can get it for you, he will. Several years ago, he and I had a long talk while we were picking blueberries. He told me that he wanted to live in the kind of world where people worked together for the common good."

"Like a utopia," I say. "I'm not sure how realistic that is."

"Billy chooses to practice what he believes in. He says it's important to live by example."

"But don't most people just disregard him as a homeless man?"

Aunt Ruby seems to be really thinking about her response before she says, "Most people around this area know Billy's philosophy and even while they may not agree with it, they respect his right to live his own life. He doesn't need to have a house to be important to our community."

"After so many years of living in New York City, I guess I just assume the homeless are in the situation they are because of addiction or mental illness."

"Billy is the sanest person I know," she says. "I've only seen him drink the occasional beer. As far as drugs go, he once told me that he'd had too many friends go down that path and it held no interest for him."

I'm not sure what else to ask about Billy, so I change the subject and explain my initial ideas for the cottage. We discuss her budget before Aunt Ruby tells me to start putting my ideas into motion. Then she says, "Buy whatever we need up here while you're in town and I'll reimburse you. I'd love for this cabin to be a prototype before you leave."

Little does she know, I'm hoping it's done long before that so I can enjoy the comforts for myself.

She interrupts my thoughts. "Ask Chris at the front desk for the keys and she'll tell you where the Jeep is parked," she says.

"Aunt Ruby, about Brogan …" I start to say.

"What about him, dear?"

"Doesn't he have to go home to work or something?" The thought of him being up here the whole time I am is more than a little disconcerting. Also, if he leaves, I can go back to the lodge with him none the wiser.

"Brogan likes his solitude, so I can't imagine he'll be a bother. You let me know if he gets in your way though, and I'll tell him to keep his distance."

He's a bother all right, bothering me by being so darn attractive. When he pulled me into his arms after the close call with that cougar, I wanted to snuggle in and never leave. There's no way I should be having feelings like that for Brogan Cavanaugh, at least not before I get my revenge on him for past misdeeds.

While I like to think my attraction to him is nothing more than my need for physical contact, I worry that it could be something more. There's something compelling about him that draws me in like a moth to a flame.

I focus on Billy's ideas for retribution and realize my need to get even has to supersede any attraction I feel. Even if I did allow my baser nature to take over, nothing could come of it. Brogan lives in Oregon and I live in New York. As soon as I win this stupid bet, I'm going home and never coming back here.

Chapter Thirty

The Mothers

Libby: Do you want any tulip bulbs? I know they're your favorite.
Ruby: You're in the Netherlands and you're thinking about buying me flowers? Go play with your husband.
Libby: They've got burgundy Breeders and Duc van Tol.
Ruby: I want a dozen of each.
Libby: Flowers have always been your love language.
Ruby: You know me too well, my friend. I love you.
Libby: When it comes down to it, Rube, love and friendship make the world go round. As long as we're both alive, I'll always be there for you.

Brogan

I'm dying to drive into town to find out what Addie is up to today. But there's no way I can chance an accidental meeting.

She'd know I was stalking her. So, I decide to go over to James's farm.

I pass field after field of hay bales waiting to be picked up. This time of year always makes me think of Monet's *Haystacks*. There's something so poetic about the way the sun filters through the blue sky and frames a field of freshly cut hay.

If I were a painter, I'd sit in those fields from July through September. Life in its purest form is art, and there's nothing more fundamental than growing things that sustain life. I admire James's pursuits more than I can say.

The entrance to my brother's land is his farm stand, Poppa's. He named it for our grandfather. Our dad's dad was the man who fed our connection to the earth.

Camping with Poppa was a way different journey than camping with our parents. Our grandfather believed that nature gave you everything you needed to succeed. As such, we didn't pack anything more than we could carry.

He taught us how to harvest pine nuts for protein, and then turn the pine needles into a tea that was high in Vitamin C. We learned which mushrooms were safe to eat and which were poisonous, which plants had healing properties, and which to avoid. Our grandfather was a treasure trove of information.

James is nowhere in sight when I walk into Poppa's. The cash register is being manned by the high school students that my brother employs every summer.

I spot Jeffrey Wilkens, who is the son of my high school friends Cheryl and Damian. "Hey, Jeff," I call out.

"Mr. Cavanaugh, how are you?" he asks. Jeffrey is an all-American looking kid: tall, strong, and always sporting a big smile. He's got enough of Cheryl's dark skin that he's not quite a dead ringer for his dad, but there's no wondering at his parentage.

"I'm doing well," I reply. "Do you have any idea where my kid brother is?"

"Probably in the peach orchard. He's adding a bunch of new Suncrest."

James and I always used to volunteer to pick peaches for the lodge. During the month of August, our chef made enough peach butter and peach jam to last the whole year. Peach cobbler and peach shortcake were also on the menu if a fresh supply was available.

I swear we managed to eat nearly as much as we picked. We always came home feeling bloated and sick, but we never seemed to learn our lesson. It's no wonder James has two full acres of peaches on his farm.

Walking out to the orchard, I can't help but be impressed by all he's been able to accomplish here. Even though this was a working farm when he bought it, the previous owners were an elderly couple who had gradually let things go. There was a lot that needed to be done to bring the land back to its glory.

When the property went on the market, James borrowed money from our parents for the down payment. He paid them back in only a few years, but he practically puts every penny he earns back into the farm.

I pull a peach off a tree and hurry to take a bite. It's so sweet and juicy I have to stop walking so I can fully concentrate on my enjoyment. James sees me and calls outs, "I hope you came to work."

"Nope. I came to hang out with my brother."

He hands me a shovel. "The price for conversation is hole digging."

I point the shovel into the ground and do what I'm told. "You've done an amazing amount of work out here."

"The earth gives back what you put into it," he states plainly. "There's no downside to hard work."

"Mom doesn't seem pleased that I'm here," I say, changing the subject.

"She's still not fawning all over you, huh?"

"No, and don't make light of it. You know how she is. This is very disconcerting behavior."

"Go pick her some flowers. I've got black-eyed Susans, daisies, hydrangeas … you name it, the flower garden is heavy in bloom right now."

"I'll grab them on my way out, thanks." I decide to pick an extra bouquet for Addie, too. She may claim she doesn't want to see me, but I've never met a woman who doesn't melt when handed a gorgeous bouquet of flowers.

"Did Mom tell you what she's planned for Dad's birthday this year?"

"No." Our dad died two months before his birthday last year, so no one was in any place to celebrate while we were so deeply mourning our loss.

"She wants us to go on a family hike around the property and sprinkle him in all of his favorite places."

Emotion chokes me as sure as if someone put their hands around my throat and started to squeeze. "That's really nice," I manage, though my voice is strangled. It's not rare to spread a loved ones ashes in locations that held meaning for them. But every place my dad loved, we still love. Every spot is sure to be so full of happy memories that the juxtaposition of why we're there may be my undoing.

James and I continue to dig holes quietly for several minutes, both of us lost in our own thoughts. Mine include the fact that at only thirty-five years old, I'm the old man of the family. More and more I feel the need to take care of my mother even though she doesn't particularly seem to care that I'm around.

"Do you ever wonder what's going to happen to the lodge when Mom gets too old to run it?" I ask my brother.

"I figured Chris would take over."

"Chris is only a year younger than Mom," I remind him.

"We'll find someone. Unless you're thinking we should sell it."

"How can we sell it? That land is our history. It's our heritage. Every event that formed us into the men we are took place there." After a moment, I add, "I guess there's time enough to decide later. I just don't want Mom working herself into an early grave. I'd like for her to travel or just relax if that's what she wants to do."

"The only thing that woman wants is grandkids to spoil," James says.

"You'd better get busy then," I tell him.

"Me? I don't have time to meet anyone, let alone date them. Plus, you're older than me. No sir, if grandkids are in the cards, you're the one who'd better get busy."

I love my family. I love kids. I just never spent much time thinking of myself in terms of being a dad. After Emma left, even the idea of marriage left a sour taste in my mouth. But after three years, maybe James is right. Maybe I should open the door to a new relationship and who knows, fatherhood might follow.

I've had friends who've wanted to set me up with various women since my break-up, but I've never been interested. Truth be told, I'm not interested now because the only face that pops into my mind when I think of romance is Addison Cooper's. But that's insane. Not only is she holding the mother of all grudges against me, she lives in New York. Nothing about the two of us together makes any sense.

Chapter Thirty-One

The Mothers

Libby: Do you ever think it might be beneficial to join a grieving group.
Ruby: I've thought about it, but I think I'm doing okay now.
Libby: I just hope you're not holding your emotions inside.
Ruby: Hardly. The first three months after Bob died, I had panic attacks that nearly had me ripping my hair out. They were awful.
Libby: Why didn't you say anything?
Ruby: Because my doctor gave me a lovely little pill that took the edge off. I'm working my way through this, Lib. Don't worry.

Addison

Spartan is like one of those towns you see in Hallmark movies. It's tiny and charming and every store I pass makes me want to go inside and buy things. I walk by a beauty parlor with a sign in the window that says, "Get your beaver waxed here!" I stop dead in my tracks as a burst of laughter ripples out of me. Oregon is the only state where they can borderline get away with something like that.

My first stop is the Quick Stop Market. I need to pick up some earplugs. My reasoning is that if I can't hear anything, I won't have anything to worry about. Sure, a bear might still break in and maul me in my sleep, but the chances are slim because Billy promised to sleep on my porch for a while longer.

A smiling woman about my age calls out, "Welcome! Let me know if you need any help."

I could walk around the grocery store for a month in New York City and no one would randomly offer to help me. "Thanks," I reply. "I'm looking for earplugs."

"Ah, you have a husband that snores, huh?"

"No husband," I assure her.

"Noisy cat?" she asks.

"Nope."

She puts down the folder she's holding and says, "I give up. What's making so much noise you can't sleep?"

"I'm staying up in one of the cabins at the Willamette Valley Lodge."

"And? Surely there's nothing making any noise up there."

"You've got to be kidding me?" I reply. "The owls hoot up a storm, other creatures sneak through the woods snapping branches, and I don't know if you've heard, but there are cougars in the woods."

She starts to laugh. "Where are you from?"

"New York City."

"Do you sleep with earplugs there?"

"I don't need them there. I know what every sound is that I hear in the city."

She walks over to me and stretches out her hand. "I'm Cheryl Wilkens. And you are?"

"Addison Cooper," I tell her. "My mom and Ruby Cavanaugh were college roommates and have been best friends ever since."

"I'm pleased to meet you, Addison. We don't see a lot of folks from New York City in these parts."

"I'm an interior designer. I'm helping Aunt Ruby work out what to do with some cabins." I suddenly realize I could really use a local brain to pick. One that doesn't have the last name of Cavanaugh.

"If you're not too busy, Cheryl, would you mind if I asked you a few questions?"

"Not at all." She sounds pleased by the prospect. "Come with me." I follow her into the freezer aisle where she already has one folding chair set up. She pulls another off one of the units and unfolds it. "Have a seat," she says while using her chair to prop open a freezer door.

I release an awkward laugh and ask, "Do you always sit in the freezer aisle?"

"I had a complete hysterectomy last year which threw me right into menopause. The hot flashes are like something out of a barbecue in hell." She fans her face to help illustrate her comment.

"I'm sorry." I'm not quite sure how to respond to a stranger telling me about her female problems.

"Don't be. I already have my kids, so there are no worries on that end, and my husband left, so I'm not too concerned about the full beard I have coming in." She brushes her hand against her chin.

I spontaneously snicker before saying, "I'm sorry about your husband, and you do not have a beard."

"I pluck it every morning," she confesses. "Now, what kind of questions do you have?"

"Do you enjoy camping?"

"Damian, that's my ex, and I had a fifth wheeler that we used to take out quite a bit. We slept in it and put the kids in a tent outside."

"Did it have a bathroom?"

"Darn straight it did. I love camping, but I'm not going to dig a hole to do my business for anyone. If God wanted me to relieve myself outdoors he would have made me a squirrel or something."

"Thank you," I tell her sincerely. "Brogan makes me out to be some kind of alien because I'm uncomfortable using an outhouse."

"You're friends with Brogan?"

"Hardly. He's been picking on me since we were kids. He used to go out of his way to make our joint family camping trips a living hell for me."

"You're not Honey Bucket, are you?" she asks excitedly.

"I don't think so. No one's ever called me that before."

"That's good. Brogan used to tell us about this prissy girl his family used to camp with. Lord, the things he did to her!" She bends over as hilarity rips through her.

The image of me washing my hair in honey pops to the forefront of my brain.

That loser! He used to brag about the pranks he played on me? "Cheryl," I confess, "I think I am Honey Bucket."

She valiantly tries to stop laughing but fails miserably.

I give her a moment to compose herself before saying, "I'm not prissy. It was simply hard to enjoy camping when two idiot brothers went out of their way to make every waking minute miserable for me."

"Oh, I bet. I know some of the pranks they pulled on you. Why in the world are you up there now, after all of that?"

"Like I said, I'm here to help Aunt Ruby. I had no idea Brogan would be in the vicinity."

"Girl, you need to get even. You know that, right?"

"You're the second person today who's told me that." And when more than one person tells me something, I start to feel a consensus afoot.

Cheryl jumps up and orders, "Follow me." She walks down the spice aisle to the condiment aisle. Picking up a bottle of clam juice she says, "Brogan hates clams. Like seriously the taste makes him gag. Why don't you invite him to your cabin for dinner and lace all the food with this?"

"While I love the idea, I don't particularly love clams myself. Not enough to eat a whole meal tasting like them."

She shakes her head. "Ask him to kill a spider or something. While he's busy, just sprinkle it on top of his food."

"Cheryl, why are you helping me like this? I thought you and Brogan were friends."

"Oh, we are, but I know the horrible stuff he did to you.

Sometimes karma can use a little help."

I take the clam juice with a big smile on my face and say, "I'd better do some shopping while I'm here and pick up some things for dinner."

Chapter Thirty-Two

The Mothers

Ruby: I just saw Brogan in the wine cellar. He was picking up a bottle of wine to take to dinner.
Libby: Fascinating.
Ruby: It is when you know where he's having dinner.
Libby: No! There's no way Addie would cook for him.
Ruby: All I know is what he told me.
Libby: Either hell has frozen over, or my daughter has something up her sleeve.
Ruby: I'll keep you posted.

Brogan

I spend the afternoon in my hammock reading a book. I don't read nearly as much as I did before becoming a writer myself, and I miss it. I must have fallen asleep though, because when I open my eyes Addison is standing over me.

On the off chance I'm not dreaming, I say, "Hey, I didn't hear you."

"I'm pretty stealthy when I want to be," she jokes. I love it when she smiles. I'd like to be the cause of her doing a lot more of that.

"What can I do for you?" I might sound a little surprised but only because I am. The last time I saw her, she was showing me the door.

"I came by to see if you wanted to come to dinner tonight."

"Really?" I'm so shocked I practically roll onto the ground. When I asked her to my place she made it sound like she'd rather lick the outhouse floor than eat with me.

"How about if you come up at six. That ought to give me enough time to cook one of my specialties."

"I'd love to," I tell her. I don't even care what Addison's cooking abilities are. The meal is the least of the reasons I'm looking forward to having dinner with her. If I'm lucky, I'll be able to convince her what a great guy I've become.

"Great, I'll see you then." She turns and walks away, affording me a very nice view. Even in shorts and a t-shirt, Addison Cooper looks like she just walked off the pages of a fashion magazine.

After she leaves, I run up to the lodge to grab a bottle of wine. I also stop at my mom's and take a hot shower. As much as I told Addie how invigorating cold showers are, I still prefer getting clean in hot water.

At five forty-five I leave my cabin with a bottle of wine, a bouquet of flowers, and a shopping bag carrying a surprise gift. Billy is sitting on the porch drinking a beer when I get there. "Hey, Bill, what are you doing here?"

"I stopped by to check on Addison and she invited me to

dinner. What are you doing here?"

"She invited me, too." *So much for a romantic evening.*

"She's in the kitchen cooking if you want to tell her you're here."

I drop the shopping bag between two trees before going inside. I immediately notice the changes that have been made since this morning. For one thing, there's a dining table with four chairs that is nicely set with a tablecloth and dishes, all way nicer than the ones in the fishing cabin.

Addie is standing in the kitchen wearing a pretty sundress and an apron. "Something smells good," I tell her.

"It better. It's strange cooking without an oven, though." She turns around to greet me.

"For you." I hand her the flowers.

"How nice, thank you!" Her skin flushes prettily.

"I also brought wine."

"I hope you brought a wine opener, I haven't been able to find one. Otherwise you'll have to settle for beer," she says.

I pull a wine opener out of my pants pocket and announce, "Once a Boy Scout, always a Boy Scout."

"The Boy Scouts were big wine drinkers, huh?" she teases.

"Only the classy ones." I pull the cork out and offer, "Chardonnay?"

"Sure, thanks."

I walk around her to the kitchen and pull open a cabinet in search of tin coffee cups. I'm surprised to find four long-stemmed wine glasses. "Where did these come from?"

"There's a cute little kitchen shop in town. I picked up some stuff while I was there," she says.

"Camping with wine glasses. That's not something I've heard of before."

"I'm not camping, I'm glamping." She has a smile on her face that positively takes my breath away.

I pour a glass and hand it to her. "To glamping."

She takes a sip and replies, "To New York."

"You really don't like it out here, huh?"

"It's only my second night. Once I get things situated, I'm sure I'll like it just fine. But that doesn't mean I don't long for the comforts of the city."

Billy pops his head in and asks, "Do I have time to go get some berries?"

"You have thirty minutes," Addie tells him.

"I'll be back." He hurriedly walks down the path.

"That was nice of you to invite him to supper," I say. I don't add that I wish she hadn't.

"The more the merrier." She takes the lid off the frying pan on the camp stove and gives everything a quick stir. "I hope you're hungry. I normally only cook for myself at home, so I quadrupled my recipe. I think I have enough food for eight people."

"Good thing I skipped lunch then. I'm starving." After a moment I bravely ask, "Do you have someone special waiting for you at home?" I'm guessing not because if she did she would have never raised the stakes on our bet.

"I'm not seeing anyone right now," she answers plainly. "What about you?"

"Free as a bird," I tell her before saying, "It must be hard to date when you're traveling all the time for work."

Instead of answering the question directly, she shrugs her shoulders and says, "A lot of people travel for work."

"I'm glad I'm not one of them."

"Don't you go on tours when you release a new book?"

"I do, but I don't look at that as work. That's more like celebration for getting the work done." Then I ask, "How is it that you've never come to any of my signings in New York City?"

"You've got to be kidding," she says. "What kind of masochist do you take me for?"

"Addison, I'm truly genuinely sorry for all the pranks I played on you when we were kids. I wish you'd believe that," I tell her for what feels like the millionth time.

She shrugs her shoulders. "While I appreciate the apology, I still have the memories. Words alone can't wash those away."

"What can I do to make it up to you?"

"I'll think about it and get back to you," she states. I don't like the look she gives me when she says that.

Chapter Thirty-Three

The Mothers

Libby: No word from Addie, and I've been gone for two days.
Ruby: She asked what time your birthday dinner was scheduled for Wednesday night. 😳
Libby: Uh-oh. What did you tell her?
Ruby: I said that I was just finalizing everything, and I'd let her know as soon I was done. What are you and Bob going to do to celebrate?
Libby: We're ordering room service. 🍾
Ruby: I'd do the same in your shoes. Enjoy every minute. ♡

Addison

"Why don't we sit outside while we wait for Billy to come back," I suggest. This cabin is small but it's positively suffocating with Brogan in it. Not only is he physically a big guy, but his aura is humongous.

"Sounds nice," he says as he steps back to lead the way.

"Bring out a chair with you if you don't want to sit on the porch. There's only one seat out here."

"I have a better idea." He reaches to take my hand. "Come with me."

I tentatively put my palm in his. The reaction is the same as shuffling through thick carpeting before touching a light switch. I wonder if he felt the zing, too. My skin is positively prickling from it.

Brogan leads the way toward the woods and abruptly stops next to a large shopping bag sitting up against a tree trunk.

"What's that?"

He hands me his wine so he can pull something out of the bag. "I brought you an extra hammock that we had stored at the fishing cabin. I thought you'd like to have it."

"Thank you!" I'm more excited than I should be considering I don't plan to spend too much time outdoors. I still have bears and cougars on the brain.

He opens it up and immediately gets to work strapping it first to one tree trunk then to another. He clearly already scoped out the perfect location. Once he's done, he takes both of our glasses and says, "You sit down first."

I can't wait. I practically jump on top of the thing. I'm sorely tempted to lie down on it and start swinging, but I don't want him to see how excited his gift makes me. Once I'm situated, I take the wine glasses while he gets settled.

I'd forgotten that when two people sit side by side on a hammock they both tend to roll toward the center, making for a very cozy situation. I'm starting to wonder if that's why Brogan brought it for me.

I try to scoot over but make very little progress in the elbow room department. Gravity is not on my side. "It was very nice of you to bring this, but I don't think it's built for two."

"You're wrong. A hammock is a great place for two people to lie down and take a nap together." His eyes are twinkling like napping is the last thing on his mind.

"We're not exactly lying down."

"We could be," he shrugs his eyebrows up and down looking like that old-time comedian Groucho Marx.

I try to stand up, but he pulls me back. "I was just kidding. If you want more space you have to do this." He lifts one leg over and straddles the hammock. "This way we can face each other."

We could, but if we both sit like that and slide together our lady and man business would be in dangerous proximity to each other. So, yeah ... no. "Move your leg back," I tell him.

"Snuggling it is," he says, while doing my bidding.

As soon as he's settled, I bring my feet up and turn them toward him so I'm pushing against his leg to get some space. He makes a sad face. "Do you ever sleep in a hammock overnight?" I ask.

"Not anymore," he tells me.

"Why not?"

"Last time I did that, I had a half-eaten protein bar in my pocket. It attracted wildlife."

"What happened?" My brain goes right to a bear attack.

"I woke up to sharp jabs coming from the underside of the hammock. A raccoon family was down there poking at me. I'm guessing if I didn't wake up when I did, they would have torn through the fabric to get the goods."

"Oh, my gosh!" I have no other words.

"The key is to not sleep outdoors with food in your pocket, but the experience soured me on nighttime hammock sleeping, nonetheless. It's still a great place to nap though."

"I'm afraid I'd have to have someone keep guard to even do that."

"Just let me know when and I'll happily volunteer my services," he says with a twinkle in his eye. There's no way I could fall asleep with Brogan watching me.

When I don't answer right away, he adds, "You don't trust me, do you?"

"Not for a second."

"Addison, we're adults now." His tone is laced with an emotion that almost sounds like longing. My body responds by sending out a heavy pulsing sensation that spreads through my extremities like the aftershocks of an earthquake. *Yikes.*

"If we were still kids, there's no way in hell I'd be sitting next to you. You'd probably be working out a plan to tie me up, slather me with honey, and offer me up to the bears."

"Black bears are predominantly plant eaters," he says like he's giving a lecture. "When it comes to meat, they prefer fish or small mammals."

"Whatever you say, Mr. Science. My point is that you were not trustworthy when we were kids. The jury is out on what I think about you now."

"Let's play twenty questions," he suggests. "That way you can get to know me better. Ask anything you want."

I think for a minute before asking, "Why were you such a butthead to me when we were growing up?"

"Truthfully, it was kind of fun to see how easily we could upset you. Again, I'm sorry." Before I can ask another question, he says, "My turn. Where is your favorite place to vacation?"

I thought he'd want to know something provocative like whether or not I slept in the nude. I'm pleased to discover a thoughtful question. "I love the old cities in Europe. I like to walk the streets of Paris and imagine what it was like two hundred years ago."

"Two hundred years ago, those streets were probably flooded in human waste that was being tossed out of windows."

"Yuck."

"It's the truth though. The past is nowhere near as romantic as *Masterpiece Theater* would have you believe."

"Where is *your* favorite place to vacation?" I ask.

"Machu Picchu."

"Peru? Why?"

"James and I were avid alien hunters when we were kids. I saw a show once that said the mountains of Peru were notorious for UFO sightings."

"So, you go to South America in search of aliens?" Ew.

"No. Well, yes at first, but I was only twenty then. I go now because the experience is downright mystical. It's the only place in the world where I feel like time doesn't exist. The hours are no more than a cycle of the sun." Seeing my look of confusion, he says, "It's like being inside the most beautiful song you've ever heard. But it's a song with no beginning or end. As long as you're there experiencing it, it just escalates until you think you must be in heaven."

"Brogan Cavanaugh, you're a poet," I tell him, more than a little surprised.

"I'm just passionate about things that are important to me." The look he gives me is smoldering.

I can't seem to find my voice for several moments, but finally manage to tell him, "I've never been to South America."

"I'd be happy to recommend places if you ever decide to go."

"Thank you." I hope Billy hurries back. It's starting to feel like we're on a date instead of an evening fueled by revenge. I have to remember to keep my focus if for no other reason than to settle an old score.

"Addison ..." Brogan begins.

He sounds serious, so I interrupt, "I should check on dinner."

I scoot around trying to figure out how to get off of the hammock but am not very successful.

"Put your feet over the side again," Brogan says. Once I do as I'm told, he hands me his wine glass and pulls me onto his lap. Holy. Crap. I'm sitting on Brogan Cavanaugh's lap and guess what? I'm not hating it. Before I can nestle in, because I'm thinking about it, he puts his hands under my butt and pushes off until I'm standing up. Wow and wow.

My knees feel weak and it's all I can do not to crumple to the ground. Brogan hands me our wine glasses and stands up with relative ease. He doesn't look the least bit affected by our recent contact and it makes me want to take my shoe off and hit him with it.

Brogan Cavanaugh is a flirt and I'm sure a total playboy. I'm going to have to watch myself with him because I'm guessing he's the kind of man to play fast and loose with a girl's heart.

Chapter Thirty-Four

The Mothers

> *Ruby: I wish I was a fly on the wall so I could watch Addie and Brogan at supper tonight.*
> *Libby: No.*
> *Ruby: Come on, you have to be curious about what's going on up there.*
> *Libby: I am, but I can wait to hear about it after the fact. BTW, Addie just texted to say that she wants to take the car out again tomorrow. Apparently, she's having lunch with some gal she met the other day.*
> *Ruby: Thanks for the heads-up. I'll make sure to give her a set of keys to my car. Hopefully she won't ask any questions. 🤞*
> *Libby: Good luck with that.*
> *Ruby: I got this.*

Brogan

Billy walks into Addie's cabin carrying a bucket of blackberries. "I brought dessert," he announces.

"I bought the can of whipping cream you asked for this morning," Addie tells him. Clearly the two of them are hanging out when I'm not around. I don't know why that bothers me, but it does.

It's not that I'm jealous of Billy, but if I were being honest, it's probably because I don't like the idea of anyone helping Addie but me. She makes me feel territorial.

Addie says, "You both sit down while I dish up."

"It smells delicious. What are we having?" I ask.

"Swedish meatballs on egg noodles. I don't have that many recipes that work without an oven."

"I'm so hungry I could eat the whole pan," Billy says.

"Good," Addie replies. "You can come back tomorrow night for leftovers."

Addie serves me and Billy first before bringing her plate over. "I figured we'd have our salad after the entrée."

"Very continental," Billy offers.

Addie raises her glass in a toast. "To a simple meal in the woods with friends."

She looks at Billy when she says "friends." He raises his beer bottle and adds, "May your neighbors respect you, trouble neglect you, the angels protect you, and heaven accept you."

The only toast that I can even think of is, "Here's looking up your dress," but I don't dare say that, so I merely respond, "Here, here." Then I take a sip of my wine.

Billy takes the first bite and immediately releases a grunt of pleasure. "I can't remember the last time I ate something so good."

I eagerly cut a meatball in half with my fork and take a bite.

I nearly spit it out, but Addie is watching for my reaction. I don't know how she managed it, but it tastes like—what is that? Clams? Who ever heard of swedish meatballs tasting like clams?

I chew it quickly and wash it down with a gulp of wine, but it's so nasty there's no way I can keep eating it.

"Will you be coming back for leftovers tomorrow night, too?" Addie asks me.

"That sounds lovely," I tell her, "but I promised to meet up with James tomorrow night."

"You could invite him along," she suggests enthusiastically.

While I would love for James to get a load of Addie's cooking, that's not going to happen if it means that I have to eat it again myself. "We need to talk business. Maybe another time." Maybe at my place.

I sit and watch while Billy and Addie practically lick their plates clean. How are they doing that without wanting to puke? Even if you like clams, it should not be the predominant flavor in a non-seafood-based dish.

"You're not eating much," Addie says to me. "I thought you said you skipped lunch."

"I did. The heat must be affecting my appetite."

"It's not hot right now," Billy comments while continuing to scrape his plate for any microscopic traces.

"Maybe I just need something lighter. That salad sounds great."

"I'll get it for you," Addie offers.

"I can get it myself." I move to stand up, but she beats me to it.

"Nonsense. You're my guest."

She brings back a beautiful plate with garden greens, avocado, pine nuts, and feta cheese. If I eat three helpings of it, it might fill me. "Thank you," I say as she puts the plate in front of me.

"There's more if you want it." It's like she's reading my mind.

I stab a big chunk of avocado and cheese with my first bite and greedily put the fork in my mouth. I can't stop my gag reflex. I immediately begin to heave like I'm going to throw up. How in the world can a salad taste like clams?

"Oh, my," Addie says, "you don't like my salad either?" She's guessed about the meatballs and looks hurt.

"I must be coming down with something," I tell her. "My taste buds seem to be off."

"You poor thing." She pats my hand like she's my mother. "Maybe you should head home and try to sleep it off."

I don't want to leave; I just don't want to eat anything she's serving. "Let me just sit here for a bit and see if my stomach settles."

"You don't know what you're missing," Billy says in between bites. The man is eating like it's his first meal in a month.

"Doesn't it taste a little bit like clams to you?" I ask.

Billy looks at me like I've lost my mind. "It's ground beef, man. How can ground beef taste fishy?"

I wish I knew.

"Clams?" Addie asks. "You *must* be under the weather." Then she takes another bite of her food.

I'm positively starving but the thought of eating makes me want to hurl even more. "I think I'll try some of your blackberries, Billy. Maybe the sweetness will refresh my palate."

He stands up and says, "I'll get you a bowl."

"You two are making me feel like a king serving me like this."

"Don't get used to it," Billy says. "I'm only being this nice cause you're sick," and then he dramatically adds, "and there's a lady around."

Addie smiles at him. "You are a dear man, you know that?"

I'm about to throw up on multiple counts now. Bill opens the cabinet and retrieves a bowl before scooping some berries into it. "You want some whipped cream on it?" he asks me.

"Yeah, give me a lot of that." I briefly fantasize about spraying the whole thing directly into my mouth. I've got to do something to get rid of this clam flavor.

Billy goes to town with the whipped cream and then drops my bowl in front of me. "Eat up," he says.

I pick up my spoon and fill it with one of Oregon's finest foods. Then I put it in my mouth ready to let the sweetness overpower the sweat sock flavor that's lingering there. Holy mother of... "Blech!" I spit out the partially masticated food right back into the bowl I scooped it out of before running outside. I barely make it to the side of the cabin before throwing up.

Billy follows and chastises, "Boy, you're not being very polite to your hostess."

When there's nothing left inside me, I reply, "How can blackberries and cream taste like clams?"

"You best make yourself an appointment with the doctor. Something's wrong with you."

I can't think of one ailment that makes things taste like the dreaded clam, but clearly there is something wrong with me if I'm the only one reacting to the food this way.

Addie walks out onto the porch. I make my apologies, "I'd better head back to my place." I sway on my feet from my recent exertions.

"Do you need Billy to go with you?" She sounds concerned.

"No, no, I can get there by myself. I'm sorry to cut the night short," I tell her sincerely.

"No worries, I'm here for a month. I'll have you over another time."

"Next time it's my turn to treat you," I tell her. If I don't turn out to be sick, the thought that goes through my mind is, *There is no way I'm going to let you cook for me ever again.*

Chapter Thirty-Five

The Mothers

Libby: I figured out why Addie invited Brogan over for dinner.
Ruby: Why?
Libby: Revenge. She used to talk about all the things she wanted to do to Brogan and James to get revenge on them.
Ruby: You think that's the only reason?
Libby: Without a doubt. And Rube, I hate to say it, but I think her need to get even is going to supersede any attraction she feels for Brogan.
Ruby: The need for vengeance and love aren't mutually exclusive emotions. Did I ever tell you about the time I put eye drops in Tom's drink?
Libby: Um, no. Why did you do that?
Ruby: Remember that big fight we had junior year? I saw him flirting with Cindy Johnston at a frat party and I didn't like it. With the help of Jason Farmer, I got a couple eye drops into his drink. He was so busy running to the toilet he didn't have time to

make eyes at anyone else.
Libby: Why didn't you ever tell me this?
Ruby: I wasn't exactly proud of myself. Plus, I didn't think you'd approve.
Libby: At least it all worked out.
Ruby: And it will between Addie and Brogan as well. Just you wait.

Addison

I agree with Don Corleone, *"revenge is dish best served cold."* Like gazpacho.

Billy and I enjoy the rest of our meal after Brogan leaves. We have more than one laugh as we reminisce about his expression when he tasted the clam juice in all his food.

Billy confesses, "I spread a thin layer of honey on the seat of his outhouse when I went off to get the blackberries."

I find the thought of Brogan getting honey all over his butt and having to take a cold shower to wash it off positively vindicating. I ask, "What else can we do to him?"

"You'd better pace yourself. That boy is nobody's fool and if too many things happen too quickly, he's going to suspect you."

That's a good point. I want to get even with Brogan, but I don't want to inspire retaliation, especially when I have so much time left here. I ask, "Do you think he'll blame me for the honey smeared all over the outhouse seat?"

"If he asks I'll tell him I saw some kids up here or something. But I didn't put enough on that he'll easily be able to tell what it is."

After cleaning up, Billy gets himself settled on the porch and I head off to bed. I sleep remarkably well, considering I'm still on a rollaway cot from the lodge. Aunt Ruby promised to have a king-size bed brought up sometime tomorrow.

The first thing I do after getting out of bed is to pop my head out to see if Billy is around. He's not. I figure this is the best time to take my first outdoor shower. I'm not at all pleased by the prospect, but I feel emboldened by my revenge against Brogan last night. I'm going to prove to that man that I can do anything he can and not complain about it.

I venture outside in my flip flops and robe, hoping not to run into any wildlife on the way. So far, so good. After turning on the spigot, I wait for a solid minute while all kinds of dirt pours out of the pipe. Yuck. Once it's clear, I take my robe off and pull the curtain closed.

Holy freaking heck, the water is cold! There is no way I can wash my hair in here. My brain would freeze and probably stop working altogether. I hurry and quickly rinse off my body without bothering to use soap before putting my robe back on.

There's no way I can shower here again. That's when I remember Aunt Ruby telling me to pick up any supplies I might need. Even though I'm pretty sure Brogan expects me to rough it while I'm here, my job is to turn this place into a glamping site, not to keep it a horrible rustic sorry excuse of a camping shelter.

I hurry up and get myself ready for the day before heading to the lodge. Billy showed me the way on a map again last night and swore up and down I wasn't in jeopardy if I followed his instructions. For some reason, I trust him. So, while I'm nervous,

I'm also fairly certain I'll arrive unharmed. I carry my mace pointed out in front of me just in case though.

I text my mom as soon as I exit the woods and get into the clearing, but she doesn't respond. She's pretty much gone MIA the last couple of days, probably afraid I've gone into full lunatic mode. Even so, she's the only reason I'm here and she therefore owes me her emotional support.

I message Aunt Ruby next and ask her to tell my mom that I need the car. She responds that I should pick up keys for the Jeep from Chris at the front desk. That might actually work out better if I wind up buying a lot of stuff.

"Hi, Chris," I greet as I walk into the lobby.

"How's it going up there?"

"Better than expected," I tell her.

"Good for you," she exclaims emphatically.

"I'm not loving it," I assure her, "but it's not getting the best of me."

"You'll show Brogan."

"You know about the bet, too?" I'm not sure why I'm surprised, but I kind of thought this was a private thing.

"Your mom told me stories of how those boys used to terrorize you. You let me know if I can help in any way."

"Thank you," I tell her before asking, "Are there any antique stores in town?"

"Sure are. Herman's and Old Stuff are both on Main Street. You can't miss them."

I nod my head. "I'll be back later this afternoon with the Jeep."

"No hurry, honey. Nobody needs it today."

Driving out of the lodge I can't help but appreciate how beautiful this place is. Would I rather be in Grand Cayman? Heck, yeah. Still, there's something special happening here. I pass families on horses and more on foot. Looking out to the river there are even more of them on boats. All these families are giving me ideas for the glamping sites.

I'm meeting Cheryl at the market for lunch today to update her on how well dinner went last night. I couldn't have done it without her insider information about Brogan's clam aversion. His reaction was so extreme I started to wonder if it was more of an allergy than a dislike. Luckily he didn't swell up or anything.

Before I meet Cheryl, I stop off on Main Street. I'm in the market for a bathtub.

Herman's looks more like a junkyard than an antique shop from the street, so I start there. I'm hoping the haphazard collections and lack of appealing displays means there are good deals to be had.

A man about my parents' age is sitting next to the cash register when I walk in. He has on wire frame glasses that are perched on the tip of his nose. He's staring down at his phone and yells out, "Syzygies, boom!"

Then he stands up and dances around in a circle. "Triple word play with a double letter on the Z, one hundred and twelve points, baby!"

He stops when he sees me and asks, "You a Scrabble player?"

"Yahtzee's my game," I tell him.

"Huh. Never got into that one. You need any help?"

"I need a bathtub, but not something fancy or expensive. I'm going to use it outside."

"You putting flowers in it?" he asks.

As if. "Nope. I'm putting water in it and using it as a camping tub."

"You gonna take it camping with you? That don't make a whole lot of sense," he says.

"The campsite is permanent, so the tub won't be moved."

He nods his head like the idea has some merit. "You using it year round or just in the warmer months?"

"Year round," I answer, although I don't know who in their right mind would want to bathe outdoors in the middle of winter.

"Uh-huh, okay." He starts to walk around bent over at the waist looking under piles of piles. God knows what's all there. He suddenly stops dead and declares, "I got just the thing! Follow me."

I trail behind him as he walks out a back door through a parking lot full of everything but cars. He stops when he reaches the fence line and makes a wide flourish with his hands. "What do you think?"

"Is that a Houston double slipper cast iron tub?" I ask in complete shock. You don't find those anywhere but designer showrooms.

"Sure is. It could use a little sprucing up on the outside, but the inside is rust free and ready to roll."

The claw feet are pristine even though the rest of the exterior looks a little rough. I'll probably just sand it down and paint it with an automotive primer before spraying it with an oil-based gloss coat. I cross my fingers behind my back and ask, "How much do you want for it?"

"Two hundred and twenty-five bucks, cash on the barrelhead."

That's it? Even if I could find one, I couldn't get this for under fifteen hundred in this condition in New York City. "Done," I tell him before asking, "Do you deliver?" There's no way I'm going to be able to haul this thing by myself. Cast iron weighs a ton. It also keeps the water hot a lot longer, which is a giant plus if this is going to be used in cold weather.

"I'd have to pay my grandson to help and he charges fifteen dollars."

"No problem," I tell him. "I'm going to look around some more, if you don't mind."

"What else do you need?" he asks.

"I need a king-size bed frame. Maybe something wood."

He tilts his head back and forth and asks, "How about wicker?"

"Let me see it," I tell him.

I wind up calling Cheryl and inviting her up to my cabin tonight instead of meeting for lunch. I spend a total of three hours at Herman's and just over five hundred dollars, but I get so much great stuff I can't wait to start placing it.

Before heading back, I call Chris and ask, "Can I drive the Jeep up to my cabin to unload before I return it?"

"You shouldn't have any problem. It's four-wheel drive, after all. I can send someone up to help you if you want."

"I should be okay," I tell her. "I'll bring it back around suppertime. I'm hoping to see my mom."

Chris says, "Hang on a sec, honey." I hear muffled talking like she's put her hand over the receiver. When she comes back, she says, "Your mom and Ruby are going into Salem for dinner tonight. They say they'll catch up with you soon."

"Okay." If not for my excitement to get the cabin set up, I'd be more than a little mad they didn't invite me to join them. "Do you know if the king-size mattress got delivered?" I ask before hanging up.

"Sure did. There wasn't room for it in the bedroom, so they left it in the front room by the fireplace."

I cannot wait to see it. After today's purchases, my victory is only an arm's length away. That's not to say I'll ever go glamping by choice. But you never know, if this project turns out as well as I expect it to, I'll definitely use the pictures in my portfolio and I might become a go-to glamping interior design expert. But let's not put the cart before the horse.

Chapter Thirty-Six

The Mothers

Ruby: You would not believe the number of boxes that have arrived for Addison.
Libby: Oh, yes, I would. In fact, no matter how many you have, I guarantee the number will more than double.
Ruby: She's a shopper, huh?
Libby: Let's just say she likes her comforts. I'm guessing she panicked when she saw that cabin.
Ruby: I can't wait to see what she thought she'd need. I'll let you know when I get back.
Libby: Godspeed, my friend. 🙏

Brogan

I managed to keep a sandwich down when I got back to the fishing cabin last night. I actually used to like clams until that night with Cheryl and Damian in Newport. One bad clam and there was no going back.

Not only have I not been able to get the taste of regurgitated seafood fully out of my mouth, but I've been scratching my backside all night. There was something sticky on the outhouse toilet seat last night, but it was so dark out there I couldn't tell what. Whatever it was though, it seems to have attracted a host of vermin who attacked while I was asleep.

I eat an unusually large breakfast, relishing the fact that everything tastes exactly as it should, then I head out to the falls for a swim. I end up staying for hours, letting my mind drift. I come up with some great ideas for my next book, make a mental list of things to do for my new house, and even take a cat nap against a big tree trunk. More and more, I appreciate the appeal of Billy's natural lifestyle.

On my way back to my cabin, I see a truck pull up the path heading to Addie's. Who in the world could be coming up to visit her? That's when I recognize Herman Benting and his grandson, Otto.

The back of Herman's truck is packed full which leads me to believe Addison has been shopping. I start to jog after them and arrive just as Herman steps out of the truck. "What have you got there?" I ask by way of greeting.

"Just some stuff for Miss Cooper. You want to help us unload it?"

The only reason I do is so that I can see firsthand what all she bought. "Is that a bathtub?" I ask in shock.

"Looks like it," Herman says.

What is that woman thinking? There's no hot water up here.

Addie comes running out looking fresh and well-rested. She claps her hands together and exclaims, "You're here!"

"I told you we would be," Herman tells her. Then he extends

the ramp off his truck and asks, "Where do you want the tub?"

Addie runs over near the outdoor shower and says, "Right here."

Herman pulls some plywood sheeting from the flatbed and lays it on the ground leading to the area Addie indicated. "What are you doing?" I ask him.

"Have you ever lifted a cast iron bathtub?"

"No."

He informs me, "They're usually three hundred pounds or so. I put this baby on wheels so we can just push it into place. I'll remove them after that."

Smart thinking. Addie spots me and offers a pleasant enough wave. "How are you feeling today?"

"A bit better," I tell her.

"You want me to heat up some leftovers for you?"

"No!" I shout before softening my answer. "I'm meeting James tonight, remember?" I wave my hands toward the back of Herman's truck and say, "Looks like you've been busy."

"Just doing my job," she answers with a smile.

While Herman and Otto roll the bathtub into place, my mom pulls up in a golf cart full of shipping boxes. "What are you doing here?" she asks me as she gets out.

"I got curious when I saw Herman drive by. Looks like this little glamping experiment is going to cost you a pretty penny," I tell her.

"It takes money to make money." Another familiar adage from childhood.

Addie comes running over and hugs my mom. "Looks like my purchases have started to arrive."

"Are there more?" my mom asks her.

Addie inspects the shipment and answers, "Definitely."

"Brogan," my mom addresses me, "please take these into Addie's cabin. I want to get a closer look at that tub. It's positively gorgeous!"

"I can't believe you bought a bathtub," I tell Addie. "Who in their right mind would want to take a cold bath?"

"It's not going to be cold," she says. "Follow me." Mom and I trail behind as she walks over to her new purchase.

"I bought an old cauldron and tripod so I can heat water over an open fire right next to the tub. Then I bought some plumbing tubing at the hardware store that fits over the shower spigot so I can fill the cauldron and add whatever cold water is needed to the bath."

Her idea is ingenious. Of course, I don't tell her that. Instead, I say, "You're kidding?" A horrible itch overcomes me just then, and I give my butt a vigorous scratching.

My mom looks appalled. "What are you doing?" she demands.

"I got bit up something fierce last night," I tell her.

"By what?"

"I have no idea."

Addie lets out a delighted giggle, so I ask, "What are you laughing at? The same thing could happen to you too, you know."

"I'm sure it could," she says. "I'm merely laughing because you're not making camping look like the kind of fun you say it is."

"I'm not complaining, just itching." I walk off and start the lengthy process of unloading the golf cart for my mom. I can't imagine what's in all of these boxes.

By the time everything is unloaded and we're standing inside the cabin, I can't help but think it looks like Addie is trying to turn this place into a proper home. "Why in the world do you need a headboard?" I ask her.

"Glamping is about making things as luxurious as you can while still roughing it in nature," she explains. "A headboard is merely one of those luxuries."

My mom sits down on the bed and asks Addie, "If the bed is going to be out here, what are you putting in the bedroom?"

"I'm going to turn that into the closet. I'll put a rod up for hanging clothes and Herman brought up a highboy so your guests can unpack their stuff into drawers. That way the main living area won't be junked up with suitcases and the like."

"What a good idea," my mom tells her. "I can't wait to see it when it's all done. When do you think that will be?"

"Give me four days," Addie announces. "I should be eighty percent done by then."

"Let me know if you need me to send any maintenance people up to help."

"I can always come over, too," I interject.

My mom scoffs, "Please. You just make sure you have your checkbook ready to pay off me and your brother."

"You make sure you're ready to sign over Cheater's Ridge to me," I tell her. Although, by the looks of things, Addison might just make it a full month up here. I briefly consider resorting to some old tricks to make sure that doesn't happen. But then again, the longer Addie's here, the more I get to see her. I certainly have a lot to think about.

Chapter Thirty-Seven

The Mothers

Libby: How did it go?
Ruby: I think Addie has bought enough stuff for ten cabins. That girl of yours seems to have her eye on turning her current residence into a mini Taj Mahal.
Libby: I warned you.
Ruby: The question is, do you think she's going to win the bet?
Libby: If I know my daughter, she'll do it. She wants to put Brogan in his place.
Ruby: I wish you were still here.
Libby: I feel safer being across the globe right now.

Addison

After Aunt Ruby and Brogan take off, I get busy unpacking. The first thing I take out is a pop up tent. I figure it'll be perfect for couples with kids old enough to want the full camping experience. It'll also give the parents a bit of privacy, so win-win.

I bought a green tent that will blend into the forest. True to its advertising, I have the thing out of its box and up within ten minutes. Nice.

Next, I unpack yoga mats for the flooring and unroll sleeping bags on top of that. An air mattress can always be added, depending on the degree of comfort the children require.

Several battery-operated lanterns are next. They're all on one remote control so once I get some help stringing them up in the trees, they should be good to go until the batteries need to be changed.

The reason I set up the tent first is so that Billy has a place to sleep. I know he says he likes sleeping out under the stars, but he's getting old and I can't imagine the hard ground is as comfortable as it once might have been.

While I'm working on the outside of the bathtub, Cheryl pulls up. Pick-up trucks must be the Oregon state vehicle. Everyone seems to have one.

"Heya!" she calls out. "I brought wine."

"Welcome," I reply. "I have dinner warming up on the camp stove. You want to go in and pour us a couple glasses while we wait? I'll be right in."

I hurry and finish up the primer coat on the tub. I plan on spraying the topcoat after dinner so that I can have a bath in the morning. I can't wait.

As I walk inside the cabin, Cheryl hands me a glass and says, "Girl, you've been busy."

"I have gotten a huge amount accomplished today. Thankfully, I didn't have to cook dinner because I'm serving you leftovers."

"Food always tastes better the next day," she says with a smile.

"That's what I tell my kids when they complain about the same meal two and three days in a row."

"Would you mind helping me move some boxes? I figure once the bed is situated and made, you'll get a better vision of what I'm doing."

We spend the next half-hour setting up the headboard and bed against the wall adjacent to the fireplace. Once the linens and duvet are on, Cheryl stands back and appreciates our efforts. "This is going to look great."

"I know." I walk over to the corner and start searching through the pile of things that Herman brought up until I find a beautiful old quilt. I throw it across one of the Adirondack chairs I bought to put in front of the fireplace.

Once the candles on the mantel are lit, Cheryl gasps. "I could live here."

"It's all about the lighting," I tell her. I explain how the outside lanterns are on a remote. "That way if you have to use the outhouse in the middle of the night, you can flip the lights on so you can see where you're going."

"That's seriously brilliant," she says. "But you know you can get a toilet seat that fits on top of a bucket if you want something for inside the cabin at night."

"Really? What a great idea."

"Yup. Just pick up some biodegradable plastic liners for it and then you don't have any cleanup to speak of. Just throw the whole thing down the hole in the outhouse."

"I don't suppose there are fans propelled by gerbils running on exercise wheels?" I inquire hopefully.

Cheryl looks at me like I'm a lunatic. So, I explain, "I had a gerbil named Herbie when I was a kid. I swear he was training for the rodent Olympics or something. He never got off his wheel and I used to think he'd be just as effective as those giant windmills in the desert."

"You may have to invent that yourself," she says. "But seriously, this place is going to look amazing when you're done. I'll have to rent one of these for a couple nights and bring the kids up here."

"Is your ex in the picture at all?" I ask. I wouldn't normally ask such a personal question so soon, but there's something about Cheryl that makes her already feel like a friend. After all, only a friend would rat out another friend to facilitate my revenge.

"He sends child support and calls the kids regularly, but his early mid-life crisis doesn't allow for more than that."

"What's his crisis all about?" I ask.

"It stemmed from living in the same town his whole life and marrying his childhood sweetheart. He claims to have had no real-life experience. That's why he took off for Los Angeles. Apparently, that's where real life happens." She rolls her eyes while shaking her head.

"How long has he been gone?" I ask.

"Ten months. I cyber stalk him on social media and have discovered that Nubian goddesses like myself are no longer his type. He's developed an interest in skinny blondes with boobs that need their own zip code."

"I'm sorry. That must really hurt."

She shrugs. "He's not the only one who wondered what else was out there. The difference is that I knew I loved him, and he and our family were my priority. I would have never walked away from him out of curiosity of what I was missing."

"Men," I bemoan for lack of knowing what else to say.

"How about you? Any love interest in your life?"

"There was someone I was hoping to date, but I wound up here and my best friend Elle seems to be staking a claim."

"That's horrible!" she exclaims.

I tell her the whole story about Grand Cayman, so she doesn't think poorly of Elle. "I gave her my permission. It would have probably only been a vacation romance, if that."

"What about Brogan?" she asks. "He's a good-looking guy with a great job. And he loves his mother. Those qualities aren't a dime a dozen these days."

I'm obviously attracted to him, but I don't know that I'll ever feel like I've evened the score card with him. "He lives in Oregon and I live in New York. I travel enough for work without adding that kind of complication."

"But he's cute, right?" she persists.

"If we didn't have such a sordid past, I would definitely do a double take," I confess.

After eating swedish meatball leftovers, Cheryl keeps me company while I spray the finishing coat of paint on the bathtub. "Are you going to hang a curtain?" she asks.

"I wasn't planning to. I mean if you're so into nature that you want to glamp, why not soak in a bubble bath and enjoy your surroundings?"

"What about people who are traveling with kids or friends?" she asks.

"Good point. Maybe I'll get a privacy screen that can be

brought out for them."

"You'd be fine taking a bath without one?" She sounds unsure.

"I want to see what's out there, so I know whether or not to get up and run for my life."

"That makes sense. Our fifth wheeler had a shower. I love nature as long as I'm clean. You know what I mean?"

"Um, yeah. Why do you think I'm so motivated to get this tub ready?"

"You could light some candles and drink a glass of wine. It could be downright romantic out here."

She's right. One of the cabins could be marketed as the bridal suite for nature lovers. A large family could rent them all out for a family reunion. I start to get excited thinking about all the marketing possibilities for the Willamette Valley Glamping Resort.

Billy wanders into the clearing and stares at us for a long minute before asking, "Girl, what are you up to?"

I give him my whole spiel and wait for him to share his opinion, but he doesn't. He just looks around until he spots the tent. "What's that for?"

"You," I tell him. "I know you like to sleep out under the stars, but I thought it might be nice to have some shelter at night." I jump and run over to it, all the while explaining, "It's got window flaps you can open so you can have a nice cross breeze, and you can keep the front flap open all night if you want."

Billy still doesn't comment on my improvements. Instead, he turns to Cheryl and says, "Tell your dad thanks for the worms.

They worked like gangbusters."

"He was hoping you might want to fish with him sometime. He says you haven't been at your usual spot in a while."

Billy replies, "Tell him I'll head back there for a couple days if he wants to meet me."

"I'll pass it on," Cheryl says.

"There are leftovers in the kitchen if you're hungry," I tell Billy. "We already ate."

He nods his head and walks toward the cabin. "Sounds good."

Once he's gone, Cheryl asks, "Is he staying out here with you?"

"He's protecting me," I explain. "He showed up the first night and slept on the porch, so I didn't have to worry about anything."

"He's a good egg. He and my dad have been fishing together since I was a little girl."

"Do you ever think he'll move into a real house?" I ask.

"I think Billy plans to carry on as he always has. But I worry about him now that he's getting older."

We sit quietly for a while, both lost in our thoughts. I wonder a lot of things about Billy Grimps, but mostly I'm just grateful to him for helping me out. Maybe by the time I leave I can help him find a more permanent situation. Not that I think he needs to be like everyone else, but the truth is that we all need people.

Chapter Thirty-Eight

The Mothers

Ruby: Happy Birthday, my friend! 🎉
Libby: I remember being a little girl thinking that I'd be in my forties in the new millennium. I couldn't imagine ever being that old. And look at me now.
Ruby: There's only one way to stop the hands of time, and believe me, I don't recommend it.
Libby: Life sure does become more precious doesn't it?
Ruby: It's achingly sweet. I just want to make sure my boys get to experience the better parts of living for as long as they can. 🐨
Libby: You're doing your part, Rube. They're either going to fall in line or not, but it won't be for your lack of trying.

Brogan

Addie's cabin has become Grand Central Station. There are trucks driving by right and left. Last night, I swear I saw Cheryl

Wilkens while I was on my way to the outhouse. I have no idea what that's all about, unless Addie has figured out a way to get the market to deliver groceries for her. I wouldn't put it past her.

I decide to head into the lodge for a shower and breakfast that I don't have to cook for myself. I'd never say this out loud, but the thrill of the fishing cabin is losing some of its appeal. In other words, I like my luxuries as much as the next guy.

Once I'm clean and seated in the dining room waiting for food, I pull out my phone to check for messages. There are a bunch of people trying to sell me stuff, my agent, and—surprise, surprise—three voicemails from Emma.

The first two simply ask for me to call her back. In the third, she says, "Brogan, this is juvenile. You're a grown man and you owe it to me to return my call and hear what I have to say. Please."

Where in the world did she get the idea that I owe her anything? There's no way I'm going to call her. I try not to let my irritation ruin my breakfast, but it sure doesn't do much for my digestion.

Halfway through my waffles, my mom comes into the dining room. She likes to walk around and make sure everyone is happy. When she gets to my table, she demands, "What are you doing here?"

I motion toward my plate. "Eating."

"Why?" she demands.

"I'm hungry. Isn't that why people usually eat?"

"Don't be smart," she says. "I mean why are you eating here and not at the cabin?"

"I wanted waffles," I tell her.

"I see. So, Addie can't eat here or use any of the facilities, but you can?"

She makes it sound like I'm the one breaking the bet. "We already know I can rough it. The wager is based on whether or not Addison can."

"Uh-huh." She doesn't sound convinced. "I think that in good faith you should prove you still have what it takes to make it out in the woods. I think maybe you've gotten soft."

"That wasn't what the bet was all about, Mom," I hurry to defend myself.

"Scared you can't do it and Addie will show you up?"

"No." *Pleeeeaaase.*

"Then you need to walk on out of here and prove you're as tough as Addison Cooper."

What's going on here? "Mom," I try again, "you bet me five thousand dollars that Addie could stay out there, not me."

She shakes her head. "I'm invoking my parental right to add a stipulation to the terms. You need to do everything you expect Addison to do. Fair is fair."

"Can I at least finish my breakfast?" I ask, thoroughly annoyed.

She reaches over and picks up my plate. "No." Then she walks away.

I don't know if there's a full moon or Mercury is in retrograde, but the whole world feels screwy right now. First, my mom starts acting all weird, then Addie shows up, followed by Emma. If I didn't know better, I'd think the universe was gunning for me.

I throw some money down on the table before leaving.

Passing the front desk, I call out to Chris, "Hey." She waves, but she's busy with a guest, so I keep on walking out the front door.

Today is going to be a hot one for sure. Within five minutes, my t-shirt is sticking to me like a second skin. I decide to head up to the falls for my daily swim.

For some reason, I feel an agitation that I've never experienced when staying in the cabin. I played solitaire for hours last night before unwinding enough to fall asleep. Also, my butt itches like crazy. It must look like a real sight with the way I've been scratching it.

After changing into some shorts and a dry t-shirt, I grab a towel and an energy bar. Then I head out again. I miss my waffles.

On the path to Copper Creek, I pass Addison. "What are you doing out here all by yourself?" I ask her.

"Good morning to you, too," she says brightly before adding, "I'm not alone. Billy is just up ahead."

"What are you doing?" I repeat. It looks like she's tying colorful ribbons to tree branches, but that makes no sense at all.

"I'm tying ribbons on tree branches."

"Why?"

"I'm marking my paths so I can learn which way leads to where. Hot pink is for the falls and citron green will take me to the lodge. Billy is tying the royal blue ones. I don't know where those lead yet."

"Addison, there are trail maps to help you find your way. Ribbons kind of take away from the rustic feel of the forest."

"They shouldn't. They're made out of bamboo," she tells me. "Totally natural."

I just shake my head when she adds, "I wanted to use wind chimes, but Billy talked me out of it."

"Have a nice day," I say as I walk by. I realize that Addie is part of the reason I'm feeling restless and that knowledge unsettles me even more.

"Someone's grumpy today," she says to my back.

"I'm hot. I need to cool off," I reply as I keep moving. I can't quite hear how she responds because she mutters it, but it sounds remarkably like, "I'm pretty sure you'll still be hot even after your swim."

Is she referring to my mood or my rugged manliness? Could Addie have finally decided I'm more than the boy who used to make her life difficult? If that's the case, maybe she'll cut me some slack and let me court her. *Could I really be thinking about starting up something with Addison Cooper?*

I force the thought of romance onto the back burner, but I walk with a renewed spring in my step, nonetheless. I continue on with my morning plans, but interesting nighttime activities keep darting through my mind.

Chapter Thirty-Nine

The Mothers

> Libby: I left a message on Addie's phone telling her that I decided to spend my birthday with Bob.
> Ruby: I'm not sure she'll get the message.
> Libby: That's why I'm texting you.
> Ruby: Thanks a lot. Please read that with the appropriate amount of sarcasm. 😳
> Libby: Will do.
> Ruby: I think I'll have Brogan break the news to her.
> Libby: How will that work to our benefit?
> Ruby: She might be so upset she throws herself into his arms for consolation.
> Libby: Either that or she'll kill the messenger.

Addison

I keep thinking about what Cheryl said about Brogan being handsome. It's not like I haven't noticed that for myself, but there's something about another woman saying it that makes me feel ... what's the word, territorial? Ick, that's an uncomfortable emotion to be having regarding Brogan.

Once Billy and I finish tying ribbons on the trees, we head back to my cabin. "As soon as it rains, those ribbons are going to fall off," he tells me.

"Do you think it's going to rain in the next month?" I don't remember rain in Oregon during the summer.

"Probably not," he concedes. "Do you need any help around your campsite today? I was planning on going fishing. I'll cook supper tonight if you want."

"That sounds wonderful, but I'm going up to the lodge to celebrate my mom's birthday." Surely Brogan doesn't expect me to miss that because of our stupid bet.

"I'll put the leftovers in the refrigerator for tomorrow then."

Billy and I have sort of become roommates. I'm not sure what he gets out of the deal, but I get a sense of security and someone to talk to, which I appreciate beyond measure. "Would you mind showing me how to build a fire to heat my bathwater before you go?"

He nods his head. "A bathtub in the woods. Who would have thought? I'm pretty sure I haven't been in a real tub since I came to Oregon." I can't tell if he sounds wistful or just confounded by this new development.

"I can't wait to have a soak. Why don't you take a bath tonight while I'm up at the lodge?" I suggest.

He appears to be considering my suggestion but doesn't verbally acknowledge it. Instead he says, "I slept in that tent of yours last night."

A ripple of happiness flows through me. "What did you think?"

"It was strange." He doesn't say anything else, so I don't push.

He starts to pick up twigs and a few thin branches, handing some off to me as we go. "You're not looking for a long-term flame, so you'll probably only need one log. This kindling ought to get it going long enough for it to catch."

Once Billy gets the fire started, I attach the hose to the shower nozzle before turning it on to fill up the cauldron. "Pretty clever, huh?" I ask like I'm begging for his approval.

He just stares at me like I'm a foreign life form. "You're gonna need some kind of bath mat so your feet don't get muddy when you step out."

"Stay right here," I tell him before running inside to grab another shipping box. When I come out I open it up and pull out a mat made from river rock that's been cut in half and attached to a rubber base. "What do you think?"

"Looks like you've thought of everything," he replies. I decide to take it as a compliment.

"How do you plan on draining that thing?" he wants to know.

"What do you mean? I'll just pull the plug and let the water run out."

"The whole area will get muddy if you do that. It'll kind of defeat the purpose of getting clean," he says.

Darn it, he's right. "Any ideas?"

"Why don't we dig a moat around the tub, and partially fill it with gravel to prevent soil erosion? That'll keep the moisture where we want it. Then we could lay a couple boards to use as a bridge."

"We could call it Bathtub Island!" I clap my hands in excitement.

"Okay." He doesn't seem as enthralled by the idea as I am.

"I wanted to take a bath today though and I don't have any shovels." How disappointing.

"Go ahead and have your bath, just don't pull the stopper. I'll pick up the shovels from the maintenance crew and start digging when I get back from fishing."

"You're the best, Billy!" I run inside to grab my bubble bath and towels. When I get back out, he's already gone. Once the first pot of water is heated, I pour it into the tub and immediately get the second one going. The only downside so far is that it takes nearly an hour to heat all the water I want to use. The good news is that the boiling water stays hot in a cast iron tub.

I add the bubble bath before pouring in the last pan of hot water, then I slowly add just enough cold water from the shower to make it tolerable.

After surveying the area to make sure I'm alone, I gingerly step into the tub before dropping my robe and sinking in. It's pure heaven.

Lying back, I let the warmth envelop me as tension slowly seeps out of my muscles. I don't understand people's love of hurrying the cleaning process by taking showers. The first thing I did when I bought my apartment in New York was to install a bathtub.

Gradually I become comfortable enough to close my eyes and really let myself go. At least until I hear a twig snap somewhere nearby. "Hello?" I call out. "Who's there?"

"Just us cougars," Brogan replies.

I make sure there are plenty of bubbles covering my naked bits before replying, "Ha, ha, ha. I'm taking a bath, so if you don't mind …"

I regret saying those words the very second they're out of my mouth. Brogan breaks into the clearing in a near jog. The smile on his face says it all. He's got me just where he wants me. "Don't you look cozy," he drawls.

"Why are you here?"

"I was going to ask you over to my place for supper tonight. Looks like you'll be smelling nice and sweet."

"I hate to break it to you, but you won't be smelling me tonight. I'm going to be celebrating my mom's birthday with her."

"That's going to be a little difficult with her being in Amsterdam."

"What are you talking about?" I demand. "My mom is up at the lodge with your mom."

He shakes his head. "After you wagered that you could stay out here for a month, she decided to meet your dad at his convention in the Netherlands."

She wouldn't do that to me, would she? My mom usually goes along with my dad when he has business in places she likes. She didn't go this time because it conflicted with the opening of Bainbridge Caribbean. Then Aunt Ruby needed her and here we are, in Oregon. At least, here I am …

Thoughts swirl around in my head like a Category 5 hurricane. I'm about to deny her abandonment again when Brogan says, "So I should expect you at six for supper? I just need to pop inside your place and pick up the wine opener I left here."

I reply, "I guess so," although I'm not sure I really mean it. He's kind of caught me off guard by catching me in the tub and then telling me my mom has abandoned me.

As Brogan walks into my cabin, I start to wonder if Mom and Aunt Ruby are up to something and I'm just a pawn in some demented game they're playing. *The only question I have is, what game?*

Chapter Forty

The Mothers

> *Ruby: I had one of the groundskeepers take a note up to Brogan about your birthday party being canceled.*
> *Libby: Why didn't you tell him yourself?*
> *Ruby: Because at some point those two are going to figure out what we're up to and may decide to rebel by going out of their way not to see each other. I figure the more I can throw them together before they find out, the better.*
> *Libby: Did I mention how happy I am not to be there right now?* 😁
> *Ruby: Several times.*

Brogan

Is it my birthday? Catching Addie in a bubble bath in the middle of the woods is exactly what I would have asked for, too. I give my writer's brain free range to imagine all the possibilities, savoring each and every one while I hurry inside Addie's cabin to get the wine opener.

I'm going to fry up some fish on my little camping grill. I might even head up to the lodge to pick up a decadent dessert, something with chocolate and whipped cream.

The first thought that hits me when I walk inside is that this place is starting to look more like a resort than a campsite. The king-size bed by the fire is fully rigged out with a plush comforter, throw pillows, and is that mosquito netting? There's even a trunk at the foot of the bed for storage with an antique lamp and picture frames perched artistically about. I pick up one of the frames but there's no picture in it yet. On my way to the kitchen, I wonder if she's replaced the silverware with sterling.

I briefly wonder what it would be like if the fishing cabin looked like this and realize it would be nice to stretch out in a big bed by the fire. Maybe after I win the bet, I'll make an upgrade.

The wine opener isn't in plain sight, so I open the cupboard to look. That's when I see it. A half-full bottle of Pacific Island clam juice. *Oh, no she didn't.* Who in the world told Addie about my aversion to clams? Wait, I saw Cheryl's truck last night. Those two must have met earlier in order for my childhood friend to betray me the way she did. Why would she do that?

Pacing around the kitchen I try to decide how best to handle this. Clearly revenge must be administered. I can either go outside and pour freezing cold water over Addie's head right now or I can hold onto this information and retaliate in kind. Secretly.

I put the clam juice back and finally find the wine opener on the dining room table before strolling back outside. Not only do I avert my gaze, so Addie doesn't think I'm a lech, but I don't want her to see the anger that's surely radiating from my eyes.

Vomited clam is by far the most disgusting thing I've ever tasted. I can't even think about blackberries now without having a flashback. That woman ruined one of my favorite fruits for me. This means war.

"I'll see you at six," I call out, not waiting for an answer as I walk toward the path leading to my place.

I decide to head into town to see if I can figure out why Cheryl ratted me out. Of course, I can't ask her directly without risking her telling Addie, but at the very least, I can gauge her reaction. What in the world did I ever do to her that she'd put me through that nightmare dinner?

On the way to town, I stop off at my brother's house to tell him what's going on, and to warn him that he might be next. After all, I didn't perpetrate all of those pranks on my own, and if Addie was being fair, she'd remember that.

When I get to James's place, he's arguing with a woman at his farm stand. She's asking him, "Is your produce certified organic or not? A simple yes or no will suffice."

"It's not a yes or no question," he tells her before explaining, "Certifying organic requires tens of thousands of dollars to get the official seal. Most farmers can't afford that, so we use the term 'No Spray' to indicate organic practices. I'm 'No Spray.'"

"So, the answer is no, your produce is not certified organic," she replies sassily.

If the look on James's face is any indication, he's about to blow a gasket. He stomps over to a pallet piled high with fresh corn. "Pick up any ear you'd like," he practically yells.

She joins him before bending over and making her choice.

James grabs it out of her hands and pulls back the top part of the husk before shoving it into her face. "What do you see?" he demands.

"A worm," comes her quick answer.

"Every ear of corn worth eating has a worm on top. That worm couldn't be there if I sprayed pesticides or used genetically modified seed. Got it?"

She shakes her head at him. "So, you don't spray but that doesn't mean you're organic."

"Woman," my brother shakes the ear of corn at her, "go buy your produce somewhere else!"

"Should I tell my friends to do the same thing?" she asks obviously ready to give as good as she gets.

"If your friends are as big of a pain as you are, then yes."

"Well, I never!"

"I'm sure you don't, and maybe that's your problem," he shouts after her.

She knocks into me as she storms by, and I can't help but laugh. "You need to work on your customer service," I tell James.

"That woman has been coming here all summer and every single time she interrogates my workers about why we aren't certified organic. I'm sick to death of it. Let her go to Market of Choice and spend a dollar an ear if she needs it certified. She could get four ears for the same price here that are fresher and just as pesticide free. Those city folks need to stay in the city and quit moving out to the country. They make me crazy."

"Are you done?" I ask with a smile on my face. James is rarely this worked up over anything.

He inhales deeply before answering, "Yeah, I'm done. What

brings you out here?"

I tell him what I found in Addie's kitchen and he starts laughing. "What's so funny? You might be next, you know," I tell him.

"While I appreciate the warning, brother, I'm pretty sure Addison Cooper hates you way worse than me."

"How do you figure?"

"I didn't bet her that she could stay out in the woods for a month."

"I didn't either. She came up with that on her own."

"Either way, I'm clearly on her side. That five thousand you wagered me is going to help me get my new hay baler."

"I was just warning you," I tell him testily. "Why do you think Cheryl told her about the clam juice?"

Jeffrey Wilkens walks over and announces, "My mom is kind of down on the male species as a whole ever since my dad left."

"Do me a favor and don't tell her that I know," I ask him. "I want to keep Addie in the dark long enough to get my revenge."

Jeff shrugs. "It's none of my business."

I look at my brother and poke him in the chest. "Don't you say anything either. Now that I know you're betraying blood to be on Team Addison, I'm not sure I can trust you."

"Please," he says while rolling his eyes. "You don't think I have my own crap to deal with? I've got crazy city girls wanting to pick fights over corn. Clearly, I've got my own female troubles."

I change the subject and ask, "Did you know that Aunt Libby left?"

"I thought she was staying for her birthday."

"Me, too. I'm not sure what's going on, but I think Mom is up to something."

"What?"

"I don't know," I tell him. "Just keep your eyes open, will you? I feel like every woman I know has decided to turn on me and it's making me a little nervous."

"If you ask me, women are more trouble than they're worth."

"I think you might be right," I tell him. Yet my mind zooms right back to seeing Addie in the bath in the woods and I wonder if she might not just be worth any amount of trouble.

Chapter Forty-One

The Mothers

> Libby: You realize that even if Addie and Brogan get together they might not get married.
> Ruby: What's your point?
> Libby: I just don't want us to get our hopes up.
> Ruby: They could still give us a grandchild without getting married.
> Libby: Ruby, what kind of thing is that to say? 😳
> Ruby: There are no guarantees in life, Lib. I just want our kids to find happiness. The ring is secondary.
> Libby: It's a whole new world out there, isn't it?
> Ruby: I've never realized that more since losing Tom.

Addison:

What the heck? I can't believe my mom has left me to rot in the wilderness while she goes off with my dad. I know I changed the game with my wager against Brogan, but we could still have spent time together. As soon as I get within range of a phone signal, I'm going to send her a thousand and one texts expressing my extreme displeasure at being abandoned.

The good news is that now that I have a bathtub, I know I can win this bet with one hand and one foot tied behind my back.

Speaking of the devil, should I have dinner with him tonight? I could stay home and eat with Billy, but I told my sort-of roommate I was going out and that he should give the bathtub a try. I don't want to get in the way of his experiencing his first deep cleaning in thirty years. Also, I kind of told Brogan I'd come.

After changing into palazzo pants and a pretty over-the-shoulder top, I decide to go ahead and let Brogan cook dinner for me. I briefly toy with the idea of taking the clam juice along and trying to find a way to put it in his food, but it's not worth the risk. *What if he caught me?* There aren't many places to hide the bottle in my current ensemble.

Just before six o'clock, I look in the mirror and apply a bit of lipstick. I tell myself that I'm doing it because it feels good to get dressed up, but the truth is I want to look my best—or as close a proximity as I can without electricity. My hair has definitely increased in volume without the means to straighten it.

It's nice to be appreciated by an attractive man and I'd be lying straight out if I said I didn't find Brogan attractive. Very attractive. Mind blowingly, toe curlingly attractive. Not that anything can come from it.

While I don't particularly feel comfortable walking in the woods by myself yet, I do feel more at ease now that I have my ribbon system set up. And my mace pointed straight out. I also bought a whistle on a rope that arrived in today's mail. I'm wearing it around my neck like a high school basketball coach. You know, so if a cougar walks by, I can blow it and yell, "Foul! You're out of the game!"

Brogan is stoking a fire out front when I arrive at his cabin. He's wearing cargo shorts and a white t-shirt. He looks yummy. "Hey," I call out.

He turns around and lets his eyes slowly devour me. The way he's scanning me from head to toe makes me feel positively naked. Heat pours through me when I remember I *was* naked the last time he saw me. *Thank goodness for bubbles.*

"Hey, yourself," he greets. "I hope you're hungry."

"It depends on how good of a cook you are," I tease.

"I promise nothing will taste like clams."

I guiltily look down at my feet before asking, "How are you feeling, anyway? You doing better now?"

"I'm great, thanks. Must have just been one of those things."

"So, what are you making?" We need a change in topic, stat.

"I'm grilling some steelhead over mesquite chips. They'll give the fish a nice smoky flavor." He takes a few steps closer to me and my stomach drops like I hit a dip in the road going sixty miles an hour.

"Would you like a glass of wine?" he asks, his voice as thick as honey and as smoky as the fire he was just stoking.

"Please," I squeak, sounding like my answer was churned out by a rusty crank.

"Come on in." He gestures for me to follow him inside.

I've already been inside Brogan's cabin, so I know what to

expect. But when I cross the threshold, I see some marked changes. First, the table is set with a tablecloth and cloth napkins. There's also a jug with wildflowers in the center and candles that are ready to be lit.

"Everything looks very pretty," I tell him.

"You're worth the effort."

My knees tremble as his compliment washes over me. "Thank you."

"After all, you went out of your way to make such a nice meal for me, and how did I thank you? I threw up." He shakes his head when he adds, "I hope you don't have the same bug I had."

That kind of sounded like a threat. Yet how could he know what happened? I start to panic when I remember he went into my kitchen this afternoon to get the wine opener, but I know the clam juice was in the cabinet tucked behind a canister of tea bags. Surely, he didn't see it. Or did he?

Brogan pours me a glass of chilled white wine and says, "I went with a *viognier*. I thought it would pair nicely with our fish." He raises his glass and toasts, "To old friends."

I clink glasses and correct him. "To new friends."

He smiles endearingly before asking, "Would you like to sit outside while I put dinner on?"

"I could stay in here with you," I suggest. You know, just in case he really is going to poison my food.

"I'm grilling outside," he reminds me. I follow along so closely I might as well be tethered to him.

Sitting down on one of the Adirondack chairs on his makeshift porch, I comment, "You can get nice cushions for these chairs online."

"I like them the way they are," he tells me. "Rustic, like I'm living in the woods."

"Living in the woods doesn't have to feel rustic."

"I suppose not. But that's the way some of us like it." He changes the direction of our conversation and asks, "So, Billy is staying up there with you, huh?"

"I hope you aren't going to say that I'm breaking the rules of our bet."

"Not at all. The bet was that *you* couldn't stay up here. There were no stipulations regarding other people." He smiles at me in a way that makes me feel like I just ate six hot fudge sundaes—content and nauseated at the same time.

"It's crazy how Billy came out here from New York, isn't it?"

Brogan looks confused. "What do you mean? I thought Billy was from Oregon."

"Haven't you ever asked him about his life?" I ask in astonishment.

"Of course, I've asked him, but he's always evasive with his answers. I just assumed he didn't want to talk about it."

Curious. "Billy came out to Oregon to meet his father," I tell Brogan.

"Who's his dad?"

I shrug. "I have no idea." Even if he'd told me I wouldn't know who it was. The only people I know in this state are Cavanaughs.

Brogan puts the fish and ears of corn directly on the grill plate he's placed over the fire. Then he scoots his chair closer to mine and says, "Billy is a man of mystery."

It feels nice sitting side-by-side enjoying our wine while we wait for our food to cook. This is very different from dating in

New York City where you either meet your date at a restaurant after work or he picks you up in a taxi. Then it's straight to a crowded restaurant where someone else prepares your meal.

Of course, this isn't a date. I know that.

After a few minutes of quiet contemplation, Brogan gets up to turn the fish over. He offers, "We could eat out here if you prefer?"

"That would be nice," I tell him. The crickets have started their evening song and while it's not a string quartet, it's still quite pleasant.

He goes inside to get the table and chairs. When he brings them out, he places them directly in the clearing under a large elm. He even brings out the jug of flowers and candles. The scene looks like it could be on the cover of *Glamping* magazine, which I know is a thing because I've done my research.

Brogan fetches a bowl with the salad next and places it on the table. Then he offers me his hand, "Will milady join me?"

I let him lead me to the table and against my better judgement, I realize this could be a date if I let it. I have to force myself to remember this is Brogan Cavanaugh, perpetrator of childhood terrors, and not a gallant gentleman. Having said that, we're not kids anymore. If I can let the past go, there's no telling what might happen between two consenting adults. The thought causes the detonation of a thousand little explosions throughout my nervous system.

Brogan serves my fish and corn before fixing his own plate. I take some salad from the bowl but decide to wait until he has a couple bites before I try it. After all, it's the one thing I didn't see him make.

Once I'm fairly certain the food hasn't been tampered with, I dig in, and it's delicious. I say as much. "You have quite a flair in the kitchen."

"I've been cooking for myself for enough years that I've learned a thing or two," he replies modestly.

We continue an amiable banter until we hear the distinct sound of a vehicle coming toward us. "Are you expecting company?" he asks me.

I shake my head. "You?"

"No." A shiny SUV that looks distinctly out of place in the woods pulls up. Then the door opens, and a long slender leg emerges. *What in the heck is she doing here?*

Chapter Forty-Two

The Mothers

Ruby: No word from either Brogan or Addie. I've decided to take that as a good sign.
Libby: If you say so. I'd go up and check on them, just in case.
Ruby: I don't think so. They might be making us a grandbaby at this very moment. I don't want to risk breaking the mood.
Libby: You can't possibly think they've jumped into bed already.
Ruby: Maybe not, but you can't stop me from hoping.
Libby: This feels like highly inappropriate speculation.
Ruby: Don't be a prude.
Libby: I'm not, but two people who've just met need to take some time to get to know each other before they do that.
Ruby: First of all, Addie and Brogan have known each other their whole lives. And secondly, what

planet do you live on?
Libby: If this is going to turn into the kind of relationship we hope for, they're better off taking things slowly.
Ruby: You mean like you did with Bob?
Libby: Shut up.

Brogan

I stand up so quickly my chair falls over behind me. Candidly, I ask the intruder, "Emma, what are you doing here?"

She creeps toward me like a hunter trying to get the jump on its prey. "You wouldn't return my calls. How else was I going to talk to you?"

"Some people might have assumed that if their calls weren't returned it was because the person they were calling didn't want to speak to them."

She belatedly seems to realize she and I are not alone and turns toward Addie. "What are you doing here?"

"Eating," the sassy Miss Cooper replies drolly.

Emma addresses me again. "I thought you said she was just a friend."

"I remember saying it was none of your business."

Emma takes turns staring death daggers at me and Addie before finally settling her gaze on me. "I'd like to talk to you privately, please."

Addie doesn't look like she has any intention of getting up. In fact, she puts her silverware down and leans back like she's watching a particularly interesting play.

"Whatever you have to say, you can say it in front of Addison," I tell her. Not because I want her to air any dirty laundry, quite the opposite. I'm hoping she'll just turn around and finally take the hint that I'm not interested in her anymore.

"I don't want to talk in front of her, Brogan," Emma points at Addie.

"Then you should go." She can't possibly expect me to care what she has to say after all this time, can she?

Emma looks torn. She finally stands in front of me with her back to Addie. "You and I used to talk about having children. Do you remember?"

Of course, I remember. It's a topic of conversation engaged couples regularly cover. "I don't remember," I lie.

"Brogan, we were good together. You have to admit that."

"I think you'd better get yourself a dictionary, Emma. When a couple is good together, one of them doesn't take a job across the country without discussing it with the other. They don't cheat either."

She has the good grace to look away when I say that. Then she seems to gather up steam and announces, "I want a baby."

Addie full-on spits her wine across the table when she hears that.

I wipe some of it off my cheek before telling my ex, "I can't imagine what that has to do with me."

"I'm thirty-five years old and I'm not getting any younger, Brogan. I sat down and made a list of traits that I want the father of my child to have and you are the only man I know who possesses all of them."

"I don't want to have a baby with you," I tell her in no uncertain terms.

"I think you're misunderstanding me. I want a baby, not a father for my baby."

"What in the hell does that mean?" I ask, totally confused.

Addie answers for her. "She wants a sperm donor."

Emma turns around and snaps, "Stay out of it. This is none of your business."

"Is this why you're here?" I demand.

"I don't want your money," she hurries to say. "And you don't need to be a part of the baby's life at all."

"Why in the world would I agree to this?" Also, what kind of man does she think I am that I would participate in creating a life and then not take responsibility for it?

"But our child could be your legacy if you want it to be."

"Emma, if I want a legacy, I'll create one with somebody I love."

"You loved me once," she says, sounding desperate.

"Past tense," I remind her. "I don't love you now, nor will I ever again."

"Are you saying no because of her?" She points to Addison.

Addie decides to join the conversation and says, "I'd make a way better mom than you."

"How dare you!"

"I dare because you appeared out of nowhere, uninvited, and you're interrupting our dinner," she answers. On the back of a dead stare only a New Yorker could hold, she tells Emma, "For another, I know what a wonderful man Brogan is, and I would never cheat on him."

She makes eye contact with me when she says this, and I decide in that moment that come hell or high water I'm going to kiss Addison Cooper tonight.

"Don't judge me." Emma takes a step toward Addie.

Addie takes a slow sip of her wine. "You have a lot of nerve coming out here."

"What are you gonna do about it?" Emma demands as she looms over Addie.

Addie looks like she's about to lose her cool, so I intervene. "Emma, you need to go, now."

"Brogan, please," Emma begs. "If I'm going to have a baby I need to do it now. I'm having some female troubles and I don't have time to find someone else."

"Go to a sperm bank," I tell her.

"Brogan ..." Emma sounds so pathetic I actually feel sorry for her.

But not enough that I don't say, "Not if you were the last woman on earth and it was the only way to repopulate the planet."

"It *is* because of her, isn't it?" Emma points again at Addie.

I begin to say, "It has nothing to do with her ..."

But that's all the farther I get because Addison interrupts, "Of course it does." Then she turns her attention to Emma and says, "Brogan knows I couldn't possibly want to see your face at birthday parties and school functions after we have our own family."

Even though she's being sarcastic—or is she?—for her to even joke about such a thing makes it clear she's thinking of me in a different light.

Emma turns her back to Addie and begs, "Please think about this, Brogan. If I ever meant anything to you, please help me."

I just shake my head and say, "No." I watch as Emma slinks away before turning to Addie apologetically for our dinner being crashed. Am I wrong or is there a light in her eye that doesn't seem to have anything to do with anger?

Chapter Forty-Three

The Mothers

Libby: Do you remember that time Brogan and James put plastic wrap under the toilet seat of the outhouse?
Ruby: Which time? As far as I recall that was a pretty standard prank.
Libby: The first time, 2 a.m., when Addie was the recipient and she screamed like she was being murdered.
Ruby: Ah, yes. The people in the neighboring campsite came running and nearly shot us.
Libby: They thought we were being attacked by wild animals.
Ruby: What brought that memory up?
Libby: I might have asked Chris to help Addie get even before I left.
Ruby: Why would you do that?
Libby: I thought it would help Addie get her need for revenge out of her system so she could focus on romance. ♡
Ruby: Libs, what have you done?

Addison

You know those bizarre dreams where you stand up in the middle of a high school football game and proceed to run down the bleachers to start cheering along with the cheerleaders? The crowd starts laughing and whistling so loudly that you look down and realize you're stark naked? That's what I feel like right now.

I cannot believe I just told Brogan's ex that he and I were planning to have a family. What was I thinking?

After Emma spins her car tires, tearing away, leaving us in a cloud of her dust, Brogan smiles at me and asks, "How about some dessert?" His tone suggests he has something more than food in mind.

"What did you make?" I ask, trying to get this conversation on the right track.

"I picked up some chocolate mousse from the lodge. They have a new pastry chef who's kicking things up a notch."

"Chocolate mousse is one of my go-to desserts. It's great with raspberries … and cherries … and cookies …" I reason that the longer we discuss dessert, the sooner he'll forget my comment about, you know …

"This is a bourbon chocolate mousse served with pistachio *tuiles* and candied rose petals."

"Yum! Count me in," I tell him.

Brogan clears our dishes while I try to regain my dignity. I slam back the rest of my wine and even reach over to refill my glass. Liquid courage. When he comes back, he places two beautifully decorated plates down on the table.

I gingerly pick up my spoon and get ready to fill it when Brogan says, "That was quite a conversation with Emma …"

I unceremoniously drop my spoon with a clatter on the table. "I'm so sorry," I tell him. "That was a completely inappropriate comment. I shouldn't have said anything but I really don't like that woman. I mean, who comes groveling back to their ex looking for a baby daddy?"

"Apparently, Emma does.'

"Were you two together for long?" I ask.

"Three years."

"I should probably offer my sympathies, but the truth is, I think you dodged a bullet."

"I most definitely did." He's staring at me so intently I'm glad to be sitting down.

I hurriedly lift my spoon to give my mouth something to do other than talk. The mousse is so divine, I nearly groan out loud in pleasure as the flavors burst on my tongue. "This rivals any dessert I've ever had, and I've eaten at some pretty fabulous places."

"The new pastry chef came from a Michelin-rated restaurant in Los Angeles."

"Why in the world would she leave there to come here?" From what I know of the restaurant business, which isn't much, I do know that working in a Michelin-starred restaurant is the dream no one walks away from, unless they're opening their own place.

Brogan shrugs. "I don't know. I haven't met her yet. But a lot of people love Oregon. They don't think it's as backward as you seem to think it is."

"I believe I've already mentioned that I have nothing against the state," I reply before taking another bite of mousse.

"I could apologize again, but clearly that doesn't seem to work with you."

"Brogan, I accept your apology, I really do. But it doesn't rewrite history. I can't forget you did all of those horrible things to me."

He reaches across the table and tenderly takes my hands. He squeezes them and says, "If I were you, I'd try to get even with me. Happily, you seem to be much more evolved than I am." *If he only knew.*

"Childish games have never been of interest to me." Which is generally true except for that little clam juice and honey on the toilet thing. Although something seems to be happening and revenge no longer feels as important as it did just a couple of days ago.

Is this attraction I feel so strong that I'd willingly give up retribution in hopes of something more interesting happening between us? As I contemplate the idea, Brogan scoots his chair closer to mine. The tiny hairs on my arms stand up straight like antennas looking for a signal in outer space.

Brogan leans closer to me and practically purrs, "I'm very happy that our paths have crossed again, Addison. Incredibly happy."

"Yes, well ..." I'm not quite sure how to react so I say, "It's nice to see you, too."

"Even if it means being stuck in a cabin in the woods for a month?"

"I love a good decorating challenge," I tell him honestly. "The truth is, now that I have a bathtub, you'd better get your checkbook out."

"You seem pretty sure of yourself."

"As long as you play fair, I've got this."

"What do you mean by that?"

"As long as you don't resort to previous childish behavior, I think I've conquered all my worries," I explain, while purposely pushing the image of clam juice out of my brain.

"I haven't pulled one prank since you arrived."

"But you wagered that I couldn't stay out in the woods," I remind him.

"You weren't honor bound to accept that bet."

"No, I wasn't." Drat that man using logic against me at a time like this.

He leans in again and I know beyond a shadow of a doubt that he's about to kiss me. I want him to, but I need a moment to collect my thoughts, so I push my chair away from the table and say, "I'm just going to use the bathroom."

He waves his hand toward the outhouse. "My outhouse is your outhouse." I take a candle off the table so I can see what I'm doing in there. On the way, I realize how badly I have to go.

Once I'm situated and get down to business, a pleasantly warm sensation hits my butt. I don't realize what it is until it starts to run down the back of my legs to my ankles.

Oh. My. God. Someone plastic wrapped Brogan's toilet. I am once again the recipient of the plastic wrap on the toilet gag. I have no words. Okay, I have words, I'm just trying to find them in the red-hot swirl of anger that's forming in my brain.

Did Brogan do this? Yet why would he wrap his own toilet

seat? Unless of course he did it knowing that I would use his toilet before he did. Men have the ability to pee on a tree with no additional effort. Of course, it's just as possible that Billy did this trying to help me get my revenge.

I quickly wipe up as much of the mess as I can before pulling up my wet pants. Even before I find out the truth, I need to get out of here and change my clothes. Unfortunately, that means I have to pass the dinner table where Brogan is still sitting.

"Addie, what's wrong?" Is that genuine concern in his voice?

"I need to go," I tell him before turning and practically running down the path to my place. I'm so upset that I don't immediately realize all the lanterns I bought for my cabin have been hung in the trees and are fully lit. I don't recognize this until I step into the clearing and surprise my friend Billy in the bathtub.

Chapter Forty-Four

The Mothers

> *Ruby: Did I ever tell you about the time Brogan broke his leg and had to be in a cast for two months?*
> *Libby: I vaguely remember hearing something about him falling out of a tree.*
> *Ruby: He was trying to put a baby bird back into its nest and he lost his footing. James was a nightmare during that time. He knew he could get away with all kinds of stuff because Brogan couldn't chase him.*
> *Libby: Why are you telling me this now?*
> *Ruby: I have a feeling James might be in collusion with Chris to prank Brogan. I saw my younger son this morning in a golf cart on the path heading to the fishing cabin. 😳*
> *Libby: And?*
> *Ruby: There were 3 full bags in the back that look like the ones our landscape folks use to collect leaves.*

Libby: Maybe he was taking up some old clothes or blankets or something.
Ruby: Really, that's the best you got?
Libby: He'll blame Addie. 😳 Just like he will if Chris pranks him.
Ruby: The whole point was for him to blame and confront her so they could have a heated moment that led to something more. But if too many people get in on this, it might backfire.

Brogan

What just happened here? One moment Addie and I are on the verge of romance and the next she's tearing down the path toward her cabin. *What happened inside that outhouse?* I get up to inspect the premises hoping to gather some clarity and start laughing when I see the plastic on the toilet seat.

Talk about a blast from the past, someone plastic wrapped the toilet. I can only think of one person who might have done that and it's the same one who fed me the worst meal of my life.

The question is, why would she have wrapped the seat herself and then used it? That's not something a person is likely to forget doing. But if Addie didn't do it, and I didn't do it, who did?

I should go after her, but I realize she's probably embarrassed and wouldn't welcome the company. I sit back down at the table and eat both desserts as it looks like that's the only kind of sugar I'll be getting tonight. I make a mental note to tell my mom how great her new pastry chef is. She's well worth whatever she's being paid.

I continue to replay the evening in my mind, spending a little extra time on the scene where Addie basically told Emma that she didn't want their kids to share a father. This leads me to wondering what Addie's and my children would look like. I'm assuming they'd be gorgeous like their mom, while hopefully having my aptitude for the great outdoors.

What in the world am I doing? Addison Cooper and I aren't going to make babies together. We can't even enjoy a meal together without something going drastically wrong. Babies are the last thing that should be on my mind.

I wonder why Emma would ever think I'd be open to having a kid with her. I feel bad she's in the position she is, but it's in no way my doing. Had she stayed faithful, we would have been married by now and probably already had our first child. As far as I'm concerned, she got caught up in the karmic wheel. She's stuck in a mud puddle of her own making.

After cleaning up the dinner dishes and securing the leftovers in the refrigerator for tomorrow's lunch, I decide to call it a night. The bedroom is small enough that I don't need a lantern to light my way. So I disrobe and climb into bed, ready to succumb to the sandman.

I'm not even fully reclined before I know something is wrong. The sheets up here might not be the softest in the world, but they don't crunch when you lie on them. *Is that a pinecone jabbing into my back?* Ouch!

My bed is full of a combination of dried leaves, wet leaves, pinecones, pine needles, and any assorted organic matter that was attached to them. I'm not amused.

After getting out of bed, I turn on a lamp to witness the sheer amount of nature that's piled on my mattress. Shaking my head, I open the window and begin the process of returning it to where it belongs. If Addie did this, she's acting like a real child and while I get her being angry about the past, this is taking things a little too far.

Once my bed is cleared, I put my clothes back on before crawling back in. I close my eyes and try to fall asleep, but my sheets smell funky, like there might have been something else mixed into that pile. Gross.

Grabbing my pillow and blanket, I decide to sleep on the couch, which I know will only be marginally more comfortable than lying on the hard ground. Needless to say, it isn't the most restful night.

I wake up with a stiff back and crick in my neck from sleeping with my head propped up on the arm of the sofa. It was that or have my feet stick so far over the edge that I hyper-extend my knees. It seems I was slated for discomfort no matter what.

I snap, crackle, and pop like that breakfast cereal from my childhood as I begin the slow process of unfolding myself and stretching out. After taking three ibuprofen, I put on an extra-large pot of coffee, then I sit down to think about what I'm going to do regarding Addie.

Should I go up and confront her about last night's pranks, or should I let her enjoy the feeling of getting even? I'm still not sure which direction I'll go while I walk down the path to her place.

All seems quiet as I step into the clearing by Addie's cabin. I hear some rustling coming from the tent she set up and am shocked to see Billy emerge as though he just woke up.

"Sleeping in?" I call to him.

"What time is it?" he looks concerned.

"Eight fifteen," I tell him.

He shakes his head. "That girl went and bought me an air mattress. It's the most comfortable thing I've slept on in my whole life."

"She's turning you soft, huh?"

"I guess so. Thought I was content the way I was, but I'm worried it's gonna be hard to go back to my camp."

"Why don't you just move down here then?" I ask him.

He doesn't answer. Instead he heads toward the outhouse. I wait for him to emerge before asking, "Did Addie tell you what happened last night?"

"No, sir."

I'm not surprised she didn't say anything. I decide to change the subject and ask, "What do you make of a bathtub in the middle of the woods?"

"I hate to admit it, but I think it's a fine addition. I took a bath just last night."

"Addison Cooper is having a surprising effect on you, old man," I tell him teasingly.

"I'm not the only one she's having an effect on," he replies smugly.

"There's something about that woman that's starting to get to me. But just when I think things are about to get interesting, she wraps my toilet in plastic and dumps a load of leaves on my mattress."

Billy starts to laugh. "Boy, if that isn't life coming full circle, I don't know what is."

"Yeah, yeah, yeah, I'm getting mine. What I can't figure out is how she's managed to do it without me noticing."

Billy shrugs. "Women are mysterious creatures."

"Were you ever married?" I ask. It seems that Billy has been opening himself up to Addie quite a bit and I wonder if he might do the same with me now that the pump has been primed.

"You want some coffee?" he asks, totally ignoring my question.

"Sure." I follow him into Addie's cabin.

He puts his finger to his mouth to keep me quiet as he points. Addison is sound asleep on the king-size bed in the living room. She looks delectable all snug under the covers with a frilly sleep mask covering her eyes. She doesn't at all look like somebody up to no good.

I finally peel my gaze away from her to see that she's made a number of other changes to the cabin. There's a nature scene hanging over the mantel as well as candle sconces on either side of it. She's even hung curtains from the windows.

I shake my head at all the things she thinks are necessary for glamping. This place is starting to look more like a home than a campsite. I walk closer to the bed to watch her sleep. Darn, she's sweet looking when that brain of hers is at rest. I make a note to tell her that when a scream pierces the air that nearly has me hitting the ceiling.

Chapter Forty-Five

The Mothers

> *Libby: Remember that Ken doll that Addie used to have?*
> *Ruby: The one she renamed Brogan and used to string up from the tree so she could hit it with tennis balls?*
> *Libby: That's the one.*
> *Ruby: What about it?*
> *Libby: I dreamed about it last night. It made me worry for Brogan.*
> *Ruby: Do you think Addie's going to beat him up or something?*
> *Libby: Not necessarily, but it still might be a good idea to check on them today.*

Addison:

I open my eyes to find a large shadow looming over me, so I do what any normal person would do in the same situation. I scream.

The shadow doesn't retreat like you'd expect, though. It moves toward me, menacingly. I reach over and grab my pepper spray from the nightstand, then I point it and let it loose.

"What in the hell are you doing?" it shouts. *Uh-oh, it's Brogan.*

"What am *I* doing? What are you doing? You shouldn't stand over someone while they're sleeping. That's creepy."

Billy comes running in from the kitchen with a bowl of water. "Splash this in your eyes," he says.

Brogan does as he's told before asking, "Does she have any milk in there? If so, can you bring that next? It'll decrease the burning."

"Been hit with pepper spray before have you?" I ask somewhat worriedly, seeing how much pain he is in.

"I'm a writer. I research all kinds of crazy things," he says with his jaw clenched so tightly, the words come out sounding more like a growl than a conversation.

"I'm sorry I sprayed you," I tell him truthfully. "But you shouldn't sneak up on a person while they're sleeping."

"I wasn't sneaking," he says, sounding anguished.

Billy calls out, "Come in here, boy, and let's rinse your eyes out good."

I hear the splashing sounds coming from the kitchen when Billy walks in and says, "I was just going to make a pot of coffee, if that's okay."

"Go ahead," I tell him. Then I get out of bed and put a robe on before joining them in the kitchen area. While Brogan flushes his eyes with milk, I demand, "Why were you standing over me? Up to your old tricks again, were you?"

"You mean like filling your bed with leaves?"

"I particularly hated that one," I hiss. "Is that what you were going to do? Dump some in here with me?" The nerve of this man!

"*You're the one who* put the leaves in *my* bed last night. Did you do that before or after you plastic wrapped the toilet?"

"I didn't do either of those things! Why would I plastic wrap the toilet and then use it without removing the plastic first?"

"Woman, I have no idea why you do anything you do," he says.

I chance a glance over at Billy to see if he might have been the responsible party, but he shrugs his shoulders innocently.

Brogan opens the cabinet in front of him and pulls out the clam juice. Guiltily, I admit, "Okay, I pulled one prank on you, but that's it."

"Clam-flavored blackberries with whipped cream." His face contorts as though he's vividly reliving the experience.

A tiny thrill of victory shoots through me and I ill-advisedly start to laugh. "I'll never forget the way you ran out of here."

"Why would you do that?" he asks incredulously.

"Why wouldn't I?" I counter.

He shakes his head like a parent scolding a child. "You know you declared war when you did that, don't you?"

"Don't you dare do anything else to me! Do you hear me?"

"I'm supposed to let you execute all these stunts and just take it?"

"I only pulled one prank on you, so don't go blaming me for your bad behavior. Even if I duct taped you to your bed, slathered you in honey, and then left the doors open so the bears could get you, we wouldn't be even. Am I clear?"

His look softens and I'm afraid he might be about to make a grab for me, so I step back. He flirtatiously drawls, "I think you have a kinky side, Addison Cooper."

"What?" Of course, he'd think that. I want to beat my fists against that thick skull of his and knock some sense into him. I want to stomp my feet and throw mud pies at him. I want to throw myself into his arms and see if they're as strong as they look. *Where did that come from?*

Billy walks out the door like nothing heated is occurring. He says, "If you two stand closer to the pot, the water will boil quicker."

Things *are* getting hot in here. "Please leave so I can get dressed," I tell Brogan.

"Don't do it on my account." His gaze scorches over me. He makes no effort to leave.

"Go!" I yell at him. This time he offers a wink and saunters slowly toward the door. Before exiting, he says, "I'd be happy to call a truce, if you want."

"You're a big baby, do you know that?" I ask. "I pulled *one* prank on you compared to the dozens you've pulled on me and you can't handle it."

"Addison, I've already lived my past. I don't need to repeat it. I've apologized to you again and again. If the only way you can heal your demons is to seek revenge, go for it. Just know that I'm not going to sit back and take it."

"Are you threatening me?" I demand.

He shakes his head slowly before answering, "Not in the least. I'm just telling it like it is."

"Okay, big man, if that's how you want to play it, that's how we'll play it. But you can't do anything to me if I don't do anything to you. Am I clear?"

"So far you've attacked three times and I've taken it. I think I have some lost time to make up for," he says with a smirk.

With my hands on my hips and what I hope is death lasers shooting out of my eyes, I correct, "I did one thing to you. ONE! Get it straight."

He merely turns around, but not before getting in the last word. "Watch your back," he says in such a way the hairs on the back of my neck stand on end.

Chapter Forty-Six

The Mothers

Ruby: I talked to Chris and she claims she didn't do anything.
Libby: It sounds like you don't believe her.
Ruby: I've known Chris a long time, and while I would guess she's technically telling the truth, I think she may have asked somebody else to help.
Libby: Who?
Ruby: Her husband, her daughter, who knows? You'd better get in touch with her directly and call off whatever plans she has for the future.
Libby: I'll do it right now. But you need to talk to James and nip that situation in the bud. ✂
Ruby: I'm on it.

Brogan

Does Addison think she can lie to my face and I'll just buy it? She's not that good of an actress.

My brain churns with ideas as I stomp through the forest

toward the fishing cabin. I could do any number of things to her to get even, starting with taking the door off her outhouse. Then I could fill her ridiculous bathtub with worms, and crack eggs all over her sheets ... I'm channeling all of my best adolescent pranks.

I enjoy each and every scenario before talking myself down. Maybe Addie needs this revenge to finally get over it and move on. Would it be so horrible to just suffer through and let her get it out of her system? In all honesty, I do have it coming to me.

I wrestle with my options and am so absorbed in them that I don't realize there's a golf cart heading straight for me until it's nearly upon me. "Mom, what are you doing up here?" I ask before I see that the back of the cart is full of packages.

"Just making a delivery. How are you doing, honey?" she asks. Then looking closer she adds, "You don't look so good. Have you been crying?"

I don't mention the pepper spray, instead, I tell her, "I didn't sleep well last night."

"Would you like a nice, big, king-size bed sent up to your cabin, too?" Her tone suggests I'm turning into Addie—too soft for my own good.

While I'd like nothing more than to stretch out in a big bed, I'm forced to reply, "I'm just fine the way I am, thank you."

She eyes me like she just won a point against me. I start to wonder if I'm at war with every female in the area. "Do you want to have lunch today, Mom?" I ask, hoping that spending time with her will get her firmly back on my side. Or as much on my side as she can be with our current wager in place.

"Sorry, honey, I've got plans."

"Are you even a little bit happy that I'm home?" I ask bluntly. I mean seriously, if she's not, I could just leave.

She smiles at me fondly and answers, "I always love to see you, dear, but it's our busy season. I promise to make time for you as soon as possible. In fact, I was thinking about inviting you and Addie to the lodge for supper, if you think you can break your rule for one meal."

The thought of putting on some nice clothes and eating at a restaurant sounds wonderful right now. "When?"

"Let me check my book and get back to you," she says before tooting her horn and driving off.

If Addie and I are both at the lodge, I can spend time with her without worrying she's up to something. We'd have to be on our best behavior in front of my mom. The more I think about it, the more I like the idea. Maybe Addison and I just need a reboot and then all will be well.

Or so I think until I put my hand on the doorknob to my cabin and try to open it. It's covered in vegetable shortening and my palm slides all over unable to get a grip. How did she manage to do this while she was sleeping? *She must have someone else helping her.* But who? Billy was up at her place the same time I was. Also, why would he plot against me? I've been nothing but nice to him.

I finally use my shirt to wipe the doorknob so that I can get some traction and open it. I walk in, thoroughly ignorant that the perpetrator also decided to grease the floor. When I put my foot down, I go shooting across the wooden planks like a bowling ball on its way to a strike. What in the fresh hell?

With the backache I already had from sleeping on the couch,

this fall does nothing to ensure my comfort. I eventually run out of greased floor and roll over so I can bring myself to my knees. Ouch.

After scrubbing the mess as best I can, I sprinkle some salt on top to cover any lingering areas. Vegetable shortening does not wipe up easily. Once I'm done, I inspect the rest of the cabin to make sure there are no more unpleasant surprises lying in wait.

I once again feel bad about the things I put Addie through as a kid. But seriously, it's one thing for a four-foot-tall, sixty-pound girl to slide and fall, and quite another for a six-foot three, two-hundred-pound man.

I decide to head into town to buy a degreaser to finish cleaning up the mess. I don't want to call housekeeping on the chance that they'd tell my mom what happened. It's best to keep her out of this as much as possible. Not because she'd be upset on my behalf, but because it might give her ideas about helping Addie win the bet.

Cheryl is working at the market today, and as soon as she sees me, she calls out, "You're back. I don't see you in months and then I get the privilege twice in the same week."

"Cheryl," I say rather curtly.

"You having a bad day?"

"You could say that."

"Brogan Cavanaugh, what bug crawled up your butt and built itself a condo?"

I wasn't planning to say anything to her about the clam juice, but I can't make small talk with her without knowing why she told Addie about my aversion. I turn to my old friend and demand, "Why in the world did you tell Addison Cooper how much I hate clams?"

Instead of denying it or trying to act evasive, Cheryl laughs right in my face. "Well, gee, Brogan, I don't know." Then she says, "Remember those stories you used to tell us about *Honey Bucket?* You told them in such a way that made it sound like the girl had it coming. Then I meet her and she's as sweet and lovely as they come. I figured it wouldn't hurt you a bit to reap a little of what you've sown."

She's got her hands on her hips and her head is wobbling back and forth like I'd better not contradict her in any way. "What else have you helped her with?" I ask.

"I brought her some wine the other night."

"That's it?" I demand.

"Yup. Are you by chance telling me that she's found some other ways to get even with you?" The look on her face is one of sheer delight.

"That's what I'm telling you. Man, you'd think I was the devil or something."

Cheryl softens her body language. "Sometimes you just have to accept the payback and move on." Which is exactly what I had been thinking. She adds, "I can't imagine Addie going anywhere near the lengths you used to."

"You don't know how mad she still is at me," I tell her.

"Yes, I do. But I also know she's a lovely woman."

"Well, someone else is out there pranking me. Who would it be if not Addie?"

Cheryl shrugs her shoulders. "You got me. That's a question you need to ask yourself."

I walk to the cleaning aisle and do just that. I decide I have one more stop to make before I go back to the cabin.

Chapter Forty-Seven

The Mothers

Libby: Remember how we spent my birthday our first year at college?
Ruby: We went out with those guys from the second floor and then we ditched them as soon as Bob and Tom showed up.
Libby: I used to feel kind of bad about that?
Ruby: Love is a battlefield, girl. Plus, we just went out for pizza. It's not like they'd invited us out for a nice dinner or something.
Libby: You're right. Maybe we should just let Addie and Brogan fight this thing out. You're the one who keeps saying love and hate are opposite sides of the same coin.
Ruby: I do say that, don't I? Okay, I'll back off and we'll let the prank chips fall where they may.
Libby: If things work out, it'll be part of their ♡ story.

Addison

After Brogan leaves, I hurry to put on a pair of cropped pants and t-shirt. I don't mind Billy coming in and making coffee while I'm asleep, it's another thing entirely for Brogan to just walk in and lurk about. My blood still feels like hot lava flowing through me. Unfortunately, this isn't a reaction to anger. It's pure lust and I'd kick myself for it if I could.

Before I can pour a cup of Billy's freshly brewed coffee, there's a knock on the door, followed by Aunt Ruby's voice calling out, "Good morning, I brought the mail."

I love shopping in person where I can touch and smell and feel everything before purchasing it. Having said that, there's a thrill that comes with buying online that makes it seem like Christmas when all the boxes start to arrive.

I open the door quickly and greet, "Good morning! How did you sleep?"

She gives me a hug before walking in. "As well as I ever do." Then she asks, "Why was Brogan here this morning?"

She must have seen him on the path. "I guess he had to talk to Billy about something. I was sleeping until just a minute ago."

She eyes me up and down like she's trying to decide if she believes me. Then her gaze wanders around the room. "It looks beautiful in here!" she says, clapping her hands together in rapid fire.

She inspects everything from the pine green raw silk lamp shade with the crystal beads to the basket of river rocks. "I thought it would be nice to have a small stash of art supplies on hand for guests with children. I collected the rocks thinking they could paint them," I explain.

"What fun," Aunt Ruby enthuses.

"They can take them home as a souvenir, but I thought it would be nice to have them paint one rock that they leave here. You can ask them to share it on social media with a hashtag of your choosing. Something like #WillametteLodgeGlamping.

"That's a terrific idea!"

"You have a Facebook and Instagram page for the lodge, don't you?"

Aunt Ruby looks sheepish when she answers, "We have them, but we don't do much with them."

"You're missing the best free advertising in the world," I tell her. "You need to post at least weekly if not more often, and make sure to encourage your guests to post their pictures. I promise you'll have a waiting list a mile long."

"Should we mention the glamping or wait until it's all done?" she asks.

"I'd start building the excitement now and post pics of the renovations as they take place. Either way, you should be promoting the existing lodge and activities."

"You have a real knack for this, don't you?" Aunt Ruby asks me.

"I love all aspects of preparing a great vacation spot. People should be able to leave their cares at home and enjoy unparalleled escape when they go away."

"Have you ever thought of opening your own place someday?" she asks.

"I haven't." But now that she's mentioned it, I realize the idea has merit.

"When you get married and have kids, it might be nice to not have to travel so much." She picks up a pine cone that I found during one of my walks.

"I haven't spent a lot of time thinking about getting married and having a family," I tell her. "I've been primarily career driven for the last several years."

"I'm not saying that you're running out of time or anything," she lets the comment hang in the air like a thick mist before adding, "I mean you're only, what, twenty-eight?"

"Thirty-two," I tell her. She arches her eyebrows and makes a funny cringey face that suggests my eggs are passing soft boiled as we speak.

Patting me on the arm, she says, "It's not my place to say anything. You kids need to live your own lives without busybody moms getting involved."

"I'll meet someone someday and, God willing, have a family." Why do I feel like I have to defend the choices I've made? I know I'm getting older, but I haven't felt my biological clock start to tick yet. Have I?

"Why don't you come outside and see what's in all your boxes? There must be ten of them," she exclaims excitedly.

I follow her out the door and, sure enough, the back of her golf cart is loaded down. I hurry to look at the return address labels and discover the top three are from a fabric outlet online. "Wait until you see what's in here," I say eagerly.

Once we get them all inside, I start to open the identically sized oblong boxes. Aunt Ruby stands over my shoulder as I pull out the first of many bolts of fabric. "What in the world is all that for?" she wants to know.

"I bought a ton of canvas," I tell her before explaining, "I figured that as long as you look at this place and see so much wood, you're going to think 'cabin.' While there's nothing wrong with that, if you're selling people on glamping then they should feel like they're camping. I'm going to drape this fabric on the walls and ceiling, in the main room, cutting holes for windows, doors, etc. so when they're inside for the night, they'll feel like they're in a tent, not a free-standing structure."

Aunt Ruby looks at me like I'm an alien who just stopped by to borrow a cup of sugar. "Addie Cooper, just when I thought you couldn't have another great idea ... I can't wait to see how this is going to look! Do you need help?" Before I can answer, she says, "Helena up in housekeeping is a whiz with a sewing machine. We've put her in charge of mending whatever needs mending up at the lodge."

"I'd love for her to come and get some measurements. She can take the fabric back up and get working on it as soon as today, if she has the time."

"I'll tell her the very minute I get back up to the lodge," she says, looking as full of anticipation as I am. "What else do you have in those boxes?"

We spend another fun hour opening the rest of my purchases. The final and heaviest box is full of books that I bought from a used bookseller. There's everything from Steinbeck's *Travels with Charlie* to *The Shining* for adults and *The Little House on the Prairie* series and *The Adventures of Huck Finn* for kids. I put them on the small bookshelf I bought from Herman's store in town.

Aunt Ruby's eyes are positively glowing when she exclaims,

"You've thought of everything. Have you tried the bathtub yet?"

"I have and it's amazing. I never would have thought bathing in the outdoors would have been my thing, but it's strangely relaxing." I don't tell her that Brogan walked in on me mid-bath, but the memory alone is enough to speed up the beating of my confused heart.

I have got to figure out what in the heck is going on with that guy. How could I possibly feel any attraction for a man who's just threatened to start pranking me again?

Chapter Forty-Eight

The Mothers

Ruby: I may have just reminded Addie that her biological clock is ticking.
Libby: How did she take that?
Ruby: At first she looked alarmed like she'd never thought about it before but then I pointed out that she has loads of time being that she's only twenty-eight.
Libby: She's thirty-two.
Ruby: I know.
Libby: Your strategy could backfire you know.
Ruby: Yeah, but it's not going to. I dropped the subject as soon as I brought it up. I just needed to plant the seed. Also, I've started to think Addie is the perfect person to take over for me when I retire.
Libby: She'd never!
Ruby: Never say never, my friend. I have a feeling about this ...

Brogan

I'd bet my last dollar that James is helping Addie exact her revenge. Being that both the prickly Miss Cooper and Billy were with me when my doorknob and floor were greased, somebody else has to be on her payroll. I'm willing to bet the down payment on a new hay baler is all the motivation my brother needs.

The ironic part is that I'd buy James a hay baler right out if he'd let me, but he's got too much pride for that. Not enough that he wouldn't swindle it out of me though.

The lot at Poppa's is full when I pull in, so I drive a little farther and park in James's driveway. His weathered farmhouse lies just beyond the farm stand. I walk over to Poppa's to see if my brother is there and find him fighting with the same woman he was arguing with the other day.

I didn't realize it before, but she looks really familiar. I just can't place where I know her from. I hear James exclaim, "Why do you keep coming back here?"

She responds, "I'm looking for a new supplier for my work and you have good stuff. If you'd only certify it, I could bring you a lot of business."

"Why are you looking for someone new? Wait, let me guess, your old source quit because you're such a ginormous pain in the butt." My brother glares at her like he's trying to bore holes into her skull.

"For your information," she answers, "my current supplier's produce is wonderful, but their prices are a bit steep. I'm trying to increase my company's profit margin." I briefly wonder if she works for the market in town. It's either that or a grocery chain.

James better think twice before he passes up an opportunity like that.

"Lady, I need you to walk out of here and never come back. Do you understand?"

"How in the world do you expect to make a living with such poor people skills?" she retaliates.

"People love me," he assures her.

"I can't imagine," she retaliates.

"Why is it so important that your supplier be certified organic," he asks, sounding truly bewildered. "Folks around here understand the term 'no spray.'"

I intervene before the two of them start ripping each other's hair out at the roots. "Hey, brother, what are you up to?" I ask him. "Been greasing any doorknobs lately?"

He turns his attention toward me and demands, "What are you talking about?"

"I was just wondering where you were earlier this morning."

His nemesis offers, "He's been here being unpleasant to me for the last three hours."

"Three hours?" I ask, shocked.

"Fine, twenty minutes," she says. "But your brother is so annoying and pig-headed, it feels more like three hours."

James doesn't even respond; he merely turns and walks away. I run after him. "Dude, you need to hold your temper with that woman. What if she's the buyer for Willamette Valley Grocery or something? You could be giving up a lot of business."

"I don't care if she buys produce for the royal family. I can't afford to be certified organic and even if I could, I wouldn't waste the money on it." He stops walking and turns to me before asking, "What's this about greased doorknobs?"

"Someone oiled my doorknob and floor leading into the cabin this morning. I know it couldn't have been Billy or Addison because I was with them when it had to have happened."

James starts laughing. "You're kidding? Looks like you've made more than one enemy, huh?"

"I don't have *any* enemies," I tell him, although I briefly wonder if Emma might consider me such, now that I won't father her child. I haven't shared this information with James yet, so I take the opportunity to do so.

"Emma Jackson wants you to be her baby daddy? That's pretty ballsy, all things considered," he says. "You don't think *she's* pranking you, do you?"

"How in the world would playing practical jokes on me help her end game?"

James shrugs. "You got me. So, you think it's Addie, huh?" He's acting almost too innocent with hands in his pockets and that naïve Forest Gump expression on his face.

"I think someone is helping her and I had considered that someone might be you," I tell him pointedly.

"Sorry, bro, I've been here since I woke up at four a.m. I have farmhands out the wazoo who can testify to that. Ask them if you don't believe me."

I believe him, but that means someone else is in collusion with Addie and it makes me nervous not knowing who that person is. "Never mind," I tell him. "Do you want to come up and have dinner with me tonight? I thought I'd put some steaks on the grill."

"Only if you feed me early," he says. "I need to be in bed by eight."

"I can feed you at six, does that work?"

"Yup. I'll bring a six pack and some peaches and cream for dessert. You need anything else?"

"No, that sounds good." Then I ask, "Hey, do you need any help around here today?"

"Seriously?" he sounds surprised. Surely, I've helped him before. I mean, I did just dig holes for peach trees the other day.

"Yeah, I've got nothing on the books today. I'd love to stick around and lend a hand. What are you up to?"

"Spreading manure in the fields that have already been harvested. I need to get the soil ready for spring planting."

Of course, we're spreading manure. What did I expect, a nice day of peach picking?

Chapter Forty-Nine

The Mothers

> *Libby: I'm planning to be back in a week. I'll text Addie so she can come to terms with her anger at me for leaving before I show up again. She's texted me over a dozen times.*
> *Ruby: Wait until you see what she's done with the cabin. The girl has a gift!*
> *Libby: That she does.*
> *Ruby: I thought you might be interested in knowing that I got in on pranking Brogan today. I'm thinking the sooner those two have a big blowout, the better.*
> *Libby: Go team!!!*

Addison:

True to her word, Aunt Ruby sends Helena up from housekeeping. She's way younger than I expected—probably in her late twenties. She's also quite beautiful and exotic looking with her high cheekbones and wide-set eyes. I briefly wonder what led her to her current occupation.

Helena seems just as excited as I am about our project and promises to be done within the week. I can't wait to see the final results.

After she leaves, I'm not sure what to do with myself. I've done as much as I can with the cabin until more supplies arrive. I decide to change into some jeans and boots and follow the citron ribbons I tied in the trees down to the main road. I think I'll avail myself of some of the lodge's outdoor activities.

I consider my options and decide that zip-lining is something I'd want to share with a friend. I briefly wonder if Cheryl would go with me sometime while I'm here. I also feel strongly that boating and paddle boarding should be done with someone else, in case I lose an oar or something. I've never particularly mastered water sports.

I therefore conclude that I should see if the stable has a mount available for me. As outdoorsy as people claim I'm not—and there's some truth to that depending on their definition—I'm a stellar horsewoman. I've been a regular rider since I was six and even though I don't currently own a horse, I do rent one whenever I can, either in Central Park or upstate where my parents live.

An older gentleman is brushing down a mare when I walk up. He's wearing a cowboy hat and dressed in all black like the Lone Ranger, sans the mask. I imagine he cut quite a dashing figure in his day. "Hello!" I call out while offering a wave.

"Howdy." He tips his hat. "My name's Jeet. How can I help you?"

"I'm hoping you can set me up with a ride. I'd like to go out for a couple of hours."

"All I have left is this here little lady or a cantankerous old coot named Thunder Foot. We don't let guests ride him though."

"Why not?" I ask. By the looks of the girl he's brushing, she wouldn't be good for more than a slow walk, and if I have to run from a cougar I want to make sure I'll get away.

"He's unpredictable. Only man that could ever ride him without worry was the owner of this place, Tom Cavanaugh, but he's been gone for about a year now."

"Uncle Tom used to tell me about him. I'd love to give him a go."

"Uncle?" he asks.

"My parents are good friends of the Cavanaughs."

"Let me call up to the lodge and ask Ruby what she thinks about that. If she says you can ride him then I won't stop you."

While he makes his call, I walk into the barn to find Thunder Foot and make friends with him. The only horse left in a stall is as black as a moonless night with a mane so long it makes me want to braid it. Although he's so handsome on his own, he might take offense at something as girly as a braid.

I walk up to him and gently say, "Hey, big fella, what do you say, do you want to be friends?"

He whinnies in reply and stomps his back foot twice. I take that to mean he's bored and wants to run. I gently scratch behind his ears and he lowers his head to give me better access. "Why, you're just a big sweetie, aren't you?"

He bobs his head up and down as though agreeing. I grab a carrot out of the bucket and give it to him, careful to lay it on my open palm and not offer any fingers for biting. After another carrot and a scratch, Thunder Foot and I are fast friends.

Jeet comes back into the barn and announces, "Ruby says you're good to go if you want to take him out."

After finding out which saddle to use, I throw it over the horse's back. He tenses his belly so that his abdomen fills with air and I can't get the cinch tight. I whisper to him, "You and I are friends and I'm not going to upset you in the least. Relax your belly so I can get this saddle on properly."

Within a couple of minutes, he follows instruction and I'm able to get the straps snug enough that I'll be secure. Once I'm mounted, I wave to Jeet and offer, "I'll be back in a few hours," then I let my mount show me where he feels like going. I don't know the area well, so I decide to let Thunder Foot be my tour guide.

It's been a few months since I've been on horseback. The last time was when a client took me out for the day to show me her property in the Hamptons. This is vastly different from that, wilder and more carefree.

Thunder Foot starts out slowly, but quickly sets a steady pace. He definitely knows where he wants to go and while I have no idea where that is, I also know he'll head back to the stables on his own when he's had enough. The trick will be not to let him get away from me if I get off his back for any reason.

We trot up a makeshift road that starts out going through the woods, but quickly weaves out of them again, opening into a field of wildflowers. At this point, the stallion breaks loose and gallops like he's trying to pick up enough steam to fly. It's a wonderful feeling that cracks the nut of tension that's been building since I arrived in Oregon.

We gradually start to climb until we reach a ridge that overlooks the valley below. Chills prickle my veins. I feel like I've ridden back in time to an Oregon that was here before the settlers came. It's untamed and beautiful and so lush that it's hard to believe it's real.

Thunder Foot whinnies and taps his foot, like he is saying, "You see why I brought you up here?"

"Wow." It's the only word I can think of. I can see why people are so drawn to this land. I feel like a sorceress looking down on creation below. I fancy that I've had some sort of mystical transformation. Of course, I'm not going to broadcast this metamorphosis to anyone. Brogan would no doubt rub my nose in it until the end of time.

Chapter Fifty

The Mothers

Ruby: I'm going to invite the kids up to the lodge tomorrow night and see if they can play nice.
Libby: Oh, to be a fly on the wall ...
Ruby: You could have been here if you didn't chicken out and leave.
Libby: I promise Addie would already be gone if I had stayed and she probably wouldn't be talking to me. I'd be number one on her 🪦 list.
Ruby: Brogan has that honor, now.
Libby: Not for long, I hope.
Ruby: I predict dinner tomorrow night is going to be a real humdinger!
Libby: What exactly is a humdinger? I've never been sure.
Ruby: Let's call it a catalyst. I have a few tricks up my sleeve, that if needed, will ensure a chemical reaction not unlike a spark over a gasoline leak.

Brogan

I am literally shoveling cow poop. "Aren't you supposed to age this crap before spreading it?" I ask while trying to hold my breath as much as possible. The stench is about to overwhelm me.

"You can," James says, "but I figure, why bother? By putting it directly into the field, it can compost there just as easily as somewhere else. It saves me a step this way."

"The smell is noxious." A wave of nausea nearly overpowers me.

"You're a wuss, you know that?" my brother taunts. "Stop holding your nose for ten minutes and then you won't even be able to smell it anymore."

I try to do as he suggests but it's hard. After filling the back of James's pick-up with manure, we drive out into the field and unload it into several piles about a hundred feet apart. When we're done, my brother hands me a rake and says, "Just get in there and start spreading it."

"Aren't there kids you can hire to do this?" I ask. If I were him, I'd work the farm stand and let my employees have this job.

"I'd love to, but kids are soft these days. All they want to do is drive the combine or pick peaches. They'd charge me an arm and a leg for any job that had anything to do with poop. Plus, this way I get to make sure it's spread evenly."

"Isn't there a machine that can do this?" I ask, appalled that James has to perform such a task.

"Sure, but they cost money, too. I was going to buy one before my hay baler bit the dust. Now, I need to hire someone to bale my hay *and* buy a new baler. Needs must, my brother."

I bust my butt for over two hours and wind up smelling like the very thing I'm spreading. If this were my farm, I'd pay people whatever they asked.

As I inadvertently step in a pile of dung, I slide like the bases are loaded and I'm gunning for home plate. After three failed attempts to stand, I finally throw my hands into the air and declare, "I'm done."

"Go on up to the house and take a shower," James tells me.

Before I go, I say, "I'm not cooking for you anymore. I'm going to take you out to dinner. We both deserve to have someone else serve us after a day like this."

"Nice, there's a new restaurant in town I've been wanting to try."

"What kind of cooking?" I ask. "I'm not in the mood for diner food."

"Good, old-fashioned, home cooking. Beth Anne Forester finally opened a place like she's always talked about."

I didn't know Beth Anne in school because she was four years younger than me, but I knew her older brother Burt. "Sounds great. You want to meet me there or should I pick you up?"

"I'll meet you there. I have some shopping to do in town and I might as well get it done before dinner. It'll save me a trip tomorrow."

I have more respect for my little brother than I ever have before. The man works like a dog and no task is beneath him. No matter who wins the bet, I'm going to buy him that hay baler, even if I have to have it delivered and then claim total ignorance of how it got there.

James's house looks like it probably has for at least the last sixty years. The kitchen appliances are ancient, and if that isn't bad enough, they're mint green. The bathrooms are so old the toilets are rusting, and the tiles are chipped and battered.

I'm sure my brother doesn't even see that stuff though. As long as he has a roof over his head, he puts all profits back into the farm.

I scrub myself for a good half hour before I'm certain I no longer smell like the business end of a heifer. Then I go through James's drawers and put on some fresh clothes. I toy with the idea of laying down on his bed and taking a nap, but I don't want to risk him finding me like that. My pride couldn't handle it.

I decide to head back to the lodge and drive up to Cheater's Ridge. I want to visualize my future home. I might even lie down on the grass and have a snooze there.

When I get back to the main building, I give Chris the keys to my Mercedes and ask if I can trade her for one of the Jeeps. She rolls her eyes at me and explains, "The reason we have Jeeps is because they're four-wheel drive, so we can off road them and haul stuff. How in the world could we do that in your little two-seater sports car?"

"Put the top down," I tell her with a smile on my face. Then I add, "Seriously, I'd appreciate it if you didn't haul anything in it. But can I still borrow a Jeep?"

She shakes her greying head at me. "Just have it back before six. We're taking a group up to the fire pit for a pig roasting tonight and we'll need all our wheels for that."

"I'll be back in plenty of time," I tell her as I grab the keys. "I'm meeting James in town at six for supper."

"So, you won't be home until when?" she asks. That's a strange question. Why would Chris care what time I got home?

James wants to be in bed by eight so I'm sure I'll be back by then. Before I can ask her why she wants to know, she picks up the phone to take a reservation.

Chapter Fifty-One

The Mothers

Libby: Bob and I had white cake with marzipan mousse and Italian buttercream for our wedding.
Ruby: I just drooled. That was one fabulous cake. Tom and I had a chocolate cake with hazelnut ganache and a swiss meringue.
Libby: I don't think I ever had hazelnuts before going to college out there, but I've been a huge fan ever since.
Ruby: They're just one of the many things that make our state so special. 😍
Libby: Where do you think the kids' wedding should be? New York or Oregon?
Ruby: We should probably leave that up to them, but if they decide on New York then we'll still have a big party at the lodge to celebrate afterwards.
Libby: Rubes, I don't want to jinx anything, but I'm really starting to get excited about this little plan of ours. 🤞

Addison

I gingerly dismount Thunder Foot before tying his reins to a nearby tree. While he gets busy chewing grass, I walk closer to the ledge and look out. I'm robbed of breath as I stare out onto the mesmerizing vista in front of me—craggy rock formations, heavily wooded stretches, and the majesty of a distant waterfall. I try to envision what Lewis and Clark made of this state when they first laid eyes on it and I'm surprised they were ever able to leave it.

I'm so captivated I don't realize that I'm not alone until I hear someone say, "I see you've found Cheater's Ridge."

Startled, I turn around to find Brogan standing next to me. "I didn't hear you arrive."

"This land has a way of hypnotizing a person," he says while his eyes roam the magnificence before us.

We stand companionably silent for several moments before I feel the tension start to build. I finally ask, "This is where you want to build your house, isn't it?"

He nods his head. "It's been my favorite spot since I was a little boy."

"I can see why."

After a few beats, he asks, "You want a bottle of cold water? I've got a couple in the Jeep."

"I'd love one, thanks." I walk next to him to retrieve it.

He spots my mount and asks, "You brought Thunder Foot up here? My god, woman, do you have a death wish?"

"He's a real sweetie. It was his idea."

He stares at me like I've just grown a second head. "Thunder

Foot is not sweet. He's a grumpy old fart who's never liked anybody but my dad."

I veer off our trajectory toward the horse and say, "I like him." Then I scratch behind the stallion's ears while he lowers his head and taps his back hoof in contentment.

Brogan shakes his head before joining us. "Well, I'll be. I've never seen him act like that with anyone but Dad." He reaches out to scratch the horse's other ear, but Thunder Foot takes immediate offense and tries to bite him.

"They say animals are great judges of character," I tease.

Brogan laughs easily like our tense scene earlier this morning never happened. "Thunder hated Emma," he says. "I only took him out once with her, but he spent the entire ride nipping at her."

"You've made my point," I tell him with one eyebrow arched in an I-told-you-so kind of way.

"That was some scene last night. I'm sorry you had to witness it." The intensity of his gaze causes my feet to feel like they're rooted to the ground. I couldn't move if I wanted to. Good thing I don't want to.

"I'm sorry about this morning," I tell him sincerely. "I've never pepper sprayed anyone before."

"That's hard to believe," he says while stepping closer to me. "Your aim was so good, I imagined you went around New York zapping people like a Wild West gunslinger."

The humor in his voice is unmistakable but I'm too busy reminding myself to breathe to laugh. "Brogan ..." I start to say, but he interrupts.

"Addie, I'm not going to play any tricks on you. If you feel the need to keep pranking me, I won't retaliate."

"I'm only responsible for the clam juice," I hurry to tell him. "And the honey on your toilet seat," I add as an afterthought.

His eyes open widely. "No wonder the bugs bit me up so badly."

I cringe slightly as a feeling of guilt creeps in. In an attempt to regain my righteous anger, I say, "I assume you nicknamed me Honey Bucket after putting the honey into my shampoo?"

He looks chagrined. "I was a real jackass as a kid." He takes another step in my direction.

"Far be it from me to contradict you." I pick up my foot to get some space, but it feels like it weighs a hundred pounds. Stumbling backward, I narrowly escape tripping over a small boulder.

"I was going to kiss you last night before you left the table." He lets the statement linger in the air as though waiting to see how I'll respond.

Hearing his intention stated so clearly makes me hot and bothered in a way that has nothing to do with the current weather conditions. "You were?" I croak.

"I was." Another step. "I got the feeling you would have been okay with that, too." If he moves any closer he'll be standing on top of me.

I can't seem to find any words, so I just stare up at him slowly drowning in the midnight blue pools of his scrutiny. "I'm sorry about the clam juice and honey," I finally manage.

Brogan reaches his arms out and slowly puts his hands behind my waist. "I'm thinking about kissing you now."

I lean toward him ever so slightly which he correctly translates to mean that I'm game. Totally, one hundred percent on board with being kissed by Brogan Cavanaugh. Right now.

His mouth descends so slowly I have a million chances to pull back, but I don't. Instead, I meet him halfway as the soft pillows of his lips press against mine. He groans low in his throat as he deepens the connection. Holy. Hell. I'm kissing the boy that used to make my life miserable, and it's the most wonderful sensation I've ever experienced.

"Brogan," his name escapes my mouth like a plea, a prayer.

He lifts his head long enough to say, "I'm going to kiss you again ..."

I shut him up by practically jumping into his arms and instigating the next round. Seconds, minutes, hours pass. Time loses all meaning as our breath becomes one and our bodies meld together in a way that I don't know where I begin or end. I've kissed a few men in my life, but never has it felt quite like this. Like I'm coming home.

When we finally pull apart, Brogan takes a hold of my hand and leads me back toward the ledge. He sits down on a big rock and gently pulls me onto his lap. "So, what do you think of Cheater's Ridge?"

"I think it's the most beautiful spot I've ever laid eyes on." Except I'm staring at him, not the scenery.

"I'm taking James out for dinner tonight," he says as he tightens his hold on me. "Is there any chance I can persuade you to join us?"

"I'd love to," I tell him. I don't even have to think about it. I feel like we've just turned a corner where childish games have no place. Revenge is the last thing on my mind. Somewhere in the haze of my thoughts, I realize that I want something more with Brogan. But how can that be with us living on opposite sides of the country?

Chapter Fifty-Two

The Mothers

Ruby: Neither one of the kids are in their cabins.
Libby: Maybe they're together. 🤞
Ruby: Maybe, but I doubt it. I think I'll take advantage and prank them both to speed along their big fight 👊.
Libby: How do you know they haven't already had it?
Ruby: I just saw them both this morning and neither of them said anything. If we're going to succeed here we need to push them over the hump so they can get their mad out and get on with falling in love.

Brogan

I'm surprised when I look at my watch and discover it's already four o'clock. Addie and I have completely lost track of time. We covered a variety of topics including the reason I hate clams and why I became a writer instead of an astrophysicist.

I discover that not only is she a proficient horsewoman, but she also won a badminton medal in high school. I'm hard-pressed not to laugh out loud when she tells me that one. Addison Cooper is an enigma. I thought I had her all figured out, but the more I find out about her, the more I discover the error of my assumptions.

I walk her over to Thunder Foot who wakes up with a jolt as we approach. "I'll meet you at the stable after I return the Jeep to Chris. We can walk back to our cabins together."

One or six intensely hot kisses later and I'm on my way.

Addie agilely hops onto Thunder Foot's back and he doesn't give her any of the trouble he usually gives me. On the contrary, he tips his head to the side and accepts a good scratch behind the ears like it's his due before he trots off carrying the woman who has not only captured my attention, but is precariously close to capturing my heart.

I'm not one of those people who believe in insta-love or even love at first sight, but I've known Addie her whole life. Looking back, I wonder if some of my pranking wasn't my adolescent way of letting her know that I liked her. After all, aren't pulling braids and shooting spit wads classic signs of early courtship? Maybe it's the same for practical jokes.

Back at the lodge, Chris hands my car keys over when I turn in the Jeep. She says, "I didn't haul anything in that fancy pants car of yours, but I spent a half hour driving around town waving at people."

I release a spontaneous laugh. "Did you have a good time?

"I felt like Miss America sitting on a toilet paper float in a parade. Just so you know, I plan on doing that every time you come down here looking for a Jeep."

"You can do it before then if you want. Just let me know and I'll give you my keys." I wink at her and she cringes almost like there's something she wants to tell me but is afraid to. "What?" I ask her.

After a moment, she shakes her head and practically forces a smile. "Nothing. You're a good kid, you know that?"

"You sound like you're just realizing that."

"I've always known. I guess having Addie here is reminding us all of what a rotten stink you used to be though." She reaches across the front desk and pats my hand adding, "I'm proud of the way you turned out."

"Thanks, Chris." What an odd exchange. I pick up her hands and give them a quick kiss. "You've always been like a second mom to me."

At that, she smacks me away. "Go on, I've got work to do." Then she turns around and heads purposefully in the other direction. The women in my life have certainly been keeping me on my toes lately.

My heart feels lighter than it has in years as I walk down to the barn to meet Addie. I'm a thirty-five-year-old man who felt every minute of my age when I woke up this morning. Suddenly, I feel like a kid again.

Addie is riding up to the barn at the same time I arrive. Watching her fly across the meadow on the back of my dad's horse fills me with a sense of rightness.

She waves when she sees me and slowly brings her mount to a halt. Then she jumps down and hands the reins to Jeet before saying, "He was a prince. I'll definitely be back to ride him again."

"Please do," Jeet tells her. "He needs his exercise but I'm the only one he doesn't try to throw and even then, he doesn't like me that much. He's getting lazy as a result."

I walk up next to Addie and call out, "You're a natural!"

She smiles cockily. "And here you thought I wasn't an outdoorswoman."

"I stand corrected," I tell her. "Although I'm still not sure how much of a camper you are."

"Who needs camping when there's glamping?" Her eyes suddenly light up. "That would be a great advertising slogan, don't you think?"

I reach out for her hand. "I do. You make glamping look fun. I'm actually a little jealous that you're living in the lap of luxury while I'm taking freezing cold showers and sleeping on a twin bed."

"Sounds like you might be ready to pay up and end our little bet."

"Not even close, lady. If I end it now, you might pack your bags and head back to New York City. I'm keeping it alive so I can have you all to myself for the next few weeks."

Addie smiles almost bashfully before saying, "Sounds good to me."

Hand-in-hand we hike up the path to our cabins. When we see my mom heading toward us in her golf cart, we quickly step apart. We decided earlier to keep whatever is happening between us on the down low for a while yet. Being that our courtship is only a couple of hours old and our families are so close, it wouldn't be wise to let them in on anything until we know where things are headed first.

My mom toots her horn and waves. When she pulls up next to us, she says, "I just dropped off more packages for Addie."

I shake my head in wonder at how much this woman is buying. "What came today, a hot tub and sauna?"

"You get me electricity up there," she says, "and I'll bump those things to the top of my list." I don't think she's joking.

My mom interjects, "How about you kids join me for dinner tomorrow night up at the lodge. Say, six o'clock?"

Addie is the first to respond. "Sounds wonderful as long as Brogan doesn't think that's cheating on our bet." She gives me the side eye.

"I think we'd both appreciate a meal we didn't have to cook ourselves," I say.

"Excellent!" My mom claps her hands together joyfully. "I'll make sure to have the chef prepare something extra special." She drives off before there's any more chit-chat.

When Addie and I get to my cabin, I say, "Why don't you come in and wait while I change and then I'll walk you to your place?" The truth is I want to be with her for every second I can.

"You've got yourself a deal," she says while I pull her along over the threshold of my place.

Neither one of us sees what's coming until it's too late.

Chapter Fifty-Three

The Mothers

Libby: Well, what did you do to them 📎
Ruby: Oh, Libs, I think I made a mistake.
Libby: What? 👀
Ruby: I ran into them on my way back from their cabins and it looked like they were having a nice time. I might have just ruined whatever rapport they've built.
Libby: Are you saying you don't think they need a big fight before they fall for each other?
Ruby: I don't know!!! But I think they're about to have a big fight now.
Libby: Oh, dear.

Addison

"Aaaaaaaargh!" I scream as a bucket full of something obnoxiously stinky and incredibly gooey falls onto us.

Brogan looks equally shocked. He took the brunt of whatever it was and is totally covered. "It smells like vinegar, but I think it's glue?" He walks into the kitchen to grab some dish towels. One of which he throws at me.

I smell my hand and suggest, "I think there might be some blue cheese in there." Then I ask, "Who in the world would have done this to you?"

"If it wasn't you …" He pauses a moment to gauge my reaction.

I shake my head vigorously in denial. "I was out riding and then with you. I couldn't have done this."

"Then," he concludes, "it must be the same person who put leaves in my bed and greased my floor and doorknob."

"When did that happen?" This is the first I'm hearing about the doorknob and floor.

"After I came back from your cabin this morning."

"Did you see anyone?" I ask. I mean, it's not like we're in an overpopulated area rife with bored teens or something.

"Just my mom but she wouldn't do this." He looks confused before saying, "Although we just saw her again …"

"Why in the world would she be pranking you?"

"I have no idea. It doesn't make any sense."

"Why don't you rinse off in your shower and then come over to my place for a bath? We can take turns."

He shakes his head which sends a glop of whatever we're covered in running down the tip of his nose. "It'll take us hours to heat enough hot water for two baths and we'll never get the smell off by taking a cold shower. I say we rinse off at our own places, then grab some clean clothes and head to the lodge and use the facilities at the spa."

"Okay," I tell him. "I'll meet you back here when I'm somewhat clean."

He crinkles up his nose and says, "I'd kiss you goodbye but, well, you know…"

"Don't even think about it. There's no way I want any of this junk to get into my mouth." I turn to leave and add, "I'll see you in a bit."

On my way to my cabin, I try to figure out who the jokester is, but for the life of me I can't imagine. Billy promised he wouldn't do anything else before checking with me so that leaves someone else as the culprit. But who?

I let myself into my cabin and hurry to grab a towel. A cold shower holds zero appeal for me, but it's still better than being covered in this mystery goop. After turning on the shower and closing the temporary privacy curtain I hung, I strip out of my clothes and try to psyche myself up for the shock of a lifetime.

I squeal when the frigid water hits, but I persevere. Whatever this stuff is, it seems to be hardening as it dries. I hop around trying to get as much rinsed off as I can when something comes flying over the top of the shower. I immediately cover my head as several slippery-feeling things descend upon me.

I can't see what they are, so I hurriedly wipe my eyes before looking down. As soon as I do, I release a sound like I'm being attacked by, well, snakes. There are dozens of slimy-looking snakes lying at my feet.

I don't bother to finish rinsing off or even cover myself, I just jump out and run. As soon as I'm in the clearing, I dance around like I'm either trying to put out a fire or summon rain via a Native American tribal dance.

Snakes are the worst! I'd sooner cuddle a cougar than stand in a nest of snakes. Which brings me to the question, who in the hell threw snakes on me? I finally settle down enough to wrap myself in my towel and scan the area for the perpetrator, but I don't see anyone. Until I do.

Brogan is jogging up the path already showered and dressed in different clothes. "I heard a scream," he declares, heading straight toward me.

Oh. My. God. Did Brogan do this? What about the last few hours we spent together? I stare at him trying to discern whether or not he's the perpetrator, but I can't get a word out.

"Why are you looking at me like that? Are you okay?"

Instead of answering, I ask, "Did you happen to see anyone else on your way up here?"

"I thought I saw Chris's daughter Megan, but that's it, why?"

Why would Chris's daughter throw a bucket of what I'm hoping are rubber snakes on me? I quickly look over at the shower. None of the vermin have moved so they're either toys or they're dead. Either way, I release a full body shiver.

Brogan's gaze follows mine and he walks over to the shower. He bends down and picks up a snake and instead of being horrified, he starts laughing. Laughing! *Oh, my, god, he did do this to me!*

"You threw snakes on me after the afternoon we just spent?" I'm horrified. Who is this man?

"Of course I didn't throw snakes on you," he says. But he's laughing so hard it's nearly impossible to decipher his words.

"If you didn't do it, why are you laughing?" I demand, not believing for one minute that he isn't the guilty party.

"I'm just ... just ... I'm sorry ..." he keeps going.

I turn and walk into my cabin and slam the door as hard as I can. Oh, he'll be sorry.

Moments later, there's a knock on the door. "Addie, let me in." He's still trying to control his laughter, the fiend.

"If you so much as open that door, I'm going to spray you with mace until the bottle is empty. Do you understand?"

"Addie, please. I'm sorry I laughed, truly. It's just that it was a pretty common prank James and I used to pull, and it brought back memories," he says, still sounding way the heck too joyful for my liking.

"I know it's a prank you used to pull, or have you forgotten doing it to me on more than one occasion?"

"I haven't forgotten, but I swear it wasn't me this time," he says even though he's obviously still trying to control his mirth.

"Screw you, Brogan Cavanaugh!" I yell. "You'd better leave right now, or I'm going to open this door and start spraying."

"Addie …"

"ONE … TWO … THREE …"

"Fine, I'm going," he says. "Come find me when you come to your senses." Now *he* sounds mad. Of all the nerve!

If this were a movie I would pick up my bucket of popcorn and walk out. Elle is in the Caribbean starring in my romantic comedy, and I'm in the middle of Oregon reenacting *Dumb and Dumber*. I'm rapidly losing my sense of humor.

Chapter Fifty-Four

The Mothers

Ruby: Chris's daughter Megan threw a bucket of rubber snakes over the curtain while Addie was in the shower.
Libby: Rubes, no! The snakes were her least favorite prank. The summer Brogan introduced that one is the same summer Addie renamed her Ken doll and started torturing it.
Ruby: Chris texted me that she tried to stop her, but she was too late. Of course, I didn't get that text because I was up at the fishing cabin setting up my own prank on Brogan.
Libby: I'm afraid the only way we can salvage our plan is if we come clean. 😨
Ruby: OR we can wait until after dinner tomorrow night. They're coming to the lodge to meet me for dinner. I can try to orchestrate a battle and then be there to referee it.
Libby: Just tell them. Hopefully, they'll forgive us some day.

Ruby: If I tell them before they've started to fall for each other, they'll both walk away before they have a chance to. Trust me. 😊

Brogan

What in the world is going on? Someone is going out of their way to torment me, and now Addie, by trying to make it look like we're pranking each other. Emma briefly crosses my mind, but there's no way she could pull it if off without getting caught. So, the question is, if it's not Emma, and it's not Addie, who in the world is behind it? I wonder if Addie would believe me if I told her of my suspicions.

Before I walk inside the lodge, I pull out my phone to text James: *I'm not going to be able to get to the restaurant on time. Why don't you join me and Mom tomorrow night at the lodge? Six o'clock.*

When I walk into the lobby, the first thing I see is my mom and Chris huddled together. Clearly this is more than just a friendly chat as they appear very animated. My mom has both of her arms stretched out to the ceiling. Chris is covering her face with her hands while shaking her head.

I approach them slowly, hoping to overhear their conversation, but Chris moves her hands and catches sight of me. She calls out, "Brogan! What in the world happened to you?" I assume she's referencing the goop I wasn't able to get out of my hair.

My mom spins around looking what ... horrified, shocked, guilty? I can't tell which. "Honey, what's in your hair?"

I eye them both closely before answering, "I was on the

receiving end of another practical joke. When I walked into my cabin, I got hit with a plastic bucket full of whatever this stuff is." I indicate the top of my head.

"You smell," my mom informs me.

"I'm here to take a hot shower," I inform them, trying to make heads or tails out of their possible involvement. "Do either of you happen to know who was behind this?"

"Why would we?" my mom answers quickly, almost too quickly. "I don't know if you're aware of this Brogan, but Chris and I are too busy running this lodge to play childish games. Not that you don't have it coming," she seems to feel the need to add.

I look at Chris when I say, "I saw Megan up near the cabins a bit ago."

"I think she was out scouting some new areas to expand the zip-lining course. She said something about seeing if there was a viable spot near the falls. And you know, you have to pass by your cabin to get there. Well, not exactly by it, but close. Like fifty yards or so, right?"

Chris is full-on babbling. Before I can call her on it, my mom waves her hand in front of her nose and says, "Go get clean, please."

They're up to something. I just don't know whether or not it involves pranking me and Addie. *What could possibly be the payoff for them?* After giving them both a suspicious look, I head off to the men's locker room in the spa where I put my bag of clean clothes in a locker before taking the longest shower of my life.

After washing my hair three times, I finally get all the junk out of it. During the final rinse, I decide to spend some quality time in the sauna and try to figure out what to do about Addie.

While I felt a real connection with her, I'm starting to wonder if there's too much history there for us to move on to something more. *How could she believe I was behind the snake incident after the afternoon we shared?*

I pour a cup of water over the hot rocks and let the steam envelop me, hoping it will help open my mind for answers to find a way in. I've never had a long-distance relationship, not because the opportunity hasn't arisen, but because I've never been interested in having one.

Why then, have I been hoping something would develop between me and Addie, knowing that she lives in New York while I'm planning on building my dream home here in Spartan? Would I be willing to spend time in the Big Apple to see if we have a future together?

After staring at the glowing coals, I decide I would. I mean, it'll take at least a year, probably two, for my house to be finished. I could easily sell my home on the coast and make Addie's cabin home base when I'm not visiting her. I'd use her cabin because, let's face it, it's more rigged out for long-term living, and it would remind me of her.

Now, all I have to do is get her to see reason. Someone is pranking both of us and we need to figure out who that is.

After my steam, I change into clean clothes and decide to hang out for a while so that I can talk to Addie after she finishes getting cleaned up. I didn't see her come down here, but I know she was planning to, and the sooner we come to a meeting of the minds, the better.

After waiting in the spa for a solid half hour with no sign of her, I finally ask the girl behind the counter if she's seen her.

"I don't have anyone named Addison Cooper on my list," she says while smiling in a borderline flirtatious manner. "Let me know if there's anything else I can help you with. My name is Gillian."

"Thanks, Gillian. I'm Brogan Cavanaugh."

As soon as I introduce myself, she practically jumps to attention and becomes all business. "Would you like me to check and see if Miss Cooper has any appointments scheduled?"

It seems I've become kryptonite to the ladies. Either that or Gillian wrongly assumes I'm going to report her for being too friendly. "No, that's okay," I tell her.

I decide to stop off in the gift shop and pick up a sandwich from the cooler for dinner. I know I'm not supposed to get my meals here, but right now I'm almost ready to cancel this whole wager. If Addie decides to stay mad at me, I'll probably just pay off my brother and mom and be done with it.

Of course, I'll still try to buy the property up at Cheater's Ridge, but I don't know how I'll ever be able to go up there again without thinking about the afternoon Addie and I shared. I feel like I finally saw the woman she really is and I'll be damned if I want to let that go.

Chapter Fifty-Five

The Mothers

Libby: Well
Ruby: Well, what?
Libby: Have you seen Brogan or Addie since you pranked them?
Ruby: I saw Brogan. I'm pretty sure he suspects me, but he doesn't know anything for sure.
Libby: I've been texting Addie to check on her, but there's been no response. She's probably fuming up at her cabin.
Ruby: Either that or she's not speaking to you.
Libby: Aren't you just full of happy thoughts?

Addison

My mind starts to clear while soaking in a hot bath. I realize the absurdity of thinking Brogan was the one to throw those toy snakes on me. Not after the afternoon we had together. Unless, of course, he decided I was the one behind the bucket of goo over his door …

I was just so surprised and angry when he started laughing that I sort of lost my mind. It must have been nervous laughter, like the kind that erupts when you're sitting in the principal's office or at a funeral of someone you barely know.

I consider going over to his cabin and clearing the air, but I remember he was going into town to meet James for dinner. While I hate letting any more time go by with this misunderstanding between us, I also realize that we both probably need our space to think things over. *Things like, could this be my movie after all?*

If it is, what am I doing starting something up with a man who lives on the other side of the country? A family friend is not the person to engage in a fling. The parental ramifications alone are the cringiest.

Soaked, clean, and dressed, I find myself staring in the fridge, looking for something to make for dinner. Billy walks in. "Hey," he greets.

"What should we have for supper?" I ask, like it's the most normal thing in the world. The truth is Billy isn't a stranger anymore. He's an odd friend for me to have, but I feel like I really know him even though I don't know much about him.

"I'll fry up the burgers if you want to make a salad," he suggests.

"Sounds like a plan." We amiably weave around the tiny kitchen getting our meal ready. Billy seems particularly quiet, even for him, so I ask, "You doing okay?"

He's silent for several moments before answering, "I've got some things on my mind."

I don't want to seem pushy, so I merely respond, "Let me know if I can help."

Once dinner is ready, we serve up and decide to eat out on the porch. The burgers are big and juicy, and full of flavor. Right after I take a huge bite, Billy says, "I'm thinking about sharing some news with some folks, but I'm not sure if it's the right thing to do."

I hurry to chew and swallow before asking, "Why wouldn't it be the right thing to do?"

"Sometimes things are best left unsaid."

"Do you want to bounce it off of me first?"

Billy looks me dead in the eye as though he's considering it before saying, "I do, but I think maybe I should tell everyone at once."

"Who do you want to share this news with?" I ask.

"The Cavanaugh family."

"I'm having supper with them tomorrow night. How about if you join us and you can tell them then?"

"I don't want to intrude," he says.

"Intrude nothing. They already think of you as family. I'm sure they'd love to have you come." I add, "We're eating at the River's Edge at six. You can walk down with me if you want."

"I think maybe I'll meet you there," he eventually replies.

He's clearly preoccupied by his own thoughts and I don't want to pry, but there is something I want to say. "Thank you for everything you've done to help me settle in here."

"You've been a breath of fresh air, Miss Addison," he says like a courtly gentleman. "I was pretty set in my ways until you showed up. You've changed that."

"I hope that's a good thing."

He nods his head slowly. "I think it is. I'd gotten myself into such a groove up here over the years, I didn't realize I'd fallen into a rut. Don't get me wrong, I love my life. I just think that maybe there's more to living than I've let in."

"I totally get that. I've basically avoided the wilderness since I was a kid, but this trip has shown me what I've been missing. I don't think I could ever be the person I was before."

"We're all growing," he says while wearing a smirk. "Good for us, huh?"

"Yeah, good for us." I ask, "Do you ever want to go back to New York City? Not to live there, but to visit?"

He doesn't hesitate when he answers, "I'm not that person anymore. Looking back at my younger self is like I'm having someone else's memories. I don't mind it, but there's no point in revisiting it."

"What about your family?" I ask.

"My mom died shortly after I got here. She's all I had left."

"I'm sorry," I say.

"Don't you be sorry for me. I've had a good life."

"So, you're not thinking of leaving here?" I ask. I have no idea what Billy wants to say to the Cavanaughs, but I'd briefly considered he might be telling them that he's going to leave.

He shakes his head. "This is my home. God willing, it's where I'll take my last breath."

We eat the rest of our meal in silence. I assume Billy is thinking about whatever it is he's going to tell Brogan's family. Meanwhile, I'm realizing how much I'm enjoying being here.

Because of my unfortunate camping trips as a kid, Oregon has never appealed to me. But now that I've gotten to know the area as an adult, I have to say that I love it here. We all need to literally and figuratively unplug occasionally. This cabin has been the perfect place for me to do that.

It's nice to not always be checking my phone for messages. While I do miss some of the comforts that electricity provides, I also have a new appreciation for candlelight. I know I've only been up here for less than a week, but I've got three more ahead of me before this decorating job and wager are over.

How in the world will I be able to go back to the hustle and bustle of New York City after a month of decompressing in nature? I suddenly understand why Billy never went home.

Chapter Fifty-Six

The Mothers

Ruby: Tonight, is dinner with the kids.
Libby: Are you going to tell them it was you behind the pranks?
Ruby: I may have to. And FYI, it was US behind the pranks.
Libby: I'm in Amsterdam. This is all on you.
Ruby: Traitor.

Brogan

I wake up early and run down to the lodge to grab some fresh pastries. I'm going to take them over to Addie's as a peace offering while we clear the air over our misunderstanding yesterday. With apple fritters and bear claws in tow, I start to feel a renewed excitement about the possibility of us.

Billy is sitting on the porch drinking his coffee when I get to Addie's. "Good morning, my friend," I call out to him.

"Looks like you brought me breakfast." He eyes the bakery bags in my hands.

"I sure did." I hand them off so he can choose whatever he wants.

"Addie invited me to dinner tonight with your family," Billy announces.

"I hope you're coming," I tell him even though he rarely accepts such invitations.

"I am. I was told to meet you at six."

I'm more surprised than I can say. "I'll make sure there's a place set for you. And might I add, it's about time we had a meal together."

"We eat together all the time up here."

"I meant all of us." Billy is such a part of our lives I can't imagine this property without him.

"I'm gonna take my bear claw and go. I'll see you tonight."

I try to shore up my courage for whatever confrontation is about to occur as I watch Billy walk away.

But before I can knock on Addie's door, it opens. She's standing in front of me looking like a woodland nymph in her robe with her hair all wavy and mussed from sleep. "Hello!" She's clearly surprised to see me.

"Hello, yourself," I say as a feeling of contentment flows through me. "I brought pastries." I start to say, "I'm sorry about …"

She interrupts, "I'm so sorry about yesterday. I don't think you had anything to do with the snakes."

"What changed your mind?"

She shakes her gorgeous head. "I just know you would have never done that after the afternoon we shared." Her eyes plead with mine to agree.

"I think my mom and Chris were the responsible parties," I tell her.

"What? Why?"

"That's the twenty-million-dollar question. But don't worry, we'll get our answers at dinner tonight."

She looks thoroughly confused. "Why would your mom want me to come out here only to prank me? And why would she do the same to you? It doesn't make any sense."

"Why would your mom come out here only to leave you?" I ask.

"I don't think that's what she'd planned to do. I think our wager is what made her decide to leave. She probably didn't want to hang around and watch us be nasty to each other. Although believe me, I'm going to give her a piece of my mind when I see her again."

"I'll have you know that I've been nothing but gentlemanly to you ever since you got here. If anyone was being mean, it was you."

She rolls her eyes. "Fine, she didn't want to hang around and hear me complain about you."

I lean in to give her a light kiss on the cheek before asking, "Any complaints now?"

"None." She takes the bags out of my hands and asks, "Are you trying to bribe me with pastries?"

"Most definitely."

She pulls out a fresh apple fritter and declares, "It's working. These look amazing. Let's grab some coffee and we can have our breakfast in the hammock."

"Aren't you afraid we'll be too close together sitting there?" I ask with a wink. She couldn't get far enough away from me the last time we sat there together.

Addie winks back saucily. "That was my plan."

"Well, then, count me in." As strange as it is to say, Addie looks like she belongs here. Not even a week ago, she tottered into the lodge looking as out of place as a juggler in church, but now she seems perfectly at home here. While that realization takes me off guard, it also feels incredibly right.

"What were you planning on doing today?" Addie asks.

"I was hoping to spend the day with you. How does that sound?"

"Perfect! Helena is coming up later this afternoon with one of my projects for the place. I could really use your help."

"You want me to help you win the bet? I don't know," I tease.

"I've already won the bet and you know it. But I could really use your height."

"As long as you don't try to leave before the month is out, I'll happily concede that you're the winner, and I'll happily lend a hand fixing this place up."

"What about Cheater's Ridge?" she asks.

"What about it?"

"Will your mom still let you build your house there if you lose the bet?"

I release a snort. "I have no doubt. She's been after me for years to move home. She'll do anything she can to help facilitate that."

After we settle in the hammock, with Addie more than half on my lap, she announces, "I can't see you living anywhere but here." She doesn't sound happy by that thought.

"This is my home. It's where I belong."

"Brogan," she says. "I'm thirty-two. I don't want to date casually anymore."

"Okay."

She looks confused and tries again, "What I'm saying is that if I date anyone I want it to be with the hopes that it will turn into something long-term."

I nod my head. "I get it."

"What do you get?" she asks nervously.

"I get that you want more. If you and I are to work, you're going to want to make an honest man out of me so our children will grow up knowing their parents are devoted to one another."

"Brogan! I didn't say anything about marriage and kids." While she's trying to sound shocked, she also looks delighted.

"Of course, you didn't. I'm saying it." I lean in and give her the sweetest of kisses. "And if things work out, I promise to live half of our time in New York, if you promise to live the rest of the year here."

Addie instigates the next kiss. "Deal. Luckily, we have three more weeks together here to see how well we do with being nice to each other. We don't have a lot of practice with that."

"I predict we're going to do so well that we'll have some big decisions to make by the time you're ready to leave." I'm not sure how Addison Cooper snuck in under my radar, but she did, and I have no intention of letting her go.

Chapter Fifty-Seven

The Mothers

Libby: I just told Bob what we've been up to.
Ruby: And? 😳
Libby: He wonders what took us so long.
Ruby: What?
Libby: He says he knew years ago that there was chemistry between Addie and Brogan.
Ruby: Why didn't he ever say anything?
Libby: Because Addie was only seventeen. He didn't think anything could come of it then and he didn't want any awkwardness between us. But just so you know, he's 100 percent on board with the idea. Now we just have to hope the kids are.

Addison

Brogan and I spend a perfectly wonderful day together. We hike and swim in Copper Creek. He even shows me where the cougar dens are so I can make sure to avoid them when I'm alone.

When Helena brings the canvas down after lunch, Brogan

helps us hang it. "You're insane," he says once we're all done.

"It's brilliant though, right?" I ask.

Pulling me into his arms, he assures me, "It's genius. These cabins are going to be a huge hit."

I briefly pull back and say, "I've been thinking about Billy a lot. He's not getting any younger."

"None of us are."

"What I mean is, he needs the security of a roof over his head. Do you think your mom might agree to either let him have my cabin or let me make over your cabin for him?"

"Absolutely. Mom's been trying to get Billy indoors for years. Why don't we head up to dinner early and talk it over with her before he arrives?"

I pull Brogan closer and inhale the spicy scent of him. I feel more content than I remember ever being. "You're the best."

"I'm glad you finally know that," he teases.

"I need to change for dinner. Meet you at your place?" I ask him.

He drops a kiss on my cheek, that moves to my lips, that lasts longer than expected. "See you soon," I finally pull away long enough to say.

I take extra pains to look nice before walking over to Brogan's cabin. We exchange a ridiculous number of flirtatious compliments before we go down to the lodge a half hour earlier than we're expected. Aunt Ruby is nowhere to be found, so we head to the restaurant to meet her there.

Brogan orders a bottle of champagne, and once it's served, he raises his glass. "To us. May we never play a practical joke on each other for as long as we both shall live."

"Forever is a long time," I tease. "Maybe we should just agree not to prank each other anytime in the next year."

"It's a deal." His smile is so radiant I feel like I'm staring at the sun. Brogan Cavanaugh is totally sweeping me off my feet and I'm loving every minute of it.

Aunt Ruby comes over wearing an odd expression. "You're early."

"We wanted to talk to you about something," I tell her.

She looks decidedly nervous while asking, "What?"

"Sit down," Brogan tells her. She looks like she'd rather run, but she doesn't.

After he pours her a glass of champagne she starts to say, "I'm sorry about …" at the same time I announce, "I'm worried about Billy. I think he needs a real home."

"I agree." She quickly follows my lead.

Having none of that conversation, Brogan asks her, "What are you sorry about?"

"Nothing." His mom turns to me and asks, "What do you have in mind?"

"I'd like to either offer him the cabin I'm in or fix up Brogan's cabin for him. What do you think about that?"

"I think he should stay in your cabin. It's already done, so he won't have to wait. I already decided I want to make him my go-to man up there for the other cabin renovations. I plan on hiring him as the onsite glamping manager once we're up and running."

"Really?" I'm so excited I can barely stand it. Now all we have to do is convince him. "I asked Billy to join us for supper. I hope that's okay."

"Is he coming?" Aunt Ruby gasps in surprise.

"He said he'd be here at six."

"That's great!"

James shows up at six, looking freshly scrubbed and hungry. By six fifteen, Billy still hasn't arrived, so we go ahead and order.

James tells us, "That awful woman came back and bought two bushels of peaches today. I wish she'd forget my farm existed."

"What woman?" Aunt Ruby asks.

Brogan answers for his brother, "This gorgeous woman keeps showing up at James's farm to pick fights with him about not being certified organic."

"Interesting," Aunt Ruby says.

"How gorgeous?" I ask Brogan.

"About a tenth as beautiful as you are," he assures me. Then he asks James, "Why does she need so many peaches? You'd think she'd just buy them wholesale through her work."

"She said she was making jam for Christmas gifts." He rolls his eyes. "At least she didn't argue with me this time."

Aunt Ruby chastises, "James, when a gorgeous woman shows up at your farm, you should try to do everything you can to be pleasant. God knows you're not doing anything to find a girlfriend."

"How do you know?" he asks somewhat defensively.

"Because I have the whole town reporting back to me every time you do anything. How else would I know?" I think she's joking, but I can't tell for sure.

"Why, exactly, are they reporting back to you?" James asks her.

"Because, James, Spartan is a small town and as such, anything that happens to one of its citizens is considered news.

For instance, I know that Cheryl's husband Damian came home this morning to see his kids."

"What?" Brogan and I ask at the same time.

Aunt Ruby nods. "Word on the street is he wants to come home for good."

"She can't let him," I decide. "I mean, he left them. She can't just forgive that."

"She'll do whatever is right for her family. And if that's forgiving her children's dad so they can all be together again, that's what she'll do. We need to support whatever choice she makes," Aunt Ruby announces this in such a way that she expects no disagreement.

Brogan intervenes. "We'll support her all right. But meanwhile I'm going to stop in and have a talk with Damian. You know, man-to-man."

Aunt Ruby smiles at her younger son while pointing at Brogan, "This, right here, is a small town in motion. Now, do me a favor and quit chasing eligible women off your property."

"How do you know she's eligible?" James wants to know.

"Was there a ring on her finger?" Aunt Ruby asks.

"Not that I saw. But how would you know that?"

His mother replies, "Because there is only one new woman that I know of in town and she's single."

Before James has a chance to respond, a handsome older gentleman walks up to our table. There's something familiar about him but for the life of me I can't put my finger on it.

He smiles at us before pulling out a chair and sitting down. "I'm sorry to be late. I stayed in town longer than expected."

Every single one of us opens our mouths in shock and demands, "Billy?"

Chapter Fifty-Eight

The Mothers

Ruby: Not only am I sure our kids are crushing on each other, but James has met the woman I have in mind for him.
Libby: So dinner went well?
Ruby: Libs, we're half-way to becoming grandmas together, I feel it in my bones. 😍
Libby: Hot damn! I'll be there in a couple of days. What happened with James?
Ruby: Let's just say I'm #1 on his 💩 list. Oh, and you would not believe what happened with Billy. I'll tell you everything when you get here.

Brogan

We're all staring at Billy like we've never seen him before. The truth is we never have seen him like this. He's positively respectable looking.

My mom looks across the table at him and says, "You look wonderful." He does, too. His hair has been cut and his beard shaved off. He's wearing what I would guess are brand new clothes. I would have never known it was him if I didn't recognize his voice.

Billy tips his head. "Thank you. You all look quite nice yourselves."

"Do you want some champagne?" I ask him, still not totally convinced it is him.

"I think maybe I'll have a beer tonight, thank you."

I signal the waitress while my mom tells Billy, "You're quite handsome when you're all cleaned up."

He smiles shyly. "I figured it was about time. Amber down at the Style and Blow kept me a little longer than I'd planned though." He holds up his hands and announces, "She gave me a manicure."

Addie starts to laugh. "I need a manicure. Maybe we can go back next week and have one together."

Billy shakes his head. "No, ma'am, I'm good for one nail buffing in this life and I just had it. You'll have to go on your own."

The waitress brings over a selection of appetizers and takes Billy's order. While we dig in, my mom says, "Billy, I have a favor I need to ask of you."

He smiles at her. "Whatever you need."

She says, "I'd like you to move into Addie's cabin when she leaves and become my full-time glamping manager." Before he can respond, she says, "I know you've never wanted to do anything like this in the past, but Billy, I need you."

He doesn't hesitate a moment before saying, "I'd be honored to accept the job."

We are all one hundred percent stunned. Everyone but Addie. She just smiles at Billy and seems to be sending him some kind of psychic message to keep talking. So, he does.

"There's something I've wanted to talk to you all about and I'm hoping this is a good time," he starts to say.

"Please," my mom encourages. "Now is as good a time as any. And thank you for helping me out. I can't tell you how much I appreciate it."

Billy smiles at her fondly. "I don't think I've ever told you about how I came to live here." When none of us respond, he says, "My mother raised me on her own. She told me that my dad died in the Korean War."

"I'm sorry," my mom says. "That had to be hard, not knowing him."

"Well," he says, "it turns out that wasn't the truth. My mom served in Korea as a nurse. She met my dad there, but he was long gone and back to the front when she learned she was pregnant with me. She went home, planning on putting me up for adoption."

No one at the table quite knows what to say, so we remain quiet while he explains. "After giving birth, she decided to keep me. She only told me who my dad was before she died."

We're so quiet, you could hear a pin drop.

He continues, "His name was Josiah Cavanaugh."

My mom's champagne glass slips through her fingers and shatters when it hits the floor. Our waitress hurries across the room to clean the mess up as Mom says, "You're Tom's brother? I don't understand. Why didn't you ever say anything?"

"I didn't want to cause problems for your family. I surely

didn't want to cause any heartache for Elaine." Elaine was my grandmother.

"Did Josiah know?" my mom asks.

"Nothing was ever spoken out loud. I did tell him my mother's name once, and he seemed to recognize it, but my whole point in coming here was to meet him, not to upset his life in any way."

My mom shakes her head. "While that's very considerate of you, Elaine and Josiah didn't even meet until after the war. It's not like he cheated on her." She doesn't let him respond before adding, "Plus, Elaine died five years before Josiah. You could have told him then."

"For what purpose?" Billy wants to know. "We'd already formed something of a friendship and honestly, that was enough."

"But Tom would have loved to have had a brother," she pushes.

"Tom did have a brother," Billy tells her. "He just never knew me by that name."

"Half of this lodge is yours," my mom hurries to say.

"I've been living here and availing myself of the land for thirty years. That's enough for me."

"Billy," she says with tears forming in my mom's eyes, "you're our family and we never knew."

"But you always treated me like family. And for that kindness, I can't thank you enough."

James interrupts. "Why are you telling us now? Not that I'm not thrilled, I am, but why now?"

Billy smiles at Addie. "I finally realized that no man is an island. And while I've been living here on the same land as you, I've isolated myself. I no longer want to do that."

"It's nice needing people, isn't it?" I ask him while looking at Addie.

"Yes, it is. I know your family has always asked me to join in on holiday celebrations and to have dinner with you. I'm ready to do that if the offer still stands."

My mom is full-on bawling now. She stands up and walks over to Billy before ordering, "Stand up." Once he does, she wraps her arms around him and declares, "It's my greatest honor to call you my brother." Then she looks between me and James and says, "Boys, do you have anything to say to your uncle?"

James says, "Now that I know you're family, you have to help me shovel manure. No more sissy berry picking for you."

Billy laughs. "Sorry, boy, I've got a full-time job working for your mom. I don't think I'll be farm laboring anymore."

My mom says, "I'm going to call our lawyer in the morning and turn over half of this place to you."

Billy shakes his head. "No, thank you. Just because I agreed to live in a cabin doesn't mean I want to be tied down to stuff."

"But Billy, it's the right thing to do."

"If you do that then I'll just have to hire another lawyer to leave my half to your sons. Please, save me the aggravation."

My mom eventually gives in, but if I know her, she's not going to be able to let Billy continue on as he always has.

The rest of our meal is full of excited conversation about the future of Willamette Valley Glamping. Addie shares some of her ideas about fun ways to keep the kids entertained and Billy suggests giving them lessons in things like how to scale a fish and cook it over an open fire.

While an atmosphere of excitement permeates the air, I decide that now's the time to confront my mother. "Mom, I think there was something you were going to apologize for earlier."

She looks alarmed. "I can't think of anything."

I arch an eyebrow at her and say, "If you come clean, I'll come clean."

She looks across the table between me and Addie and seems to notice for the first time that we're holding hands. Normally this would be the first thing she saw, but our meal has been an eventful one.

"Okay," she announces. "I'm sorry I greased your doorknob and floor. I'm also sorry about the spoiled sour cream, glue, and blue cheese concoction."

"It *was* you!" I unnecessarily accuse. After all, she already confessed. "Why?"

But before she can answer, Addie asks, "What about the snakes? And the leaves in Brogan's bed, and the outhouse?"

"I was behind the leaves," James confesses.

"Why?" I ask.

"Why not?" he replies.

Billy pipes in with, "I put the honey on the toilet seat."

My mom adds, "Chris wrapped your toilet and Megan threw the snakes on Addie." Then she announces, "I did everything else."

"Not to be repetitive, but again, why?" I want to know.

Mom inhales deeply before spilling it. "I knew that Addie was mad at you for all the pranks you used to play on her. I figured if I could help her get revenge, she might see you for the handsome and charming man you are."

"You brought her out here to set her up with me?" I'm beyond stunned.

"What about the glamping?" Addie wants to know.

"That was just an excuse to get you here, dear. But you've done an amazing job with it."

"Was my mom in on this?" Addie demands.

"Of course. I couldn't have pulled this off on my own."

Addie and I stare at each other, totally blown away that all this game playing was done for the benefit of bringing us together.

"You're welcome," my mom says, smiling brightly. Then she turns to our waitress, who just walked over, and says, "Could you please tell Tara that we're ready for dessert?" She smiles at James and adds, "I asked her to make one of your favorites."

"Who's Tara?" James wants to know.

"She's our new pastry chef from Los Angeles," my mom announces as a very familiar face walks across the dining room carrying a giant peach shortbread on a platter.

She smiles around the table when she arrives. When her eyes land on James, she practically shouts, "You!"

James stands up like someone just poured boiling water on him. "What are you doing here?"

My mom introduces, "James, I'd like you to meet Tara. Tara, this is my youngest son, James."

James shakes his head like he's trying to get the rocks out of it. "You were trying to get me certified organic so I could sell you your work produce when I'm already the person who supplies your produce?"

"How was I supposed to know it was you? Your invoices only

say James on them. Your farm stand is named Poppa's. Nowhere does the name Cavanaugh show up."

"You wanted to replace me because I'm overpriced?" James is practically foaming at the mouth. "Do you have any idea how cheap my prices are?"

"They seem steep for being in Oregon."

"What does that mean?" he demands. "It costs just as much to run a farm here as anywhere else."

"I was trying to save your mom money." Tara looks like she's contemplating throwing the shortcake at my brother.

Meanwhile, my mom has a wicked smile on her face as she says, "Tara, why don't you pull up a chair and join us?"

"No, thank you, Mrs. Cavanaugh," the pastry chef says, "I have work to do."

Before she can walk away, Addie asks, "Are you Tara Heinz? You look just like her."

Tara shrugs her shoulders before answering, "Yes."

"Do you know her?" James asks Addie.

"Um, yeah. I'm pretty sure everyone at this table knows her."

That's when it hits me. "Heinzie, the best heinie of our generation?"

"Excuse me?" my mom demands like I've just said something untoward.

"She was a supermodel when James and I were in college," I explain. "She was known as 'the best butt in the business.'"

Mom looks up at Tara and asks, "Really?"

Tara nods her head once before saying, "I need to get back to work now." She walks away, leaving us all wondering how one of the world's most beautiful women is working as a pastry chef in Oregon.

Chapter Fifty-Nine

The Mothers

Libby pulls around the circular drive in front of the lodge. She doesn't even bother to get her suitcase out of the trunk before running inside.

Ruby spots her friend across the lobby and makes a beeline for her. "We did it, we did it, we did it!!!" she yells.

The two friends hold hands and jump around like two little girls with a secret. "Addie texted me last night to thank me for bringing her here. Can you believe it?" Libby practically squeals.

Ruby hurries to interject, "I predict an engagement by this time next year and a wedding by the following year. According to my calculations, we could be grandmas by the time we're sixty-three!"

"I should have never doubted you." Libby shakes her head in awe. "I only wish I had another daughter for James."

Ruby dusts an invisible speck off her shoulder before blowing on her fingernails. "While that would be wonderful, I'm pretty sure James is already spoken for."

"So, you think things are going to work out with him and your pastry chef?" Libby wants to know.

"James and Tara are even more at odds than Addie and Brogan were. I predict a super fast courtship with those two."

Addison

Sometimes life throws you a curveball that's so spectacularly wonderful you never see it coming. Brogan Cavanaugh is my curveball. I would have sworn up and down that he was the devil incarnate when I arrived in Oregon. Yet, through the machinations of our mothers, I realized that he's exactly what I need in my life.

It's been a week since Aunt Ruby confessed the real reason for my being here. Brogan and I are cuddled up in his hammock sharing a sweet and sexy moment. He lifts his head from where it's nestled next to mine and says, "We should go camping together."

"Real camping?" I ask in shock. "Like in a tent?"

"Yeah, real camping. I thought we could head up to Cheater's Ridge."

"So, we'd just sleep up there and come back here to eat and bathe and everything else?"

"No. Real camping implies that we'd stay up there for the entirety of our trip. We would be *camping.*" He says the last word like is Greek and I've never heard it before.

"Why would we do such a thing?" I want to know.

He nuzzles my neck. "We wouldn't tell our moms where we'd be so they couldn't keep dropping by three times a day for a visit."

"They have been very present, haven't they? But camping?

Why don't we just go away together? We could go to your place at the coast."

"We can go there next week. I want you to feel as strongly about Cheater's Ridge as I do. I want to share my dreams with you."

"Well now, that's just sweet," she says. "How can I refuse such an offer?"

* * *

The three nights Brogan and I were going to spend camping, turned into four. For the sake of modesty, I won't bore you with the details, but it's safe to say that in addition to learning how to make pancakes on a campfire and discovering how much fun it is to skinny dip in the falls, Brogan and I also forged a very real bond. We shared more than our dreams with each other, we made plans for a future that include one another.

I watch as Brogan finishes packing up his suitcase. "I'll head down to the lodge and get a golf cart so we can drive our things down," he says. "My mom is going to take us all to the airport together."

"I hope you don't mind flying to New York with my mom. I promise not to let her ask too many questions."

"I love your mom, she's my aunt Libby. She can ask me as many questions as she wants."

I reach up and give him a kiss that if we're not careful might lead to something we don't have time for. "I'll be ready by the time you come back."

After Brogan leaves, I look around the cabin that has been my home for the last month. I love it here and I'm thrilled that it's going to be Billy's home. I've made some changes with him in mind. For instance, I switched out the beaded lampshade for a leather one and I put pictures of him and the Cavanaugh family into the frames. He wasn't too keen on being photographed at first, but he stopped objecting when he realized I wasn't going to stop.

A knock on the door jolts me back to the present. "Come in," I call out.

Billy opens the door slowly. "You all alone up here?"

"Brogan went down to get the golf cart for our luggage."

"I wish you weren't going," he says.

"I'll be back for Christmas. I'm spending the whole month of December here through the New Year," I tell him.

"You know, it's all your fault that I look like a respectable person, now."

I walk over to my friend and open my arms to him. "Billy Grimps, it has been a pleasure getting to know you." He holds on tightly while I add, "You are never getting rid of me now."

"I guess being that you already feel like family, we're stuck with each other," he tells me.

"If you ever want to visit New York again," I tell him, "you have a place to stay with me."

"I don't imagine I'll be doing that," he says. "But I'll look forward to your next trip to Oregon."

Brogan isn't the only wonderful surprise I found in Oregon. Billy is the least likely person I'd ever think I'd become friends with, yet here we are. Tears fill my eyes at the thought of not seeing him every day. "I'd call you, but you don't have a phone," I tell him.

"Not much point with no reception. You could write to me once in a while and let me know how you and Brogan are getting on," he says with a hitch in his voice.

"Will you write me back?" I ask him.

"Yes, ma'am, I will."

With my arm still around him, I say, "You've got yourself a deal then. But we'll be back in a couple months. Would you mind making sure the fishing cabin is ready for us?"

"I've already talked to Herman. He's lining up bathtubs for all of the cabins. I'll make sure you get the nicest. Ruby's going to install wood-burning stoves for year-round comfort and she's got a line on solar water heaters so you don't have to wait for the water to heat up for your bath."

Billy and I sit out on the porch and enjoy a cup of tea together. "Life doesn't always turn out like you expect it to, does it?" I ask him.

"Girl, that's the biggest understatement I've ever heard. Just remember that no matter what turns it takes, your happiness is always in your hands. When you start to feel like things are overwhelming you, the only solution is to simplify your life."

"Like moving out to the woods and living off the land?" I ask him with a smile on my face.

"Just like that," he tells me.

Brogan pulls up in the golf cart and gives the horn a toot. "Uncle Billy," he calls out.

"Boy, you don't need to keep calling me uncle."

"What if I want to?" Brogan asks him.

"Then I guess I don't mind hearing it," Billy says.

Brogan loads our stuff into the golf cart while I say my final goodbye to my new friend. "I happen to think you're a wonderful man, Uncle Billy, and I thank you for taking me under your wing and keeping me safe up here."

He kisses my cheek and replies, "I don't care what happens with you and Brogan, I'm always going to think of you as my family."

Tears threaten to spill … who knew that four short weeks ago this homeless man would touch my heart so?

When it comes time to leave, we wave goodbye to each other, and I finally let the tears fall. Brogan toots the horn one last time, and I watch my first glamping experience, along with my new friend, fade into the distance. One thought pops into my head so strongly that it takes my breath away. I don't feel like I'm heading home going back to New York. I feel like I'm leaving home by leaving Oregon.

Chapter Sixty

The Mothers

Standing on the curb at the airport, Ruby says goodbye to her son and Addie. "Be good to each other," she says. "And remember, no pranks."

Brogan hugs his mom. "Thank you for being a meddling, interfering mother."

"I've always got your back, honey."

Addie hugs her next. "I love you, Aunt Ruby. I'll see you in December."

The mothers let their kids pass off the luggage to the baggage handler while they say their goodbyes. Ruby holds on to her friend like she doesn't want to let go. "So, Christmas at the lodge this year, right?"

"Bob can't wait," Libby says. "He's requested we stay in one of the cabins if they're ready."

"Billy is working full steam, following Addie's checklist. They should be done by Thanksgiving. If left on his own, I'm afraid my brother-in-law would have a much more simplistic view on what's needed for a glamping experience. Fortunately, Addie wants to see the project through."

Libby shakes her head. "Your brother-in-law. I still can't wrap my head around it. What a gift that is for you all."

"It really is," Ruby says. "I wish we'd known this years ago."

"You've got to take the blessings when they come, I guess."

"You better text me the whole way home and let me know how everything is going," Ruby says.

"I promise. And just so you know, Bob and I are going to be checking on the happy couple regularly."

"I'm glad Brogan's publisher has an apartment he's letting my son use, but is it wrong of me to say I hope he's not there very often?"

Libby laughs. "Not wrong at all, but it'll be good for our kids to have a little space from each other, too. You know that old saying, 'absence makes the heart grow fonder'? It'll be good for them to miss each other once in a while."

Ruby finally lets her friend go. "I love you, Libs. I wish I didn't have to wait until December to see you all again."

"You don't," Libby tells her. "You can come out my way any time you want."

Ruby tips her head back and forth before saying, "I know the lodge would be fine without me, but who's going to throw James and Tara together if I'm not there?"

"How in the world are you going to manage that with James being out on his farm most of the time?"

Ruby's eyes twinkle with mischief. "Don't you worry about that. I've got my ways."

Libby gives her friend one last squeeze before joining Addie and Brogan. She turns around and shouts, "Meddling Mothers one, Stubborn Kids zero!"

Ruby waves wildly and calls back, "Pretty soon that's going to be, Meddling Mothers two …"

"Go get 'em, girl. I can't wait to hear how it goes!"

Preorder Ain't She Sweet (book two in the Seven Brides for Seven Mothers Series):

Tara Heinz began her modeling career at the tender age of twelve. After spending fifteen years drooling over forbidden foods, she does the unthinkable. She enrolls in culinary school and becomes a pastry chef.

After a nasty breakup with her rock star boyfriend leads to tabloid war, Tara takes a job at a rural lodge in Oregon to escape the spotlight she no longer desires.

James Cavanaugh is a farmer in Oregon. His days are spent building his business and his nights are spend sleeping, so he can get up at four in the morning.

Ruby Cavanaugh has plans for her son that involve her new pastry chef. Of course, neither James nor Tara know what's going on until it's too late.

While you're waiting for Ain't She Sweet, check out Whitney's multi-award-winning Relatively Series!

Relatively Normal

Four Years Ago

My best friend is a vision straight out of one of those glossy bridal magazines that costs more than a macchiato and breakfast sandwich at Starbucks. She's well over six feet tall in her heels, slim as a fashion model—except she's sporting a C-cup no emaciated supermodel would be caught dead with—and her silky brown hair is currently twisted in an impossibly complicated up-do that probably required four professional hair stylists and a drag queen to execute. She's elegant beyond words.

I gasp as she spins around, so I can behold her in all her splendor. The sleeveless, beaded-bodice trumpet gown fits her like a glove. "Jasmine Marie, you're glorious!"

She giggles, which is a sound you wouldn't expect to come out of such a stunningly ethereal creature. She spins again, "I've never felt so girly! And that's saying something being that I'm this tall."

"Whoever said a month's paycheck was too much to spend on a wedding dress clearly never saw you in this one. I feel like a proud mother right now."

Jazz heaves a sigh. "Speaking of mothers, you have to do me a favor." My eyebrows raise in interest. She continues, "Watch out for mine and make sure she doesn't murder my dad's new wife during dinner."

I snort. "Puh-leeze, your mom is every ounce a lady. She'd no more commit murder than I would."

"Alas, Brandee—with two e's—the latest of my dad's spouses, has just announced she's pregnant. My mom isn't taking the news gracefully."

"You're kidding me? You're going to have a new brother or sister at twenty-nine?" Then I ask, "How old is Brandee again?"

My friend rolls her big brown eyes. "My dearest stepmother has just turned twenty-four."

"I don't know, Jazz. I think your dad is the one who needs offing in this scenario. I might be persuaded to help."

"I would appreciate if no murders were committed at my nuptials." Then she hugs me, and says, "But I love you for offering."

"Oh, Jazzy," I exclaim, "this day is going to be so wonderful. You deserve every minute of happiness. Dylan is one lucky guy."

Brushing a non-existent wrinkle out of her skirt, she declares, "Now all we need to do is find you the perfect man. Three of the groomsmen are single. You've met two of them, and the third is the one with sandy blond hair. He's Dylan's cousin, Jared, from Detroit."

"Detroit? Hard pass." The sarcasm rolls off my tongue. "I'm not looking for a long-distance love. But have no fear, I'll definitely scope out the other two. I'm not opposed to meeting the future Mr. Catriona Masterton tonight."

She beams. "People often meet their future spouses at weddings. It's a thing."

"So, it's got to be my turn, right?"

Jazz playfully punches my arm. "That's the attitude I love! I just wish you were walking down the aisle with me."

I call out to Jennifer, our assistant, "Make sure you pack up all of Jazz's stuff and take it over to her suite at the hotel. Oh, and before you go, tell Elaine to get the limos turned around out front to transport the wedding party to the reception once the ceremony ends."

In addition to being best friends, Jazz and I own a much sought-after event-planning business in Manhattan. We're the go-to duo known for stylishly executing even the trickiest parties—like weddings where the groom was once married to the bride's sister—without a hitch.

I turn to the current bride. "I wish I were walking down the aisle with you too, but someone has to make sure this shin-dig of yours goes off perfectly. There's a ton of potential business out there, so we have to make sure this is our best party yet. Now, hustle, the bridesmaids are already upstairs, and their procession starts in . . ."—I check my watch— "two minutes, which only gives you seven before it's your turn."

I pick up my friend's chapel-length train to keep it from getting dirty on the stairs. "Let's go, lady; your happily-ever-after awaits."

We arrive upstairs in the entrance of St. John the Divine Cathedral just as Emily, the last bridesmaid, starts her goosestep down the aisle. Jazz and I stand side-by-side watching her go. As Emily takes her place in the front of the altar, the first strains of "Trumpet Voluntary" fill the atmosphere like a heavenly serenade. Chills race through my body as I kiss my friend's cheek and hand her off to her father who will deliver her to her destiny, one Dylan Finch.

Once the ceremony is over and the reception is in full swing at the St. Regis Hotel, I take off my party-planner hat and put on my dancing shoes. It's go time. I have my eye on a particular groomsman, whom I've met on a couple other occasions. He's sweet and shy, but super easy on the eyes. I'm not sure we're destined for matrimony, but a couple of dances would be fun.

I straighten the skinny navy skirt of my evening dress and prepare for the chase. I take a step forward and wind up doing an unexpected split to the ground. *Ouch!* The waiter rushes over to clean up the spilled drink I inadvertently stepped in, and before I can begin the process of restoring my dignity, a pair of shiny, black shoes shows up next to me.

A manly hand stretches out and a deep voice inquires, "May I be of assistance?" He introduces himself. "Ethan Crenshaw, lifelong friend of the groom." I recognize him from the rehearsal dinner, but I didn't get a chance to talk to him. Not only is Dylan's friend chivalrous, but he has gorgeous green eyes that remind me of Maeve's, my childhood cat.

I take his hand. "Thank you. That's very kind."

"Let me help you to a chair and then I'll get some ice for your injury. It'll keep the swelling down," he announces.

Once I'm positioned at table fourteen in the main ballroom, I watch Ethan walk to the bar. He looks good in a way that suggests he's comfortable in formal wear, like James Bond. And bam, just like that, I realize I had totally forgotten about the cute groomsman.

When my knight in shining armor—a.k.a. a black tuxedo—returns, he helps prop my foot up on a chair and states, "There's a nine percent chance of getting injured at a wedding reception."

As far as opening lines go, it's not the best. Yet, his previous gallantry more than makes up for it. "That seems to be an awfully high number," I reply. "I've been to almost two hundred weddings so far and this is my first injury. If my calculations are correct, that puts my risk at point five percent, nowhere near your estimate."

"Two hundred weddings? You must be quite a popular friend."

I inform him, "I'm a party planner. I'm Jazz's partner."

"Ah, well then, surely you've had a blister, a burnt finger, or a stiff neck?"

I laugh. "If you're going to include all the mundane discomforts, I'd think you'd be more accurate to say there's a hundred percent chance of getting injured at a wedding."

He shakes his head. "No, only nine percent, unless my research is wrong." With a pointed look he adds, "Which it never is."

What kind of person researches injuries at weddings? So, I ask, "What exactly do you do for a living?"

"I'm an actuary. Certainly, not as glamorous a profession as party planning, but it pays the bills."

I've heard the job title, but I have no idea what it entails. Kind of like an ornithologist. I know it's something. I just don't know what. At my confused look, he explains, "Insurance companies and brokerage firms hire actuaries to assess the financial risk of investments and people. I currently work at an insurance company and help set rates, based on the statistical probability of natural disasters hitting certain demographics. For instance, earthquake insurance in the Midwest costs you next to nothing compared to what it does in California, for a reason."

"Huh." I can't seem to think of any other response.

"It sounds like a job that could bore the paint off the walls, doesn't it?" he laughs.

I flirt, "Lucky for me, I like numbers."

Ethan sits with me for the next three hours while I ice my ankle, ten minutes on and twenty minutes off, as per his suggestion for the best healing effects. As we get to know each other, I watch Jazz flirt and dance with the man who just promised to love her forever.

Dylan is hands down the sweetest, funniest, and most devoted man I've ever met. He adores my friend with his whole being and treats her like delicate china, even though she's not the kind of woman you'd want to sneak up on in a dark alley. Jazzy is one hundred percent Amazon with a touch of Xena Warrior Princess. She and Dylan are perfect for each other.

I was once in love with a man very much like Dylan and it didn't turn out well, which is why I'm currently in the market for someone more practical. I'm less concerned with grand gestures and flowery compliments, than in a reliable partner who will be there when the chips are down.

Throughout the reception, not only do I discover that Ethan adheres to a strictly regimented life, but I also learn he's a lovely man. He even offers, "Would you like me to see you safely home? No ulterior motives, I promise."

"It's kind of early to leave, don't you think?" And while he claims no other motivation, I wouldn't be opposed to a little romance.

He looks at his watch and explains, "I promised my neighbor,

Mrs. Fein, I'd look in on her cat while she's away. Apparently, Fifi suffers from separation anxiety and needs someone to bat her toy mouse around with her before she can go to sleep."

As the party is winding down, and I can see the staff has everything well in hand, there's nothing more for me to do. I allow Ethan to escort me home. True to his word, he doesn't try any funny business. He just gives me a sweet kiss, leaving me wanting more, and asks, "When can I see you again?"

The Courtship

When my doorbell rings, I quickly apply a fresh layer of lipstick and grab my purse. Tonight, we're celebrating our first anniversary, which happens to coincide with Jazz and Dylan's first anniversary. I'm wearing a cerulean-blue wrap-dress that compliments my blonde hair and blue eyes. I bought it especially for this occasion.

Ethan greets me with a bouquet of long-stemmed white roses. "For my beautiful lady."

I pull him in and give him a proper kiss of appreciation. "These are perfect, thank you." Even though red roses are meant for lovers, Ethan's favorite are white ones. He claims they're pure and untarnished, like me. Swoon, right?

Our dating experience has been perfect. There's no rush to jump into bed and burn ourselves out having wild monkey sex six times a day. That's not to say there's isn't any chemistry. There definitely is. It's just not some uncontrollable chemical explosion guaranteed to fizzle once the initial throes of passion are spent. It would be more accurate to conclude we're committed to an adult relationship that involves a lot of other aspects of our union, in addition to the physical. It's exactly what

I'm looking for. I've reached an age where I'm no longer interested in unpredictable and spontaneous men.

Ethan and I have a nice routine together. We eat out twice a week, taking turns picking the location. Sometimes it's breakfast, sometimes dinner, but it's always twice a week. I change up my location depending on what the buzz on the street is. I'm always on the lookout for a new adventure. Ethan seems content to stay with the same handful of locations, which is fine. There are plenty of new things for me to try, though he seems to favor a few select menu items.

We watch television two nights a week and go to the movies on Sunday. I stay over at his apartment twice a week and he stays the same number at mine. All in all, we spend a lot of time together. We also seem to have a thing for the number two.

I put the roses into a vase and inhale their fragrance deeply before saying, "We'd better run. Our reservation is at seven."

"I changed it to seven thirty. I didn't want to run the risk of being late and losing it," he replies.

That's Ethan in a nutshell. He thinks things through and always has a plan. In a world where people constantly fly by the seat of their pants, I think this is a refreshing way to live. "Perfect. Would you like a glass of wine before we leave?"

He holds out his hand. "No. We can always get one at the bar if we're early. I asked the Lyft driver to wait for us."

As we walk out the door of my Chelsea apartment, the world is my oyster. I'm celebrating a year with the same wonderful man, I have a flourishing career, and the air is finally cooling and starting to smell like a New York City fall. Contentment permeates my world.

Ethan and I hold hands in the car on the way to the restaurant. I say, "This is quite a special night, isn't it?" We don't normally eat at restaurants as expensive as Astor Court, but this is a celebration.

"It is. Since we met at the St. Regis Hotel, it's only fitting we return to the scene of the crime a year later."

Ethan guides me from the car into the hotel with his left hand placed gently on my lower back. The lobby is old-world elegant, and I feel like a princess entering a castle.

Once we're seated, our waiter, a middle-aged man wearing black pants with a matching vest and bow tie, greets us, "Mr. Crenshaw, Ms. Masterton, we're so honored to have you dining with us. My name is Frank, and I'll be taking care of you this evening." Wow, that was worth a couple hundred bucks right there. It's the little things like this that make people keep coming back.

Frank pops open a bottle of champagne and pours for us. Ethan has left no detail unattended. He's even requested the same champagne Jazz and Dylan served at their wedding, Veuve Clicquot Rosé.

After our appetizers are ordered—lobster risotto for me, and the caprese salad for him— Ethan surprises me by dropping to one knee beside me. "Catriona . . ." My heart starts to beat so loudly I can hear it pounding inside my ears. Before he can say anything else, I start the little camera in my brain clicking away to save this moment for posterity. I never suspected he was going to propose marriage tonight.

I inhale deeply and look up at the mural of a blue sky with white, fluffy clouds painted on the eighteen-foot ceiling. I observe the gold-leaf crown molding and count all six crystal chandeliers. Everything seems to be moving in slow motion.

I always thought that women who claimed they didn't know a proposal was coming were just playing up the drama for the retelling of their story. Turns out, some might really be surprised. I finally look at Ethan and say, "Yes?"

He smiles widely. "Will you do me the great honor of becoming my wife?"

First of all, there's no way I'm not going to say yes. I mean, this is storybook stuff. Secondly, I love Ethan, and thirdly, did I mention the perfection of this night? I semi-shout, "Yes! Yes, I'll marry you!" A crowd of fellow diners give us an encouraging round of applause as the waiter approaches with a ring box on a silver tray.

Ethan opens the lid and removes an emerald-cut diamond from its black velvet pillow. He places it on my ring finger while uttering a heartfelt, "Thank you."

I wish someone was recording this so I could watch it on replay. Even though I'm living it, it feels like it's happening to someone else and I'm sure to forget some detail. Once Ethan gets back into his chair, he announces, "You should move in with me. We'll be able to save more money for the wedding that way."

What he says is true. My thirty-eight hundred dollar a month apartment will add up to a hefty sum for a wedding. I ask, "When would you like me to do that?"

"I've been thinking about it since I bought the ring, and decided if you said yes, you should move in right away. I know your lease is month-to-month, and as this is the last week in the month, how about over the weekend?"

And just like that, my life as a single woman in New York City comes to an end. I've never lived with a man, and suddenly I feel quite grown up. I mean, sure I'm thirty, and have a successful business, but now I'm an engaged woman to boot. If you had told me last year that this would be happening, I would have never believed you.

One Year Later

"Catriona, would you please pass the No-Salt?" Ethan never calls me Cat.

Despite the fact that he's been asking for that god-awful substitute for the year we've lived together, I can't help but crinkle my nose. Still, I hand over his salt replacement and ask, "Why do you insist on using that?"

Over the top of his glasses, he explains, "Based on my heredity, there's a thirty-eight-percent chance I will develop high blood pressure by the time I'm forty. By not using salt to season my food and by doing a minimum of thirty minutes of cardio a day, I reduce my chances to a mere twelve percent. Those are odds I can't afford to ignore."

This is the kind of information Ethan is known for. It's a biproduct of his job, and while I suppose he's right, I'd personally rather die five years early and really enjoy my food than put up with the weird aftertaste of the fake stuff.

If we can ever get confirmation on our preferred wedding venue, I'm fully prepared for an all-out battle about serving real salt at our reception. For me, this is a non-negotiable point.

"Our flight to Chicago leaves at five thirty tomorrow night."

I say this as I grind some pink sea salt onto my scrambled eggs.

"We should have a car pick us up at eleven fifteen, then."

I perform an internal eye roll. I don't care how early Ethan leaves for the airport when he's traveling alone, but I absolutely refuse to spend my life anticipating the worst and winding up sitting at JFK for three hours before getting on a plane. "I have a lunch meeting tomorrow, so I'll have to meet you there—if you insist on going early, that is."

He gives me the look, one that suggests, "Aren't we being a little frivolous?"

I cut him off at the pass before he has a chance to say it. "I'm meeting with the Vanderhauffers, of Vanderhauffer Jewels on Fifth Avenue, about doing their daughter's wedding. The kind of money and exposure we're talking about will more than make up for the extra car fare."

I'm actually not meeting the Vanderhauffers tomorrow; I'm meeting with them today. I have a massage scheduled for tomorrow to preemptively defeat the incoming stress of Thanksgiving. I don't usually lie to Ethan, but sometimes it's just easier than having to explain myself. Also, it avoids a heated disagreement, which I'm against, as a rule.

Plus, let's be honest, there is no way Ethan will appreciate the eccentricities of my family. I firmly believe there is a widely accepted range of behavior—from straight and stodgy to certifiable—that all humans exhibit from one degree to another. Fortunately, or unfortunately, depending on how you look at it, my family is firmly lodged in the quirky range.

Take my mother, for instance. She's plagued by a disorder where kitchen gadgets actually talk to her and beg her to take them home. During my childhood, she would drag me from one garage sale to the next just to see what treasures people were getting rid of. God forbid it was a shortbread pan in a shape she didn't have or some kitchen wonder that promised to peel, slice, dice, or waffle cut any vegetable you could imagine.

She's currently the proud owner of twenty-nine shortbread pans that form every shape from flower bouquets, to hearts, to the Loch Ness Monster. In addition, she has a basket of assorted culinary oddities, which she stores in the laundry room. She doesn't know exactly what they do or how to assemble them. She just knows they might come in handy one day, and God forbid she not have them when they're needed.

Also, my mother is the only human being alive who knows how to properly load a dishwasher—knives down, forks up, and no spoon caught spooning with another, ever. Even if you follow every one of her dictates to the letter, you will still inevitably do it wrong. "Forks up only on the first twenty-two days of the month and never on a full moon!" You think I'm kidding? Don't get me started on what happens when Mercury is in retrograde.

My mother's idiosyncrasies used to bug the absolute crap out of me until I decided to find them charming. Now when she tells me about a new shortbread pan she's found or complains that after thirty-five years of marriage, my dad still doesn't know how to load the dishwasher, I just smile. I'm never going to change her, and darn if I'm not going to miss these conversations someday.

Then there's my nan, who is happily still alive at eighty, and living with my parents. She developed something like Tourette syndrome when I was eight. Up until then, she was a perfectly normal grandma. Then one day, out of the blue, she snapped.

We had all been sharing a pew at the First Presbyterian Church on Easter morning. I couldn't wait to get home and bite the head off my solid chocolate Godiva Easter Bunny, but in the meantime was covertly popping jelly beans into my mouth, slowly sucking off the semi-hard candy coating before letting the delicious gummy center melt on my tongue.

I'd just eaten two pink ones, two white ones and had started on my two yellow, when Pastor Abernathy's wife walked by us. Nan shouted out as loud as you please, "Twat!" You've never heard such silence. The entire congregation was not only rendered mute, but totally immobile by the epithet hanging in the air above them.

Mrs. Abernathy had stopped dead in her tracks, slowly turned around, and scowled at my grandmother—a woman she'd known since they were in elementary school together. She had stared her down in such a way a lesser mortal would have succumbed to the arctic exposure of her glare.

My grandmother, on the other hand, had merely smiled and greeted, "Dorcas, how are you this fine Sunday?" It effectively left everyone wondering if they'd really heard what they thought they heard or if they'd all been victims of some strange audio hallucination.

The doctor hadn't been able to pinpoint the exact cause of her change, but guessed it was the result of a series of small strokes that effectively killed the governor living in her brain. After the incident at church, Nan became proficient at saying whatever she was thinking, wherever she was thinking it. Most people decided to act like they didn't hear her. It was a weird truce between the citizens of our little town and an old lady seemingly bent on offending everyone she came into contact with.

If a proliferation of shortbread pans and curse words weren't enough, my father's quirk is a love of dead rodents. No, I'm not kidding. I only wish I were. He has other peculiarities, but this one stands out as the most glaring.

My brother, Travis, is plagued by overt-selfishness and an inability to grow up. At twenty-nine, he's unemployed, living in my parents' basement, medicating his angst over life not turning out the way he expected with anything he can get his hands on—scotch, pot, Benadryl, sleeping pills. You name it, if it can alter his consciousness in any way, he's all over it like flies on a cow pie.

Why am I telling you all of this? Because up until this point, I've managed to keep Ethan from ever meeting my family. Even with us in New York City, and them in Illinois, it hasn't been easy to keep them apart. Now that we've been official for over a year, and Thanksgiving is just around the corner, Ethan has decreed he *will* meet my family, regardless of any excuse I come up with to keep that from happening. He's also invited his mom and dad along so that we can share our wedding plans with both sets of parents at the same time.

I can only hope my particular quirk, which is an almost mystical belief that all things work out as they should, is less a Pollyanna-ish pipe dream and more a fact-based reality. Otherwise, there's no way I can see this weekend going well for any of us. Is it any wonder I'll be spending two hours with a hulking masseur? I'll probably need another two when we get home.

Relatively Normal is available now!